Because
I Have Loved
and Hidden It

Because
I Have Loved
and Hidden It

ELISE MOSER

a novel

Cormorant Books Inc.

Canada Council **Conseil des Arts**
for the Arts **du Canada**

The publisher gratefully acknowledges the support of the
Canada Council for the Arts and the Ontario Arts Council
for its publishing program. We acknowledge the financial support
of the Government of Canada through the Book Publishing
Industry Development Program (BPIDP) for our publishing activities.

Printed and bound in Canada

LIBRARY AND ARCHIVES CANADA CATALOGUING IN PUBLICATION

Moser, Elise
Because I have loved and hidden it / Elise Moser.

ISBN 978-1-897151-36-5

I. Title.

PS8626.O8425B42 2009   C813'.6   C2009-903865-X

Cover image and design: Angel Guerra/Archetype
Text design: Tannice Goddard, Soul Oasis Networking
Printer: Friesens

CORMORANT BOOKS INC.
215 SPADINA AVENUE, STUDIO 230, TORONTO, ON CANADA M5T 2C7
WWW.CORMORANTBOOKS.COM

Mixed Sources
Cert no. SW-COC-001271
© 1996 FSC
FSC

In loving memory of
Dorothy Cohen Moser
and
Albert Cohen

I write

because poetry is to the body as energy is to mass; it lives
in me as in you, and perhaps
because we have little else to give one another, you and I
because history repeats with the cocooning of secrets

because I have loved and hidden it
in cycles sure as Mississippi floods:
stupendous litany of ampersands
it swells and washes and carries the house
away

and to find it again I must describe it
to you

Have you seen the shark's eye glint on my bone-handled knife,
the lime that bleeds May?

— Susan Elmslie, *I, Nadja, and Other Poems*

SHE WAS ALL SURFACE. *All her consciousness was concentrated on her skin, every molecule of air passing over her, twitching through the fine hairs and bouncing into and out of the invisible landscape of her, triggering quakes along her nerves, sideswiping her senses. His breath was more intense still, its warmth making her shiver. She could feel his hair brush the side of her face and she knew he was lowering his head so he could kiss her neck and she thought she might implode. Then he did and she didn't die from it, but for just a second her mind boiled over. It foamed with the brief hot softness of his lips and breath. She felt her own breath catch in her throat and she heard it, a heavy wetness smacking against air. She thought she might never breathe again and she thought she might dissolve right there, with him bent against her and breathing the heat out of his lungs across her shoulder. Her nerves quivered with disbelief and a pleasure she doubted even while they vibrated with it.*

She took the heat of his body from his mouth and from his skin and she began to feel the dense textures of his hands, sculpted by work and by daily life, the strength of his muscles making his fingers and his palms and his wrists dense and hard. He held her hands down, away from them both. She could not move her hands inside his hands, her arms straining up against him. She closed her eyes, her mind moving back to inhabit the insides of her eyelids where they sealed her away from the irrelevant sight of the wall, the room beyond his head, his chest and shoulder, and she felt her collarbones suddenly spring into existence under his lips. She was grateful for the bones of her body, which had never meant anything to her before, but now received this gift, this touch, these invisible traces of moisture from his own warm skin.

⊱✦⊰

JULIA SITS BY HER OPEN window in the dark. Montreal is uncharacteristically silent — she rarely sees it during its few quiet late-night hours. Only Sunday mornings, in her Plateau neighbourhood, are equally serene. The street looks like a rare exterior shot from a film noir, deep blacks cut by occasional shining planes of light. Her chest aches with an anxiety that is salted with regret and a pinch of shame. Her lover is missing, and everything she did not say, did not do, every awkwardness and thoughtlessness eats at her now. She is embarrassed to be regretting her own defects at a moment when she ought to be consumed by thoughts of him.

He must be somewhere, his body must be somewhere even if his spirit already roams the ether; what street is he on now? If death had a street it might look like this, buildings that seem to be vacant in the stillness, empty cars rooted to black pavement. Nicholas's absence has always lived in Julia's veins; he has often deprived her of his company through carelessness or preoccupation. This absence, occurring not through his choice but possibly through some violence or grave misfortune, is much more painful. Julia's throat is tight. She rubs uselessly at her temples.

There is a movement outside, a flick of shadow — a dried leaf in invisible wind, or a cat perhaps, slipping under a car. A scrap of life, breaking the hypnotic spell of death's street.

❧❧❧

AT HER MOTHER'S FUNERAL, JULIA stood in the thick damp heat regretting that she'd worn pantyhose; they clung to her legs like evil. She hated being too hot. She'd really hoped to feel cool — composed — for this particular event.

Carol had requested that her body be displayed at the funeral home. This didn't surprise Julia on religious grounds; Carol had picked and chosen among the traditions of her forebears, forgoing leavened breads during Passover but regularly chowing down on cheeseburgers. She did find it bizarre considering the state of her mother's body post-cancer — yet it was self-absorbed in a way that was entirely in character for Carol. Julia thought she wouldn't care to see her mother, even in death, but upon entering the air-conditioned dimness of the funeral home and identifying herself to the man at the door as Carol's daughter, she was ushered immediately into the viewing room with unctuous solicitude. "Of course," he'd said, his head ducking to one side as if attached by a string to his ankle, "the Goodman party." Not much of a party, Julia thought. With the man retreating silently behind her, Julia stood before the casket. Her irritation lifted and, curious, she stepped forward.

In the coffin was a corpse she recognized as her mother only after adjusting mentally for the years of age and disease, and the effects of the undertaker's ministrations. Her mother's body, planetary in shape for much of her life, had melted away to what looked like a bundle of dry sticks; her ankles, sticking out past the hem of her dress, could have been filched from a turkey carcass. Julia pictured her mother the last time she'd seen her, crossing a windblown street with a plastic shopping bag in each hand, her grey hair wild about her head. Now she lay in her box, primly wrapped in the too-ample folds of a shiny purple polyester dress, the belt of which was pulled so tight the end had been tucked around under her back. Her hair was neatly combed back from her face and sprayed into a hard shell. Her face looked as if all the flesh had been boiled away, revealing sharp bones and gristle, the ridges of a chaotic landscape. Her mouth was oddly pursed, as if she'd been blowing someone a kiss when she unexpectedly died. Julia felt sorry for her mother, seeing Carol's habitual appearance — which Julia had found unattractive and embarrassing during Carol's life — effaced at the last moment by a stranger. She wondered if she would be so reduced when her time came.

Julia was considering the possibility of getting a coffee before the formalities began when she heard the chunk-chunk of her Uncle Paul's walker. She turned to watch him enter, dressed in a dusty black suit that hung on him like a bathrobe. He made his way slowly to the open coffin and thunked his walker onto the carpet with a determined finality. "Hi, dolly," he said to Julia, his voice low and phlegmy. He patted her hand with his own puffy one. He was more liver-spotted than she remembered, his skin slung as loose on his old skull as his suit was around his shoulders. She gave him a quick, gentle hug. "Where's Judy?" she asked. Paul waved a hand. "Not feeling too good today." Julia knew that Judy, Paul's second wife, had never really liked Carol. It was entirely like Judy not to attend a funeral simply for form's sake. Good for her, Julia thought. She wondered what negotiation had taken place at home.

They stood for a few minutes in silence. Julia had the urge to step over and hug her uncle again and, this time, hang on to him — but she felt held back, she wasn't sure why. Instead she found herself gazing at him, mentally placing a hand on his bowed shoulders, his bent head.

Uncle Paul looked up and jerked his head toward the exit. "Let's get this show on the road," he said loudly, and then picked up his walker and began to manoeuvre it around again. "I don't want to hang around in this place," he said under his breath, cocking his head toward Julia so she could hear him. "I'm gonna be back here soon enough."

⚹⚹⚹

AT THE GRAVESIDE, BEFORE HER mother's uninscribed half of the double headstone, Julia, Paul, and Paul's son, Bill, stood across the opening in the earth from a couple of people her mother must have known during her last years, perhaps from her apartment building. After Bill read a very brief account of Carol's life, Uncle Paul leaned down from his walker and picked up a handful of the moist grey earth and threw it clumsily into the rectangular hole. Julia heard it smack the wood of the casket.

"I say goodbye to my sister," Paul said, his chin raised, his arm sweeping across the open pit of the grave. "She was a good sister, and now she's dead." Julia grinned to herself privately without lifting her head. Then Paul grabbed his walker and jerked it out of the soil at the edge of the grave, where it had sunk, and began the process of turning around to leave. Julia waited until the others had all moved off and then rummaged at the edge of the pile of dirt for a pebble. She laid it on her father's side of the headstone and took a minute to think of him. Then she caught up with Paul and fell into place beside him, walking slowly to keep pace. She was dying to peel off her damn pantyhose. They walked in silence to Bill's car. Bill loaded the walker into his trunk while Uncle Paul levered himself into the back seat. "Julia, dolly, come sit here, I have something for you," Paul said, patting the seat next to him.

As they pulled out of the cemetery, Uncle Paul drew a crumpled manila envelope from the inside pocket of his suit jacket. "This is for you," he said. "Your mother gave it to me for safekeeping when she went into the hospital. But I think you should have it."

"What is it?" Julia asked, tenting the envelope to get at the paper inside, but Paul put his hand over hers.

"Don't look at it now," he said, turning his head to gaze out the window. "You don't ever have to look at it if you don't want to. I just thought you should have it."

⚜

AT HOME, SHE'D KICKED OFF her shoes before the door was even fully closed. She pulled off her pantyhose on the way to the kitchen, the nylon stretching up from her feet like hot cheese from a pizza. She poured a glass of water from the kitchen tap, sat down, and took a sip. Then she opened the flap of the envelope and shook out the contents. A single piece of paper, sepia with age; it was a birth certificate. Baby Goodman, born October 1, 1963. Sex: F.

⚜

JULIA SETTLES IN AGAINST THE pillow and pulls the duvet up to her waist, folds it over. She is readying herself for her nightly confrontation with sleep. For some, sleep is a calm and restorative companion for nights that pass away in unconscious meditation. For Julia, it is a moody and inconstant lover, ardently desired and, when it comes, welcomed with gratitude and relief — but when it refuses her, she is resentful. Waiting to see which or when it will be, she lies with anxiety.

Sleep rarely abandons her for an entire night, but often forces her to wait in a stew of unpleasant emotions while it dallies elsewhere. The sheets are cool against Julia's skin, the pillows against her cheek and neck. She has her secret rituals, meant to call sleep and convince it to visit her — to stay with her and confer its grace upon her: the clean sheets, the good pillow, the duvet snapped in the air so it floats down like a bird landing on water. Julia attempts to clear her mind.

She knows it is a false clarity. Since she fell in love, began to think constantly of Nicholas, sleep took offence and has kept its distance. And why not — what lover can accept with equanimity the thought of another, even if no rivalry is possible? The first night she tried to sleep in her now-quiet bed after having made love with Nicholas, sleep turned its jealous back completely. Since then, it has kept a wounded silence many nights, only coming to Julia when she has finally worn down the thought of Nicholas by the constant turning of her mind. She exchanges one moody and inconstant lover for another, insinuated the second into her life, giving him the cloudy jar of her mind every night. Now she has two lovers, both of whom want her but neither of whom wants to be burdened with her. Both of whom will let themselves come so close — but no closer. And sleep is not appeased by the absence, even the possible mortal end of its rival, Nicholas.

Julia tries to find a mental neutral, an emptiness that will leave her free of Nicholas, her longings for him, her anxieties. It never works; Nicholas is inside Julia whether she likes it or not. He lives in her tiny firing synapses, in sparks of electricity jumping through her brain. She'd like to find a way to dull the hot glinting slivers, make her brain a quiet place — the way the streets were quiet in the damp late night when Nicholas left her door. Then she would stand on the sidewalk, arms crossed against the cool dark, to watch his straight back recede under the streetlights, his taste in her mouth, his smell on her fingers. She wishes he smelled stronger; he's a fastidious man

— which has its pleasant aspects, to be sure. He is always clean, his white shirts spotless, his shoes well shined. Even when he says he smells, in the dense wet humidity and high heat of these climate-change summers, Julia can hardly get a whiff. He's never gamy, never rank.

There's something almost feminine about his cleanliness, while Julia, on the other hand, finds herself embarrassingly aromatic. In the summer she's afraid her underarms are rancid, her vagina strong and sticky; her skin accumulates grime. Nicholas appears not to mind. She doesn't trust what he tells her; her insecurities are too strong to be calmed by his reassurances. In the past he has embraced her, told her in the heat that he wants her slimy, slipped his hands into her underwear and pressed the lips of her together until they released their wetness, declining her offer to wash because he said he wanted her sweat and her smell. In spite of all this, she has lain in bed and wondered whether this time he didn't call her because of her smelly cunt. She knows this kind of speculation is futile and, worse, self-indulgent. She is fully aware that her feverish desire scares him much more than her over-fragrant genitalia. And she is not even sure if his erratic interest in her has anything to do with her at all. It could easily be all about him, and she could be any woman, any version of herself — twenty pounds fatter, her breasts ten years more wasted, wine dribbling out of the corners of her mouth as she laughs too loudly in public and pounds her fist on the table in some bar where he knows the bartender. Or maybe she could be taller, with smoother skin, a mind like a steel trap, tender shivering fingers that fill men with yearning at their feathery touch — and Nicholas still wouldn't call her.

Julia turns her head once, slightly, from side to side, feeling the cool pillowcase on her face, smelling the clean cotton. She feels the edge of the duvet cover, also fresh cotton, under her palms. Before Nicholas, she used to be able to touch herself to sleep, the spasm that tensed all her muscles leaving her relaxed and warm in its wake. Not anymore. Now she touches herself and imagines herself with Nicholas, and although she intends to think of them making love, to imagine him pulling the fabric of her shirt away from her waist, up so he can slide his cool dry hands around her hips, up until they cover her ribs, his fingers long and powerful as if he wanted to squeeze the breath out of her and breathe it into his own mouth, pull it down into his own lungs just because it has been inside her — even though this is what she would like to think about, and what she begins to imagine, the scenario invariably fades. Without intending it, she finds herself imagining instead some scene of rejection, disdain, inadvertent contempt. This is not what she wants to be thinking, knowing he may be in danger or worse, but he never comes to her mind, his sweet-soft skin and tender fingers, without the disapproving set to his beautiful mouth or the flicker of his eye away from her, toward something else. She invents conversations between them that have never happened, that end with Nicholas leaving her in her doorway, dignified but nursing a wound that will not stop bleeding. She knows this is her mind telling her what she does not want to know, that this is the real substance of her affair with Nicholas — but he has always been just tender enough, or just in time, to tug her back to him. He can be beautifully, meltingly gentle, a fragile curl of butter turning liquid in the heat of her inner elbow. Then his tenderness is a tiny pool of rainwater in the hollow of her collarbone — but it only happens now and then. She doesn't know how the part of him that can be so gently, warmly nourishing can be so thoroughly absent at other times.

Julia turns on her side and pulls the duvet up over her shoulder, the cover making her realize that her skin has turned cold in the night air. She lifts her knees up high, feeling the small of her back creak and stretch as the tension is tugged up like a drawstring being pulled through the neck of a bag. Only this strain will not come out, not tonight. As she lies here in her bed thinking of Nicholas and his strong hands and stern expression, the tension collects at the base of her spine and forms a ball. She can see it, a tangled ball, and then as she thinks it, it begins to move, becomes a tight writhing mass of worms. The image is revolting and she desperately tries to distract herself.

What is Nicholas doing now? Something involving wine, she hopes. Some foreign version of the way she often conjures him in Montreal, sitting in the bar he frequents, chatting up some young woman he is interested in. Only in Morocco he will be speaking French, or he will be allowing some tourist to practise her English on him. Julia knows he tells himself it must be innocent since they are in public, he and this young woman. He lets himself do it, telling himself that he has no intention of sleeping with her. The girl is complaining about her boyfriend, who will be here in twenty minutes to pick her up; they are going to a club with friends. Julia imagines Nicholas congratulating himself — see, the purity of his intentions is proved by the fact that he cannot bring this woman back to his room, by the fact that he will be sitting here with her when her boyfriend arrives, some strapping Dutch boy with a blond beard, and Nicholas will meet the boyfriend and they will enjoy the camaraderie of acquaintances, of fellow travellers. Julia sees this in her mind and smiles sideways to herself because she dislikes this part of Nicholas and is mystified by it, yet it does not stop her from wanting him, doesn't even make a dent in her wanting. It is part of him, makes him the complicated, unknowable person he is.

She wonders whether, given a good opportunity, she would sleep with someone else who came along, for the simple and fleeting pleasure of it or in the hope of love. She'd like to think so — it makes her feel independent. Yet she must admit to herself that her desire for Nicholas overwhelms any thoughts of other people, and she resents him for drawing her so strongly. She feels him a massive, powerful magnet and herself an ordinary, flimsy straight pin; she sees herself wheel through the air in slow motion and land, stuck, on his metal edge, her little flat head left jutting out over the side, winking, dull silver, in the light from the window.

She remembers the simple affection with which he gave her a farewell peck on the lips after the second time she slept with him, as they said goodbye out on a busy street where anyone — his wife, for example — could see them. Like a suburban husband saying goodbye to his spouse at the commuter train, or an elderly man dropping his wife of fifty years at her weekly mah-jongg game. Julia sighs and turns over again, kicks the duvet down to her hips, pulls the pillow lower. If sleep persists in ignoring her tonight, she will have to get up, read a book, occupy herself. Do something that she can do with her head resting on the arm of a chair — because, awake though she may be, she is very, very tired. *He never showed up at his hotel in Casablanca*, Deepa said.

⋘⋙

THEY'D EVENTUALLY SLEPT TOGETHER. "NOW we've consummated our affair," Nicholas had said, his voice still soft and husky with desire for her. Although still steeped in afterglow, Julia found this faintly ridiculous. She'd been sipping wine, cross-legged on the bed, and spat up a giddy mouthful, laughing, spattering his white shirt, which lay crumpled across the sheets. "It sounds like soup," she'd cried, unable to control her hiccups of laughter. Even while it was happening she was embarrassed at her mirthful incontinence, but Nicholas was still glazed with adoration, and only seemed to be happy that she was amused. He'd lain back, naked, his long, muscular body stretched out like a piece of fine cloth displayed for a buyer. He folded his arms behind his head and lay for a time, silent, not looking at Julia. Then he said, "I'm ... married."

Julia had despised him, just a grain's worth, for not having had the guts to say so before "consummating" with her. Then she became curious. Julia had seen his wife around town for years, and since their flirtation had entered a serious stage she'd been wondering whether he was cheating, or had some kind of arrangement; she tried to tell herself he might not even still be married to the woman. Now she knew he was still married, but none of the details. "I'd like to keep this between us," he'd said, "so as not to cause ... pain." God, Julia had thought, he can't even make himself say "my wife." But there he was, naked, warm as a fresh baguette, and he'd made her literally weak in the knees an hour earlier. She tossed back what was left of her wine, feeling the too-large mouthful dam painfully at the entrance to her throat. Why was it that liquid could sometimes be as hard to swallow as stone? She coughed and felt an unpleasant roughness behind her tongue, had to clear her throat. She looked at his graceful legs. Away from his face.

⋆⋆⋆

JULIA WAKES IN THE MIDDLE of the night after a vivid dream and feels an unpleasant buzzing in her chest. Her heart seems to lurch to a stop. She is lying in her bed in the dark and she is thinking, therefore she is still alive, so she is sure her heart has not actually stopped. She puts her hand on herself and tries to feel it beating, and cannot. Her chest feels empty. She is like a doll stuffed with crumpled paper. She probes the flesh around her sternum, lays her hand across it. Nothing. Finally she pushes her fingertips into the little hollow under her ear and finds her arterial pulse. It's plodding away, slow, like an ox in a field, the weight of the plow and the resistance of the earth pulling against its muscles with every step.

Having confirmed her continuing existence, Julia's mind turns to Nicholas. Why, at 6:20 a.m., woken from a nightmare involving her parents (as they usually do) and a plate of spaghetti (as they rarely do), her heart dull as waste within her — why then does she, without even choosing it, immediately think of Nicholas? There is a little spasm in her chest as she remembers he is missing, feels the beginnings of grief. Shaking her head, she tells herself she is too emotional, that he is simply busy, and has forgotten everyone else; he's often done that in the past. She turns on her side and thinks of his beautiful hands, imagines caressing his shoulders, pressing her face against his back while he talks on his cellphone — a liberty she has not taken in real life. Normally she folds herself up on the bed while he speaks with a kind of relaxed joviality he doesn't use with her. She imagines him finishing his call, snapping closed his phone, turning to face her and retracting into himself — and she reaches in past his reserve and pulls him down onto the futon to sit straddling her waist, where she can feel his weight. She laces her fingers through his and feels the size of his strong hands, open and wide as dinner plates against her smaller ones. This is the last thing she remembers before she falls asleep again.

❧

THE BIRTH CERTIFICATE LAY IN Julia's hand like a flake of debris wafted away from a burning house by the heat of the fire. Her first thought was: how could she have lied to me about my age? Julia felt as if she suddenly had a cataract over her mind. Seeing the simplest thing, like this piece of paper, was a struggle. Everything was opaque, unclear.

Her second thought was: Paul knew about this. *He has always known about this.* And she felt a wave of hatred rise through her, a powerful muscular seizure as if she were about to vomit. She closed her eyes, let it pass. Be reasonable, she thought, pressing a soothing palm against her disturbed stomach. Who knows what Paul knew, and when. Her eyes opened again. Although if Carol was pregnant in 1963 rather than 1965, everyone would have known it, wouldn't they? Julia's head was beginning to feel tight and painful. None of it made sense. Why would her mother have told her that she was two years younger than she really was? Julia had a moment of disorientation, as if she'd suddenly found herself in the wrong body. She caught herself thinking, that's why my breasts have shrunk, I'm really forty-two! She smiled, with a certain amount of bitterness.

≈✦≈

JULIA HAD EXPECTED TO FEEL grief when her mother died — or anger, relief, or possibly a wrenching sense of loss. This bewilderment — this she hadn't expected at all. She stared down at the paper in her hands. It was crumbly as baked phyllo dough and almost as brown, the lettering swollen with time. She was finding it difficult to understand what she was holding. She turned it over as if there might be instructions for her printed on the back, but it was blank.

Her mother's brother, Paul, had called her in mid-July. Carol was in hospital. It was "the cancer." Julia's heart had leaped painfully, but she'd kept her voice calm. How serious was it? Uncle Paul paused, sighed. They didn't know how long she had, he said. Hard to tell. At forty, Julia knew that plenty of her peers were taking care of aging parents or had already experienced a parental death. Yet she'd been completely out of contact with her mother for so long that Carol's illness — and, even more, her impending death — felt like an ambush, a strangely ambiguous one. She didn't quite know what to say to Paul; she didn't even really want to thank him for letting her know, although she did.

After the conversation, Julia had had a moment of silent rage, her temples knotted down to her jaw. Why couldn't her mother just die quickly and easily, spare herself and everyone else the anguish? Then Julia had put her head back and closed her eyes and willed her shoulders down, tried to follow her breath in, down, back up and out again.

Poor Uncle Paul. He was a good guy. He'd never understood why she didn't talk to her mother, although he hadn't held it against Julia, at least not to her face. Now he had the unpleasant job of being the bearer of this news, which must be tough for him to deal with, too. Probably tougher for him — he actually liked Carol, or at least had preserved a connection with her. Julia opened her eyes. Aside from his son, Bill, and grandson, Matthew, Carol and Julia were Paul's only surviving blood relations, and Carol was the last of his generation. He was much older than she was — twelve years (Carol had been a middle-aged accident for her mother) — and there was no other family left. He did have his second wife, Judy, who Julia actually liked more than anyone she was related to by blood. (Blood, Julia thought. What does that mean? Everybody has blood.)

Julia wondered what it would be like to be the last man standing, in a genealogical sense. She supposed it all depended on your past relations with your family. With the technical exception of Bill, who was a pleasant but distant person with whom Julia had no contact at all except at family events, she was alone in her generation. It wasn't the same, though: Paul was the oldest person in his family. Everyone who had preceded him was long gone, and he had had a reasonable expectation that his much-younger sister would outlive him. (Julia wondered what it would mean to her, really, when Paul died.)

It took Carol six weeks. Julia wished more and more fervently for her mother to be spared pain and suffering, her desire increasing in proportion to her mother's reported decline, although she didn't have any desire to take the bus across town and visit. On the contrary, in spite of Carol's worsening condition, Julia continued to feel her usual violent aversion to seeing her. Paul called weekly or more often from the Côte-des-Neiges apartment he shared with Aunt Judy to give Julia medical updates — fluid in the lungs, metastasized to the liver, morphine drip. Every time, he suggested that Julia come see Carol, but the anxiety that her mother provoked in Julia would kick in. She shut him down as nicely yet firmly as she could, one hand gripping the phone and the other, palm open, pushing against her chest, feeling the rise and fall of breath. Paul finally extracted from her a promise to attend the funeral, which Julia regretted as soon as the phone clicked back into its cradle, realizing that he was probably running back to Carol's bedside with the news already.

Well, what difference did it make? Julia went out and bought black summer-weight pantyhose, a new pair of black shoes. At home, unaccountably tired, she sat on the bed to put the shoes in the closet and found herself struck with a sort of painful, amused resignation as she leaned down and saw the lineup of black shoes, almost every pair she already owned. I've been preparing for this for years, she'd thought to herself, pressing her hands against her side where a sharp pain levered itself momentarily between her ribs.

And now this, this single piece of paper, nibbled at the edges by the decades.

NICHOLAS DOES RESEARCH IN THE field of architecture, usually architectural history. He writes, curates exhibits for museums, does a little teaching. He is a freelancer, highly respected and, while he complains, well enough paid to be able to make his living the way he wants to make it. Julia, who used to work in theatre, has noticed that it is an occupational hazard of people who are auxiliary to the arts — people who staff galleries, work in publishing, research for films or museums or universities — to feel chronically underpaid. This is because they compare themselves to the wealthy patrons who fund their jobs, or those in their fields who have achieved spectacular, highly visible success. Somehow they don't think to measure their lives against those of the women who answer the phones in their offices, as Julia once did, or the people who come in at night while they are finishing some overdue report, to empty their stylish wire wastepaper baskets, vacuum around them as they obligingly lift their feet. Nicholas is wry about his financial struggles, not resentful in the way that Julia finds unattractive in other people. The truth is he really works hard. It's one of the things Julia likes and respects in him. He works steadily, with focus, always has new projects in various stages of gestation. If he had children, Julia suspects, everything would be different. She sometimes looks at him while he is paying attention to something else, uncorking a bottle of wine perhaps, and tries to imagine what his children would look like. It's like trying to imagine a cake before it's baked: impossible, unless you've seen one made with the same recipe before.

They first met at an exhibit Nicholas had curated at the Canadian Centre for Architecture, a huge building enclosing a museum and research centre behind a long row of blank walls and windows. It lies like a huge, flat white cake along the edge of a stately lawn, tucked just behind the main streets of downtown, generously separating the edge of the city from a highway. Nicholas's display was strange, showing how the history of the design of the gardens of Europe reflected changes in the ideal conception of the state. Inside the small, gently lit rooms with their warm wooden floors was a series of panels showing dark old engravings of gardens reproduced against white backgrounds — the seventeenth-century design of the Jardin du Luxembourg, for example, or Le Nôtre's plan for the park at Versailles. The great panels were mounted between live box hedges sitting in great heavy planters, grey concrete moulded to resemble carved stone. Together they created a sort of pinked wall winding throughout the gallery. Julia drifted from panel to panel, finding herself much more interested in the plants than in the plans. Nicholas had appeared from behind one of the panels as she was fingering a glossy leaf. He slipped into her field of vision like a wraith, and when Julia looked up, startled, she found him peering at her, his gaze intense, black eyes deep and liquid. She'd jerked her hand away from the leaf, embarrassed to be found interested in the wrong thing, but he'd reached out and touched the same leaf, his finger long and elegant and his gesture graceful, and Julia had felt suddenly pulled in, like a swimmer who has stepped into an invisible, irresistible current.

She'd come back to the long, low cake within weeks, for a series of courses Nicholas gave. Architectural history for non-architects. There were six people in the evening class. Aside from Julia, there were a retired couple, ex-teachers with matching chinos and cotton crew neck sweaters in complementary colours; a technical writer who rode his bicycle to every class, rushing in each week while unclipping his helmet just as Nicholas began to speak; a young Romanian engineer who spoke little but sat back in his seat and watched everything from under heavy eyelids; and Andrea, a pale sylph, a wry smile constantly enlivening her well-shaped lips. As Nicholas spoke — his voice gravelly and deceptively hesitant, approaching and retreating and then approaching the same ideas over and over again from different angles until they gradually rose to view in multiple dimensions — Julia found herself watching Andrea when she wasn't watching Nicholas. During the first class Nicholas had showed them slides of Palladian villas, and when Andrea raised her hand he'd looked over at her and pointed at her with his chin, saying, "Yes, Andrea ... Palladio." After this he continued to address her as "Palladio," which Julia thought embarrassed the woman, although it was hard to see past her ironic smile.

The first night after class, as everyone dispersed, Julia went into the bathroom. She loved the bathroom at the CCA. The doors — set back and so discreetly labelled as to be difficult to identify, giving her the thrill of being in on a secret — led to the sleek interior, tiny golden slips of glycerin soap melting into their slight depressions in the dark stone countertop beside each swan-necked faucet. On leaving the bathroom she almost ran straight into Nicholas, carrying his box of slides and his briefcase. "Door's this way," he'd said, gesturing with his slide box, as if she'd somehow wandered into the almost-hidden bathroom by mistake instead of going down the grand staircase to the exit. They'd trotted down the stairs together,

Julia stiff with shyness, Nicholas almost seeming not to remember she was there by his side. As they approached the exit he'd stepped deftly ahead of her and held the door open, a courtly gesture at odds with his gruffness, and then as they emerged he'd turned toward the parking lot and said, "I'll give you a ride." Julia followed dumbly, appalled by his easy confidence. What made him assume she needed, or even wanted, a ride? From him? But in fact she was willing enough. They pulled out onto the street, passing the technical writer pedalling diligently on his mountain bike; Nicholas asked her where she lived and she found that her place was in the opposite direction from his, but he merely turned the wheel, letting it slide back under his palms as the car turned under them.

During subsequent classes Julia sometimes felt almost tipsy in the waves of sexual energy that sloshed around the room. The retired teachers and the technical writer seemed to be immune. Julia herself often felt she was outside it, watching the currents flow between Nicholas, Andrea, and Michael the Romanian. She could see the minuscule movements of their eyes, their face muscles twitching. She didn't feel affected, yet as the weeks passed she became more animated, more confident, growing into a larger version of herself. She didn't realize it had anything to do with the class, or with Nicholas. She heard the lively edge in his voice as he called on "Palladio" to offer an opinion — solely, Julia often thought, for the sake of being able to call the woman by that nickname, to see her large warm brown eyes turn in his direction. Andrea often glanced at Julia first as if to acknowledge Nicholas's intent, and during every class Julia decided that afterward she would walk to the metro with Andrea, to have a chance to talk to her. But at the end of each class Nicholas managed to be standing at the doorway when Julia was passing through it, and each time he offered her a ride, or simply made clear that he assumed he would be giving her one. After it happened the third or fourth time Julia let herself relax into the pattern, assuming it too — fingering a small knot of anxiety that one week she might find herself mistaken.

In the car that first night, Julia found herself bantering with Nicholas. As they discussed how much reading he could reasonably pile on his diverse class during this brief eight-week course, he said "I don't want to be cruel." Julia replied "I'm sure you're more than capable of it," shocking herself with her cheek-bordering-on-rudeness, as well as the grin she heard in her own voice. She couldn't relax her face enough to melt away the grin, and sat with her bag at her feet, wondering why the hell she'd said such a thing to a man she'd only ever met twice. He didn't seem bothered; on the contrary, he'd continued chatting as if that were a normal thing to say while exchanging pleasantries with an almost-stranger.

❧

SHE WAS WEARING HER FUNERAL outfit when she went to see the exhibit. She frequently wore the clothes; they weren't new for the return of her mother's dust to the dust of the cemetery. They were her only really stylish skirt and shirt that fit, and they were, like most of her clothes, black. The weather had turned relatively cool almost immediately after that hellish afternoon at the graveside, so she'd put on the new panty-hose and then, for the hell of it — she was going to a museum after all — the new shoes. In Montreal, she knew, it is entirely unremarkable to dress all in black; no one assumes that it signifies mourning — an association that, had it occurred to Julia, would have kept her from choosing these clothes. But it didn't occur to her, so she dressed herself, coincidentally, in the same clothes she'd worn to her mother's funeral, shrugged on her red trench coat, and went to see an exhibit about European gardens.

Julia had rarely been to the CCA; she had no more than a passing interest in architecture. Working at Le Jardinier had brought her into contact with books and images about the history of gardens, though, and she figured this would be a dutiful, enriching sort of outing on a Saturday afternoon. Olivier had given her one of the store's free passes to the exhibit, certainly a deciding factor — both in removing the financial disincentive to going and by communicating a tacit expectation that she attend. Since breaking up with Stewart almost exactly two years before, Julia had made herself go out to all kinds of things she was only barely interested in. Classical music recitals at McGill, which necessitated a trudge up the steps of the music building on Sherbrooke Street, past the doughty presiding figure of the seated Queen Victoria. Poetry readings at the Double Hook Book Shop — when there was still a Double Hook Book Shop — crammed into the basement, surrounded by children's books, plastic glass of box wine in hand; the creaking, painted woodwork gave more the impression of a favourite auntie's house than the literary institution she knew it was.

These outings were preventive measures. Julia did not go on them so much to meet people as to avoid waking up one day unable to move from her bed, with long, tenacious roots growing straight out of her jellied ass and into the mattress, nourished by an accumulating loam of old chip bags, back issues of *People* magazine, and half-finished crossword puzzles from the Saturday *Globe* or *Gazette*. She did have a very brief fling, with a woman named Lauren she met at the lesbian and gay film festival. They'd found themselves sitting side by side during a program of amateurish semi-pornography, and when the lights came up Lauren caught the corner of Julia's eye and they shared a suppressed laugh. They followed each other out of the screening room and down the National Film Board's glassed-in switchback stairs to emerge onto the corner of St. Denis and de Maisonneuve, and while the wind made their cheeks rosy and their feet cold, they discovered that they had tickets to the same seven o'clock screening. They went to grab a falafel and ended up in Lauren's bed instead, her cherry mouth moist and hot, her brilliant eyes holding Julia's gaze for days across a series of late nights and lazy weekends. During that period Julia went to a whole different assortment of things she was barely interested in — dinner parties full of chickpeas at Lauren's shared house, lingerie-draped art events at dyke bars. At the time those were meant as fertilizer for the doomed-from-the-start relationship that, painfully but mercifully, died of drought within weeks. In retrospect the whole thing took on a sadly prophylactic air.

So Julia found herself attired for her mother's funeral inside one of the well-manicured rooms of the CCA on a Saturday afternoon in September, fingering the leaf of a hedge. In the middle of long insomniac nights, her mind kept on "blend" by the pressure of wanting Nicholas so much and so painfully, she hardly remembered that on that afternoon of their first meeting she hadn't instantly known they would become lovers. She thought of it as if she had stumbled and sunk immediately into his black eyes like Alice into the rabbit hole, a journey of incomprehensible length that became, itself, the destination. She had that dizzying sensation of falling that was at once fear and freedom, movement and a strange kind of stasis.

She remembered the moment as if it were a still from a film: a close-up of his fingers on the leaf where the oils and the sweat of her fingers must still have been clinging to the surface pores of the plant. Fingers on leaf. In her dark bedroom Julia often closed her eyes, grieving the absence of sleep, trying to call it with this flimsy physical gesture of the eyelids; imprinted on the insides of her thin lids she found a pattern of leaves. From above entered two large, golden fingers, like the hand of God reaching for Adam on the ceiling of the Sistine Chapel. The thought made her want to laugh bitterly, but she was too exhausted to laugh in any way at all, so she just forced what little air remained in her lungs through her nose with a short puff. It was all the disdain she could muster toward the grandiosity of her own vision.

❧

JULIA KNEW WHO NICHOLAS'S WIFE was, had seen her in the store on occasion, although they hadn't ever actually met. She made beautiful handmade reproductions of period furniture that sometimes, apparently, cost as much as an original, were the originals to be had. She was something of a local celebrity. At one time Olivier had carried faux-Victorian plant stands of her design, although it had been years since Julia had seen her standing at Olivier's desk, car keys dangling from her hardworking hands with their calluses and chipped finger-nails. Julia was impressed that she still did her own work, still wrecked her own hands. "Well yes," Olivier said, "she's an artist. That's why we buy what she makes." He smiled patiently at Julia, who understood that by "we" Olivier did not mean him or her. She certainly couldn't afford anything made by Deepa O'Malley; Olivier probably could, but only as an indulgence, and with a professional discount. Rather, he meant the higher end of Le Jardinier's clientele, who lived either in the increasingly affluent Plateau neighbourhood around the St. Denis Street store, or who drove south from Outremont or east from Westmount to get there, combining a stroll along the fashionable shopping street or dinner at L'Express with a browse among the roses and miniature fig trees, glass vases and gargoyles of stone arranged behind the lush display window.

The first night of their affair, the night of their "consumma-tion," when Nicholas mentioned his wife, Julia had occupied herself with the sight of his legs. His feet crossed casually at the ankles, his big toes much bigger than the other four on each foot. The smallest toes on each side softly curled, baby animals asleep. He'd stayed quiet, letting her think, breathe. Finally, stroking his calves lightly with her fingertips as if to reassure herself that he was actually there, she'd looked up at him and said, "I know who your wife is. I've seen her in the store." He hadn't responded, hadn't twitched an eyelid. She supposed he could assume, as a matter of course, that anyone he met knew of his wife. Then Julia had looked up and around her little apartment. While she was looking away Nicholas got up and went into the bathroom, returning with his face and hands — and other parts, maybe — freshly washed and smelling of soap. He'd reached for the wine bottle and emptied the last slosh into Julia's glass, handed it over to her, then sat back down on the edge of the bed. Julia looked guiltily at the spatter marks on his shirt, which she'd stained with wine earlier. "Maybe I should put some salt on that," she'd said. Nicholas had waved his hand, dismissing her worry. Later, when she realized how fastidious he was, how careful of his resources, she understood how deeply he must have been infatuated with her at that moment.

⋙⋘

THE "INNOCENT" PHASE. JULIA THINKS about those first few days when everything was still unselfconscious, impetuous, full of potential. She thinks of the first time he came to her place after their first night; he stepped through the door and she fell into his arms and they kissed each other so fiercely and so deliciously that Julia thought they might just keep kissing until something, some extremity — starvation, perhaps — intervened to pull their mouths apart.

Now Nicholas puckers up for a matronly peck most of the time, and Julia's mouth is hungry. She staves off the feeling by pressing his hands to her lips, by smelling his skin, by taking his elegantly formed penis into her mouth instead. It's like animal candy, sweet and warm, perfect food that can be enjoyed forever without being consumed or diminished. She sometimes gets so involved that she almost forgets he's there on the other end of it, and she's startled when he cries out, flooding her mouth with more warmth, more sweetness.

He came to see her on his way home from teaching a course, only days after the ravenous kiss; she had a concert to attend that evening, and was just buttoning her blouse when he rang her doorbell. She'd returned to the bedroom to finish dressing and he followed her, walking up behind her and not stopping until he'd pushed her over onto the bed, his long body pressing her against the covers until she couldn't recover her breath and she pushed him off. He lay there on his side, but glued to the length of her. She propped herself up on her elbows and took deep breaths, holding one of his hands between hers. He told her about his work, his plans for dinner, and she began to smell and kiss his fingers one by one, deeply concentrated; as they talked his other hand stroked the backs of her thighs in her black pantyhose. The warmth of his blood came through his skin, through the thin nylon, making her shiver. He pushed her skirt up so he could stroke her thighs more freely and found a hole in the pantyhose she hadn't known was there. He touched her bare leg through the hole with his fingertips and it felt to her as if no one had ever touched her skin before. "Did you do this," he'd asked mischievously, caressing the back of her thigh through the unexpected opening, "so I could feel your skin?" She didn't see his face but she heard the smile in his voice. Her brain felt thick and slow, and she was ashamed of not having a quick reply for him; as she was feeling stupid she was regretting the waste, due to her self-consciousness, of this moment of warmth and pleasure. A loss that she knew was taking place only in her own mind, but which was nevertheless flat and bitter.

The truth, if she will remember honestly, is that there was no innocent phase. Innocent moments, perhaps, tiny sparks of true freedom, but rare and fleeting. From the very beginning she kept herself tightly bound, terrified of letting herself want too much, of frightening him away with her need. He retracted himself almost immediately too, like a Venus fly-trap touched, burdened by his own fears and imperatives. Julia has no idea what keeps them attached to each other. Even at the moments when they have disliked each other there has been something connecting them, and they have remained in each other's orbits, one way or another. He is vivid in her mind, coming to her consciousness at the least provocation, or none at all. She has no idea whether she occupies his thoughts when he is not with her. He must think of her sometimes, because he calls her sometimes.

One day Nicholas asked Julia to meet him that evening in Mile End — far enough from her part of the Plateau, farther from his neighbourhood of Verdun perched on the southeastern rim of the island. She found him sitting at a table in the window of the humble Romolo Café, Bernard Street's traffic passing beyond the glass, a constantly shifting parade of Hasidic women with baby carriages and their children in matching outfits, Greek matrons with net bags of groceries, students and hipsters converging on the yuppier restaurant across the street that boasted of its vast selection of rare and imported beers. A French newspaper lay in an untidy heap on the table next to Nicholas. As Julia sat down she could see he'd done the crossword puzzle in French and she felt affectionate admiration for him. She couldn't do crosswords in French herself — her vocabulary was much too limited, restricted to the words she needed for her daily life: grocery shopping, banking, selling bulbs and ergonomic trowels and hyacinth postcards. He went to the bar to buy their drinks and, returning to their table, began to speak to her in French. She knew he'd been speaking to the bartender in French and simply hadn't switched back, Montreal etiquette being that the conversation continues in the language in which it began. This happened to her occasionally too; it was strangely awkward. He caught himself as she hesitated. It was nearly dark in the bar, the music and conversation around them so loud it was almost like another wall; she looked up at his strained and shadowed face and wished she could erase the unease by leaning across and kissing him. But she knew that would erase nothing, and it gave her pain to feel so powerless, to feel her love for him so useless. It was one of those Montreal moments, that was all.

⚜

DROPPING THE PAPER ON THE table, Julia stumbled to the sink and hit the tap, overfilling her glass of water and slurping it desperately. She stuck her hand into the flow of cool wet and smeared her face with it, standing and listening to the rush of white noise pouring past her. Nothing made sense. It was as if she could no longer trust the floor to be solid. She hit the tap again to turn it off and then picked her way back to her chair.

Think clearly, Julia. What were her parents doing in 1963? In 1963 they were still in Toronto. Her father was finishing his grad degree, her mother was typing theses in their third-floor apartment to keep them in rent and cheap Chinese food. Julia remembers her mother talking about how hot it was that summer in their two airless rooms. How Julia's father would appear, breathing hard at the top of the stairs, at the end of his long day of teaching summer courses, doing his own research and writing his thesis, and Carol would send him right back down two rickety flights for bags of ice from the corner store. Julia had wondered why she didn't just go down the stairs herself. Now she suddenly understands. Carol was seven, eight months pregnant. She must have felt horribly trapped in her hot little room, her big belly wedged in behind the typing table. Someone else's thesis, interleaved with carbon pages, piled beside her.

Carol was proud of the fact that she and Raphael, Julia's father, had lived together "before it was fashionable," disguising their unmarried state with a four-dollar ring they'd bought on a vacation in Atlantic City. She used to say that, then look down, as if she was also a bit embarrassed. Julia kneaded her temples. They got married when they returned to Montreal, June 1964. Julia grew up with the photographs. The big one in the living room, a black-and-white image of Carol and Raph facing each other in profile, young and looking somehow unformed, their faces serious. Carol clutched her nosegay of lilies, her hair piled in fat curls at the back of her head; Raphael looked skinnier and sharper than Julia ever remembered him, his face all glaring white planes and hollow black shadows. "Just before we broke the glass," Carol always told Julia, her voice soft with remembering.

There were also the photos in the fat quilted album that had already started to turn yellowy-grey by the time Julia was old enough to look at it. She and her mother sometimes sat and leafed through it together, Carol telling stories about the wedding. This was a game Julia played with her mother, never with her father. Carol liked to talk about her beautiful ceremony, her wonderful reception. The three-layer chocolate cake with white butter cream frosting. The ice-blue satin dress and dyed-to-match shoes and Raph's matching cummerbund; the bridesmaids' dresses of pale orchid, the miniature pink roses and sprays of baby's breath in their hair. Julia knew her parents had really loved one another. When her father died of a heart attack in 1985, her mother had been devastated.

Odd fragments came back to Julia now, unbidden. "Why didn't you have a white dress, Mummy?" she'd asked, the album open across her skinny seven-year-old legs in their white tights. She was looking at her favourite picture, the only unposed one, of Raph pushing a fat blob of icing into Carol's laughing mouth with his finger, a bashful grin on his face, Carol's eyes liquid with adoration.

"I liked the blue one," Carol had said shortly, and Julia had understood, without having a clue why, that she shouldn't ask any more. Julia had flipped through the rest of the album without speaking then, ending on the last page. There, Julia knew there was a picture that didn't quite belong, tucked under the final group shot of the two families together. She pulled it out. It was a black-and-white picture of the lined face of a newborn baby, a shock of black hair sticking up almost comically, a faint crust of cradle cap barely visible at the hairline. "So small," Carol said wistfully, touching the picture with a finger.

"How big was I, Mummy?" Julia had asked, knowing that Carol also loved to tell the story of Julia's birth, proud that she had pushed all ten pounds of her out in under six hours.

Carol smiled and stroked Julia's face. "You weighed 'a whopping ten pounds,' according to the doctor. You were always my big girl!"

Julia, in her kitchen, looked back at the strange piece of paper in her hand. She turned it over. The other side was spotted with age. She turned it back again. Place of birth: Toronto, Ontario, Canada. Mother's name: Carol Rhoda Schneider. Father's name: Raphael Goodman. A throbbing began between Julia's eyebrows. Suddenly she jumped up and stalked into her bedroom. She yanked open the top drawer of her dresser and dug under the accumulation of stretched-useless tights and washed-out socks. There they were. Her passport. An envelope with $40 in U.S. currency left over from her last trip south. Her birth certificate. She pulled it out so fast she was afraid she might have ripped it. No, it was intact. Her birth certificate. Julia Rachel Goodman. She breathed, sinking to the edge of the futon. Born May 31, 1965, Montreal, Quebec. Mother's name: Carol Rhoda Goodman, née Schneider. Father's name: Raphael Goodman. Julia frowned. She took the document back to the kitchen and placed it on the table next to the other one, smoothing them both carefully with flat, sweaty palms. Which one was real?

✥

JULIA DREAMED SHE WAS RUNNING. She was wearing old white low-top sneakers and a big loose skirt that swished around her legs as she ran. She was young, maybe sixteen, and running through the grounds of a big, busy private school — her school, in the dream, although nowhere she'd ever really been or seen. No one seemed to notice that she was running until she ran past a man, who said to her in a low voice as she passed him, "You're running." She kept going; as she passed through a large stone archway she understood that it had been Nicholas. Though he didn't know her yet, somehow he had seen her, here, where no one else saw her. She wanted to turn back and find him but she couldn't; she had to keep running.

She woke from that dream the day he left for Spain and North Africa, where he was going to do research for a new project — and, she knew, drink Spanish wine, eat couscous. Perhaps dally with Spanish and Moroccan lovers. She didn't expect him to be faithful to her — whatever that meant, in their situation. He was already cheating on his wife, although Julia had the vague impression that they had an unusual arrangement that allowed him, and perhaps Deepa O'Malley as well, a certain latitude in their amorous lives. She'd never asked him, feeling it would be asking for an unacceptable intimacy — and also afraid to bring this sin, if it was one, out into the open between them. He was careful, but not furtive, about seeing her; he didn't appear to be required to be home for dinner every night, or hold to any other such domestic routine. So Julia was surprised early on when, in the course of their first rending argument, he'd looked away and said, "I haven't been ... a faithful lover."

It had followed on weeks of awkwardness and miscommunication. He'd offered her a pass to a panel discussion he was participating in at the CCA, and the reception afterward; she'd declined because he hadn't invited her to go with him, and she felt too awkward showing up alone — thinking, in her insecurity, that perhaps he didn't really want her there at all. Later she felt he was angry with her for not going, but he wouldn't actually say it.

A week later he was making a presentation at an architecture seminar at one of the universities. He said he would call afterward so they could meet, but he didn't call that day, or the following days. Julia stewed and wept and finally phoned him with the intention of telling him to fuck off. He acted as if it had been an inconsequential mistake. The professor had invited Nicholas to join them for a drink afterward, it got late. Julia felt sick, hearing this explanation, which was so casual that it was as humiliating as the original slight. He'd continued to talk, inviting her to dinner at a little Italian place near the Jean-Talon market. She found herself seeing his face in her mind again, wanting him with a physical urge that felt like the impulse to run through open space. He cheerfully urged her to come, asking her to help him drink a very good bottle of wine someone had given him in thanks for a favour. She'd gone, and he'd been lovely, feeding her buttery cloves of roasted garlic from his own plate, painting her lips with wine with his fingertips before kissing her in the shadows of their corner table, sipping at her lips like a hummingbird.

When they finally got down to arguing, it was all strangely oblique; there were no issues, only ragged emotions from both of them. Julia found herself mostly mute, feeling that it hardly mattered what she said if they didn't understand each other anyway. She was making her way recrimination by recrimination toward the door, intending to fling it open and demand that he leave, when he hung his head slightly, eyes averted, and said, "I haven't been a faithful lover." Julia only managed to stammer, "What do you mean by faithful?" She was genuinely curious. He didn't answer and she suddenly realized that it was the wrong question, because he was really telling her that he had fallen out of love with her. She had turned without speaking and made her way to his coat, fumbling to collect his boots and thrust them at him; then as she put her hand on the doorknob, he'd come up behind her and turned her around by her shoulders and offered her a goodbye peck, as if they'd just had a friendly game of checkers.

Afterward, stomping through the empty streets to shed some of the rattling energy that was making her hands shake, she was astonished by the utter failure of two normally articulate adults to actually say what they meant in any clear or useful way. She felt tears tracing icy tracks down the sides of her face in the February wind and hugged herself as she passed under the big trees at the edge of Jeanne-Mance Park, their long bare fingers rubbing each other, soughing in the night wind. She saw that their inability to understand each other was due to fear and she hated both herself and Nicholas for it. Her heart was a hole in her chest and she lay rigid and wakeful in her bed that night, the duvet kicked away and her skin cold, her throat raw and clotted.

A week of silence later she emailed Nicholas, brief and formal, to ask for the return of a book she'd borrowed from the store for him, and he'd set a time for her to meet him at a café situated conveniently between her work and her home. They ended up back at her place, and he left half a bottle of French Chardonnay later. Julia stood rigid by the window, watching him walk away, her underwear on inside out.

❧❦❧

BILL LIVED IN TORONTO. JULIA considered going on the earliest train and coming back that night so she wouldn't have to stay with him, but it seemed rude, so she put off going to see him. She wasn't sure why she didn't want to start by asking Uncle Paul about the birth certificate, except that he clearly hadn't wanted to discuss it in the car, and he also obviously had chosen not to mention it to Julia any time before that. She didn't know whether he'd known about this since 1963 or had only found out about it in the weeks preceding Carol's death, but it gave her a queasy stomach to think of how many people in her family might have participated in hiding something that could affect her life so intimately.

It seemed unfairly difficult, the prospect of finding out — well, she didn't know exactly what she needed to find out. That was part of the problem. It was also hard because it seemed that the story was scattered, embedded in the moments of Carol's life, and too many of them had disappeared in the same instant they'd arrived. The moment when Carol stood on the sidewalk outside the doctor's office in Toronto, the fake wedding ring on her hand, and imagined her baby, still wholly unknown, rooting itself within her. The moment when she felt the glass crunch under her ice-blue shoe, a blessing to banish emptiness. The moment when she felt Raph's hand on the milk-pale skin of her hip for the first time — or for the hundredth time — and felt that she could do anything to keep him. The very second when Carol was struck by the image of her face suspended in the bathroom mirror and saw her own weakness, and was afraid.

Julia touched her cheek meditatively with her fingertips. Here was a moment right now, and now it was gone. She was losing her own life in pale little bits like flakes of skin rubbed off by the wind, carried away and dispersed, irrecoverable.

Olivier went out to an appointment at the bank, leaving Julia alone at the cash. There were other people coming in later, but for the moment she was the only staff and the store was quiet. She was supposed to be redesigning the display area at the back, a flagstone patio they used in warmer weather to show potted trees, water garden fixtures, and so on. She found it hard to focus on something so far away as spring. She was starting her architecture course tonight and wanted to enjoy anticipating that. She knew she had to do something, take some kind of step, make some kind of decision, before this stupid birth certificate thing would stop bothering her. Anger made her grit her teeth. Her mother had found a way to reach over and twist Julia's innards from beyond the grave. She stabbed her ballpoint pen repeatedly into the notepad that lay on the glass counter next to the computer terminal that served as a cash register. It made dark little blue marks on the paper, like blemishes on a teenaged face.

Julia didn't know whether Bill knew about this whole thing. She suspected he did, because Uncle Paul hadn't shown any hesitation about handing the envelope over to Julia in the back of Bill's car with Bill sitting in the front, six inches away from them. Bill was older than she was — he would have been about ten years old already when she was born. Julia felt a twinge between her eyebrows. When she thought she'd been born, she corrected herself. Still, if he was eight years old in 1963 and his aunt had given birth, he might have heard about it, then or later. She pressed two fingertips into the tender spot and rubbed. She'd fallen asleep immediately the night before, then woken up after an hour and been unable to fall asleep again until almost dawn.

She'd lost so much sleep in the last year or two of her relationship with Stewart, she'd only begun to feel lately that she'd caught up. She knew it wasn't only lack of sleep that had made her so deeply tired, but a sort of exhaustion of the emotions. Exhaustion of the soul, she'd have said, if she believed in souls. Olivier had been very understanding, had given her a month away from the store that August, which was a very busy month for them. Stewart had gone kayaking in B.C. with his brother in July while Julia worked long days at Le Jardinier, and when he returned there was a stiffness between them that was worse than the bickering and petty sniping they'd been inflicting on each other before he left. They spent entire days in the apartment together without speaking, somehow occupying the same space without any contact, physical or verbal. Julia would come home from work, eat some toast or salad because she had no energy to cook, then lie on the couch with a glass of ice water, damp with a faint layer of sweat, and watch TV until bedtime. Then, knowing Stewart was in their bed, she wouldn't be able to bring herself to go to it. Usually she ended up beached in the dark living room in the erratic blue light of the TV until she finally fell into a fitful slumber, dried tears making her face stiff and itchy.

Stewart would wait until she'd eaten her toast and installed herself on the couch and then cook himself something. The smell of his food revolted Julia so much she'd even wondered, briefly, if she might be pregnant — but she knew she couldn't be. They hadn't had sex together since well before Stewart went away, and the last time Julia had only given Stewart a blow job, at his request. Afterward he'd let go of her hair, which he'd been holding in his fist, and simply got up and walked away. She heard him washing her saliva off himself and she'd felt sick. No risk there, she thought grimly.

She could no longer remember why she didn't leave earlier. Any point in the year before they actually split would have done, the long months of unhappy fighting and nastiness. The night of the blow job that left Julia swollen-eyed and miserable, kneeling on the floor of the bedroom by the side of the bed. Or any day during the weeks after Stewart returned, folded in on himself, nursing his own wretchedness.

Julia searched her mind. She did remember having a feeling of being utterly lost, stranded on the living room couch, simply unable to imagine where to go. That would have been depression, she supposed. Then Stewart announced he'd received a chunk of money from his mother to buy a house. He'd made an offer before leaving for B.C. and it had been accepted while he was away. He'd be leaving in two weeks, when he took possession. Julia heard this and thought her stomach might thrust itself right up and out through her mouth, it seized so violently; she hunched on all fours on the floor, because she could not stand, and retched as if Stewart himself was caught in her throat.

In retrospect she could see how Stewart was trying to keep things orderly in his life, as he always did. In his own strange way he was probably making an effort to be considerate when he chose to move, instead of forcing her to leave the apartment. At the time none of that was apparent to her, and if it had been, it wouldn't have mattered. Two days later Olivier's wife, Claudette, had driven Julia to their little condo in St-Sauveur with three bags of groceries and four bottles of wine, and Julia had stayed there, living on Aspirin, coffee, and a steady stream of Merlot, for almost a month. Olivier and Claudette phoned her every couple of days to make sure she was still alive, and she spent late night hours talking on the phone to her oldest friend, Campbell, in Halifax.

Campbell had been gently advising her to leave Stewart since before she herself understood how unhappy they were. Campbell offered to send her a ticket to come stay with him, but she knew he couldn't really afford it, and didn't have room for her in the little apartment he shared with his grad-student boyfriend. Besides, the truth was Julia didn't actually want to be with anybody. She just wanted to be obliterated for a while, as if in an induced coma, until the worst of the pain passed.

She'd thought that once she got back to the apartment, now emptied of Stewart's things (and — typically for Stewart, who was dutiful, if not nice — scrubbed clean, a full roll of toilet paper in the bathroom, a fresh filter in the basket of the coffee maker), that she'd be able to eat and sleep normally again. Instead she found herself filled up with emptiness, the quiet echoing absence. Not Stewart's absence, exactly, but the absence of a direction, of substance in her life. It took almost a year before she was able to settle into something like calm, before she could call sleep to her and have it come and stay while she passed through the night.

After that Julia slept easily nine or ten hours a night, hungrily, as if she had to make up for all the hours she'd lost in the previous year. She knew that wasn't how sleep worked but she couldn't shake the feeling — and she was glad to let more than a third of any given day evaporate in unconsciousness. Even after she started going to museums and concerts and coffee dates with friends again, the details of her daily existence seemed to be keeping her life warm until she was ready to use it again. Gradually she started to achieve some kind of balance, the ability to get satisfaction from her work, to enjoy her friends. Her sleep habits seemed to even out too, for which she was grateful. Until this.

Idly, she drew lines connecting the stab marks on the pad. She wasn't going all the way to Toronto, maybe for nothing, Julia decided. Nor was she ready to talk to Uncle Paul yet. She was going to talk to her Aunt Judy.

NICHOLAS SENT JULIA AN EMAIL a few days after he arrived in Madrid, from an internet café near his hotel. It was voluble, for Nicholas. His hotel came complete with a parakeet, which lived in the courtyard and seemed to prefer Nicholas's windowsill as its perch. A friend was taking him on a tour of Moorish landmarks, to Granada to see the Alhambra and to Cordoba to visit the Great Mosque, after which they planned to spend a day swimming in the sea and eating fish before returning to Madrid. The coarse white cotton bathrobe provided by his cheap hotel had an indelible pink stain on it; it reminded him of her.

Julia sat at the computer in the office at Le Jardinier and let the joy wash through her. In the months since they'd begun their affair Nicholas had often travelled, alone or with his wife, or in some work-related capacity. When they were feeling at ease with each other before a departure, he was especially tender and affectionate; when there was tension, he was brisk and businesslike. But he always told Julia where he was going and when he would return, and he always replied to her emails.

He was hard to fathom; she knew it was probably a mistake to read anything into the length or contents of his communications. Still it made her happy to hear from him, to read something he'd written to her — for her. She also felt glad for him because she knew he loved Spain, delighted in his research, got great pleasure from the ocean, the sounds and smells and brilliant surface of it. As much as she'd thought over and over again that she'd stopped loving him — after one of their strange, painful arguments, or one of his long silences that felt to Julia as if he had turned away from her as if from an unsatisfying meal, half-eaten — she often missed him with an ache in her chest. Yet she wished not for him to be back with her, but only for him to be content where he was, whomever he was with. She honestly didn't care if he was rolling in Spanish hay, as long as he still wanted to see her when he returned. She could imagine him frowning at the little green bird staring at him from his windowsill, its round eye fixed on his dark, liquid ones as the afternoon light turned gold and then flattened into dusk. The wine-stained bathrobe lying limp across the bedspread. Should have put salt on that, Julia thought, smiling to herself.

━◆━

ON THE OTHER END OF the phone, Aunt Judy paused. Julia thought her aunt must know why she wanted to talk to her; she waited, listening to the silence. "Come over for lunch, dolly," Judy finally said. "Come Sunday. You don't mind if Paul's out at the club?" "The club" was a group of old men who'd been friends for decades; they met at one or another's house every couple of Sundays to drink tea and kibbitz. Julia was sure Judy knew she didn't mind.

"That's fine, Aunt Judy. Actually I'll be glad to have the chance to talk you alone." She heard Judy sigh.

"That's right, dolly," Judy said softly. "We'll talk."

On Sunday, Julia took the bus over the mountain to Paul and Judy's house in Côte-des-Neiges. The day was clear as they passed the lookout and Julia saw the Olympic Stadium, with its insectoid roof, in the distance. As she passed Beaver Lake she thought of the times, early in their relationship, that she and Stewart had come up here to walk in the sun among the running children, eating french fries from the chalet in summer, stepping aside to avoid the middle-aged folk dancers who gathered under the chalet's eaves, or huddling over hot chocolate steam in winter. Once they'd crossed the road and gone into the police stables and visited the horses that patrolled the mountain, the clean smell of manure and straw perfuming the warmth that rose from their great calm bodies. She'd thought, then, that she and Stewart would come back here in their own middle age, and after. Julia looked down at her hands. How little we realize, as we live our days, that we are painting the world with our memories of ourselves. She looked up again, and gazed out over the acres of headstones that grew like a stunted orchard across the descending flank of the hill.

As the bus followed the curves of the road out of the park, and habitations and commercial buildings reappeared, Julia realized that this was the first time she'd revisited the neighbourhood, with its square attached houses and aging low-rise apartment blocks, since her mother, who'd lived in a small flat here, had died. As the bus cruised toward the familiar street, the cemetery behind her and the elegant stone tower of the Université de Montréal rising to her right, Julia felt a sudden lightness. She couldn't run into her mother by accident anymore. She wouldn't suffer the jolt of spotting Carol carrying her groceries across the street and being afraid Carol would turn and see her. Julia breathed.

Aunt Judy's house smelled wonderful. She was younger than Paul, and still spry. She'd set the table with a crisply ironed white cloth printed with garlands of purple flowers and golden leaves. It was covered with dishes of food, more than the two of them could possibly eat, and the smell of something sweet and buttery floated out of the kitchen. Julia presented her aunt with a small bouquet of purple irises with splashy yellow centres she'd bought on the way to the bus stop, and Judy bustled into the kitchen to cut the stems, reappearing with the flowers arranged in a slim cut-glass vase, which she placed on the table, moving all the dishes around to make room for it in the centre. Finally satisfied, she looked up at

Julia and pointed. "Look," she said, smiling, "it matches my tablecloth!"

They sat and ate, Julia consuming about twice her normal amount in an effort not to slight Aunt Judy by overlooking any of the multitude of lovingly prepared offerings. Judy managed to eat in spite of the fact that she didn't sit down for more than a minute at a time, jumping up constantly to bring salt from the kitchen, adjust the blinds in the dining room, put the kettle on, turn the kettle off. While they ate, Judy kept the conversation going, telling Julia about her grand-children, the play she saw in Yiddish at the Saidye Bronfman Centre, an interview she heard on the radio with Alan Dershowitz. She asked Julia how she was and Julia, in an effort to say more than her usual "Fine, thank you," described to Judy her first two architecture classes, the second of which had been the night before. She found herself chattering on and on about Nicholas, about his impressive erudition, his clever way of teaching, his magnetic presence in the class that made everyone eager to learn, to please him. Judy got up to clear their plates, returning with a saucer of lemon slices arranged in a pinwheel, went back into the kitchen, came out again with a cut-glass bowl of cube sugar, sat down and then got up again to fetch spoons, and as she disappeared through the doorway again Julia realized she was describing Nicholas's hands to her aunt's receding back. She immediately shut her mouth and, simultaneously, her cheeks went hot. Aunt Judy came out again, spoons in one hand and a loaf of still-warm honey cake in the other. Apparently she hadn't noticed.

They ate the honey cake and drank the tea, and when

they'd finished eating Aunt Judy pushed the cake plates aside and folded her hands, looking over at Julia. "So, Julia."

Julia's pulse shot through her, making her breath come short. She pulled the manila envelope from her purse. Her hands felt hard to control, as if they really belonged to someone else, and she had difficulty spreading the thin mouth of the envelope. Eventually she succeeded in pulling the two birth certificates out and laid them on the table upside down so they were facing Judy. She put her palms flat on the table, hoping the cloth would absorb some of the sweat that oozed from them, and waited. Judy didn't look down. It was as if she already knew what was there.

"Why do I have two different birth certificates?" Julia asked, hearing her voice tremble slightly.

Aunt Judy smiled calmly. "You don't, dolly. This" — she pointed at one of the documents — "is you. And this one," she pointed — "is your sister."

❧❀❧

NICHOLAS AND HIS WIFE WENT away for a vacation on Prince Edward Island. During the days he was gone, Julia thought of him frequently. In the nights as she waited for sleep to come, or in the mornings as she meditatively ate toast, her feet up on a chair, jammy crumbs sprinkling the front of her pyjama top. She imagined Nicholas standing in the screened-in porch of a freshly painted Victorian bed and breakfast, staring out at the grey-blue ocean, coffee cup in his hand.

She'd only ever seen him in the morning once, when he'd stopped at her place to pick up a sweater he'd left behind the week before. He was going to the library at McGill to finish some work and couldn't stay; she was on her way out to work and couldn't ask him in. He stood there at the door, a rather cool, damp wind blowing in from behind him as he propped it half-open with his hip. He looked sleepy and terribly boyish, his hair untidy, his wrinkled shirt open at the neck as if he hadn't quite finished getting dressed. Julia stood in the doorway and looked at him and turned liquid inside. She thought he had never looked more lovely, she didn't know why. Something about his dishevelment, perhaps.

Thinking back on it, she laughed at herself a little. It may have had everything to do with her mood and little to do with his actual appearance — but then again, maybe not. She imagined that if she'd stepped closer — pulled him against her and buried her face in his soft neck, burrowing in under the collar of the wrinkled shirt — she could have smelled the must of sleep on him, the aroma of his body marinating gently in its own oils and exudations for hours. It still gives her a sharp interior thrill to see him in her mind as he stood there that day in his worn jeans, his dark eyes hooded; bashful but firm about not coming inside. "I haven't even had coffee yet," he'd said, his voice gravelly in his throat. "I still have to have coffee."

Now that she thinks of it she can see that he'd hung back in the doorway, gazing at her, as if he didn't trust himself to come closer. His eyes had followed the line of her neck through her open collar; he'd been distracted. She'd felt the air moving against her skin, and she had blushed. Why hadn't she seen it while it was happening? How many other moments had she let pass, blinded by anxiety and self-consciousness? She remembers him again, the touch of his gaze on her collarbone, the gentle hollow of his own just visible. Stripes, Julia thinks. His shirt had stripes.

A few days after he returned from PEI they agreed to meet for a post-dinner drink at the Bar St-Laurent. When she arrived he was biting into a big, sloppy hamburger. He motioned toward a chair. "Do you mind?" he'd asked. Julia didn't; it made no difference to her if they talked while he ate. She sat in her chair and he pushed his glass of wine toward her, waving at the server across the low dark room to bring another. He chatted about his vacation. He and his wife had eaten a lot of seafood. He described the red earth and the rows and rows of bright green potato plants leading from every roadside all the way to where the land fell away to the sea. He smiled to himself as he told Julia about cycling along the narrow roads, stopping in at craft and antique shops set up in people's garages or converted from old houses, a bit of a busman's holiday for his wife. He described to Julia how a gruff old woodworker had been visibly impressed with his wife's knowledge; when he found out who she was he gave her an antique plane that had belonged to his grandfather. Julia saw the pleasure and pride on Nicholas's face and felt warm toward him. He rarely spoke about Deepa O'Malley, but when he did it was with respect. Clearly, whatever else he felt about his marriage, he basically liked the person his wife was. It pleased Julia to see this in him. She also liked that he didn't hesitate to express it to her. She had no desire to compete with another woman for a man. Especially not this difficult one.

꩜

UNCLE PAUL CAME HOME AS Julia was putting on her red trench coat to leave Aunt Judy's apartment. The sound of his keys in the lock made Julia feel like a teenager caught doing something illicit, smoking out her bedroom window or wearing forbidden eyeshadow. Paul had pushed his walker all the way over the threshold before he looked up and saw her standing there and then he blinked, startled. Julia smiled. "Hello, dolly," he said, grinning weakly at her. Julia was at a loss. Should she stay now? Paul hung his coat up and then ducked his head and began to thunk his way methodically across the floor to the living room. Aunt Judy stood in the doorway, hands clasped before her. She gestured with her chin toward the door. Julia turned to leave.

Outside in the wind, the tears that had sat lumped in her throat all afternoon burst and spilled out her eyes. Aunt Judy didn't know the whole story, hadn't been around at the time, but it was enough to shock Julia, to make her feel unsteady. Carol and Raphael had agreed not to get married until Raph had finished his M.A. "But they couldn't bear to be apart, and your mom went to live in Toronto while your dad finished his last year of studies." Julia knew her parents had really loved one another, but she found it hard to imagine her rigid, constricting mother as Judy described her: young, passionate, impulsive. She could see her mother's face during the last years they'd been speaking to each other. It appeared to her mind's eye lined with disapproval, the brow and mouth stuck in a permanent frown. "One thing led to another, I suppose," Aunt Judy said, spreading her palms as if to open the idea. Julia stared.

"What happened?" Julia asked. Aunt Judy leaned forward.

"She got pregnant, honey," she said.

"I know." Julia was exasperated. This was all so difficult to understand. She struggled to think of a way to make Aunt Judy see what she wasn't getting. Finally she said, "But what happened to the baby?"

Aunt Judy sighed. "Honey," she began. Julia felt her stomach drop a little inside her. "In those days an unmarried girl couldn't have a baby. I mean ... of course, they did, but it was very difficult. You couldn't keep that baby. And I think," Judy paused. "I think there was some concern about the reactions of the parents. So your mother gave the baby up."

Julia's stomach dropped the rest of the way; she felt ill, and wished desperately she hadn't eaten all that lunch. Aunt Judy walked briskly into the kitchen and returned with a glass of water. "Here, dolly," she held the glass to Julia's lips and rubbed Julia's back while she sipped at it. "Are you okay? You look awfully white."

Julia closed her eyes and breathed. She wrung her hands unconsciously in her lap. She couldn't think of why she should be so upset by this news. It had nothing to do with her, really, she told herself. Her stomach settled back into its normal place and she began to feel better. At least this answered her main question — she was still only Julia, born in May, 1965. There was no secret new identity, no hidden history. Not for her, anyway. She took the glass from Aunt Judy and drank off the rest of the water in steady gulps, gasping for breath when she finally put it down. In the silence that followed Julia picked honey cake crumbs off her little plate one by one, pressing her finger onto each one to make it stick and then putting it on her tongue, where it dissolved. She concentrated on cleaning her plate as she let the information settle into her mind.

"You should really ask your uncle about this. He knows more about it than I do," Aunt Judy said quietly.

"I will," Julia said, pushing her chair away from the table and standing up. But not today. Not today.

❦

JULIA EMAILED NICHOLAS ABROAD MORE frequently than she wanted to. She would have preferred to go blithely on with her life, not needing him, not thinking of him. She watched people come through the store, pretended to evaluate their suitability as potential lovers. She took herself out for coffee on St. Denis Street on Sunday mornings when the broad avenue was empty of traffic, the warm wind pushing clattering paper cups and rattling twists of paper against the curb, sunlight flashing off the plate-glass windows.

At a dinner at Lauren's she met a visiting stained-glass artist from New York who had work-worn hands and a wing of glossy black hair hanging over one eye. Julia thought she might end up in the woman's borrowed apartment at the end of the evening. Murmuring about the New York art world, the mushrooms on her plate, the artist leaned in much too close and Julia got a sudden whiff of the woman's winey breath. It smacked her with desire, the memory of the taste of Nicholas's wine-sour mouth ambushing her, the feel of his lips powerfully real to her for a confusing moment.

She ran to the bathroom to catch her breath, and when she came out she squeezed in next to Lauren on the other side of the table and sat, almost mute, until it was finally possible to leave without being too rude. She pressed the artist's hand warmly, smiling, keeping her arms extended between them. Walking home in the humid wind that seeped through her party clothes like warm breath, her sandals echoing on the sidewalk concrete, she'd ached for Nicholas — and for the loss of the softness, the warmth and attention, the pleasure that she could have had from the stained-glass artist if she'd let herself. If he hadn't come to haunt her. She stood on a street corner waiting for the light to change and pressed the heel of her hand into her side. He was probably stretched out across Spanish linen in a hotel room somewhere. Licking salt off the skin of some lush graduate student who'd carried him off to the sea to bathe him in moonlight after a day spent poring over engravings of Moorish brickwork together. At home Julia sat before her laptop without even kicking off her shoes. Her side pulled tight as she wrote to Nicholas, describing for him the way he'd been living in her senses. She struggled to make him feel the force of her wanting him without making herself sound sad and forlorn.

The truth was, as much as she missed him, the strength of her desire for him was also a kind of power. The next day she emailed him again from work first thing, before Olivier arrived, telling him how she'd wakened in the morning to the memory of that wine-taste and, lying in bed in the wash of light coming from the rising sun, she'd smiled.

※

GLOBAL WARMING HAD ROBBED MONTREAL of a real summer the year before, leaving Julia's shoulders cold in the evenings.

This year it seemed to be compensating the city with an extra month of beautiful warm weather. Julia wore her summer tank tops and dirtied her feet in flip-flops long after she thought she'd have switched over to pantyhose and ankle boots. With Nicholas away she felt sort of aimless in the evenings and on the weekends. She knew it was merely psychological, since they rarely spent more than one evening together in a normal week, and he was away so often, with his trips planned around his life with Deepa O'Malley, that often Julia didn't see him at all.

Everything seemed slightly out of sync, the evenings shortening while the temperature remained warm, the days often humid with a Montreal heaviness. River sweat, Lauren liked to call it, as if the St. Lawrence, surrounding the lizard-shaped island, was sending a veil of invisible, rank perspiration up from its surface as a way of asserting its dominion. You are part of me, the river seemed to say, I am part of you.

Julia went for a beer after work with Marie-Soleil, who worked with her at Le Jardinier. They sat and idly lifted the cold condensation off the sides of their beer bottles with the edges of their fingers; Julia wiped hers futilely across her greasy forehead. She went to the movies with Lauren, who teased her about the stained-glass artist, pinching her gently and berating Julia for being a coward; she shivered as her bare arms got really cold in the air-conditioned theatre. She wandered the streets on made-up errands, buying one stamp at a time or shopping for a birthday card she wouldn't need to send for months. Nicholas sent her one more email, very brief. He was preparing to leave on the Moroccan leg of his trip. He'd visited a walled garden the day before and thought of her as he looked at the intricately detailed mosaics adorning the walls and pathways. Julia rummaged through the books at the store until she found a picture of a Moorish garden and she imagined Nicholas there, just beyond the edge of the photograph, gazing with her at the wall tiled with geometric patterns of turquoise, royal blue, green, and pearl-white, his beautifully shaped head brushing the upward-arching branches of the olive trees, his dark hair a nimbus against their pale spiked leaves.

She walked through the city, passing sidewalk cafés full of people smoking, laughing as they drank tall glasses of beer. Table after table was littered with cheap white porcelain cups; miniature ones, the insides rimmed with dried espresso crusts, or bowls clotted with milk foam flecked with cinnamon, the people seated there engaged in lively conversations, holding each other's gazes as they argued and laughed. Julia passed along outside these little pens of conviviality and felt wistfully alone, observing what felt like a life that was beyond her, and she thought alternately of Nicholas and of her sister. She couldn't really feel that this person was her sister, although there wasn't any other word for their relationship; not ever having had a sister, she didn't know what it was supposed to feel like. Julia hated the strange hollowness that bloomed in her chest when she thought about this phantom sibling. She didn't understand why she should feel a sense of loss in the absence of someone she never knew existed.

Sometimes she thought she was simply displacing her yearning for Nicholas. Other times she was seized with teeth-clenching fury at her mother, for dying without having told Julia about this mystery person. She stood frozen in place on

St. Lawrence Boulevard, blocking the sidewalk in front of a Thai noodle shop — her breath stuck in her throat, her vision blurred by hot tears — and thought of the years she'd spent not talking to her mother. Would Carol have confided this secret if Julia had tried harder to maintain some kind of communication with her? Julia sobbed out loud, once, her fists clenched. She'd talked to Carol throughout her twenties, her early thirties. It had been like allowing her mother to hammer nails into her forehead every time, Carol's constant disapproval and sour disdain hitting Julia unerringly — and Carol had never given the slightest hint of the existence of another child.

That night she woke gasping from a nightmare in which a shrunken, distorted version of her mother clung to her back, fingernails sunk in Julia's shoulders, withered legs flapping around Julia's waist as she ran through an eerily empty city trying to shake her mother off.

❦

MARIE-SOLEIL WAS BECKONING HER, cocking her head to indicate someone at the cash. Marie-Soleil was beautiful, an aptly named golden ray of light, abundant bright blond curls rolling around her shoulders as if to cushion her precious skull from any possible harm, her smooth skin glowing through the depths of winter. Olivier liked to station her at the cash where she could bathe customers in her inner light, but it meant she didn't learn much about the rest of the business, and constantly had to interrupt Julia for some piece of information or other. Julia sighed and put down her pen. She'd promised Olivier she'd get this budget done before the end of the day.

The woman at the cash register looked familiar, but her head was bent as she examined a tray of paperwhite bulbs, and Julia couldn't see her face. A semi-regular customer, perhaps. Julia put on her managerial smile and approached the counter. "Hello," she said. The woman looked up and Julia felt her heart thud, just once, inside her chest. The woman smiled.

"Hi," she said, offering a small, work-roughened hand. "I'm Deepa O'Malley. I wanted to speak to Olivier, but apparently he's not here?"

Julia had the bizarre sensation that Deepa O'Malley could see the images of Nicholas inside her head, as if her skull were made of glass and pictures of Nicholas were swirling around inside, rippling along the inner surface. She mentally inventoried the muscles of her face. All normal. Except her eyes, which were intently focused on the woman before her, her lustrous curtain of very dark brown hair glinting chestnut under the track lighting. Julia had heard that Deepa O'Malley's mother was originally from India, her father an Irish Montrealer whose forebears had escaped the cholera and landed in Griffintown. Her eyes were flecked with gold. Her skin was barely lined, the cheeks slightly loose under high bones, the eyes crinkled in the corners; she was aging, but very gracefully indeed. Julia told herself sternly not to stare. Why, she wondered, would Nicholas ever have wanted to look at me when he could be looking at her? And then she berated herself for being foolish. History changes everything, she knew. Who — besides the two of them — knew what they had gone through together?

"I'm Julia, I'm the manager. I'm afraid Olivier won't be back today. Can I help you?"

Deepa O'Malley smiled again.

⁂

THAT NIGHT IN HER INSOMNIAC cocoon, Julia tried to imagine Nicholas and Deepa O'Malley together. Standing next to each other. He is taller, but they are both strong, upright; their muscles roll easily under elastic skin. Julia saw that Nicholas was restless, constantly moving, physically and also emotionally — his roving psyche a self-winding watch, accumulating power as it swept through space. She lay in the tunnel of her clammy duvet and thought about him. He would be in Morocco by now. Perhaps he was peeling clementines with his long fingers. Julia saw him slipping the juicy sections between his lips, piercing their thin membranes with his white teeth, the sharp-sweet juice squirting over his tongue, the rinds piling up before him on a polished wooden table. The fragrant, bitter oil of the peel spraying unnoticed across his disordered pile of notes, a handful of Moroccan coins. Perhaps his wallet, his passport. A taxi receipt.

She wanted him; the damp slick between her legs seemed like a sorry thing, mere moisture compared with the lonely yearning that balled up, a solid fist inside her chest. She wondered whether Deepa O'Malley was lying in her marital bed thinking similar thoughts. She had seemed so relaxed, so peaceful that afternoon in the store. Perhaps she was lying with a lover of her own right now, a talented young man with long blond hair and supple limbs, or someone older, grizzled with the residue of an eventful life, slow, confident hands fanning that beautiful hair out across clean linen.

Julia kicked the duvet away, pushing it down to the bottom of the bed with her feet. You know you're in trouble, she thought with half a grin, when you so miss the man with whom you're having an affair that you're thinking about his wife. She turned over and pulled the pillow down and hugged it. I wonder what Baby Goodman is doing tonight, she thought — if she's even alive. She must have a name of her own by now; whatever it is, it's unlikely to include either "Baby" or "Goodman."

How strange. The more time passed, whether or not she was actively thinking about her sister, the more real she became in Julia's mind. No, not real. She searched her thoughts. Just ... more of a fact. It was time to get some information.

At work the next day Julia was self-conscious. Although she knew the chance of Deepa O'Malley returning to the store any time soon was incredibly low, she couldn't help it. She fluffed her hair in the washroom so it sat on her head just so, she cleaned her fingernails with the little nail file attached to Olivier's Swiss Army knife after she'd potted a couple of forced amaryllis for display. She was embarrassed at herself, finally deciding that if she emailed Nicholas and told him that she'd actually met his wife, it would help her chill out about the whole thing. She puttered around rewashing glass vases until Olivier left for the day, then went into the office to use the computer.

As she typed she tried to picture where Nicholas would be sitting when he read her missive. A flyblown internet café, surrounded by European tourists and empty, filigreed tea glasses, their bottoms filled with a hardening glassy sugary sludge. Or perhaps a sleek air-conditioned hotel lobby, all dark wood, marble flooring, and brass railings. Nicholas knew about her previous relationships with women; if he were here and she told him how beautiful she found his wife, he'd tease her. But he wasn't here. When she finished her email to Nicholas, Julia opened a new email and typed "Baby Good-man" in the "To" line, and sat and looked at it for a while. Then she closed the program and called her Uncle Paul. She told him she wanted to ask him about the birth certificate, and there was a long pause. Then he said, "I know, dolly," and invited her to come for supper Friday night.

The table was set the same way it had been when she'd come for lunch with Aunt Judy. Julia brought flowers again, this time from work, a small square Japanese ceramic pot with two narcissi sitting in a bed of pebbles, about to bud. Aunt Judy had made another huge meal and as they ate she chatted incessantly, giving Bill's news (he'd got a new puppy, it chewed through the wiring on the DVD player), offering more food, jumping up and down to answer the phone. Bringing a serving spoon, making tea. Finally the dishes were cleared, and the dishwasher churned in the kitchen. Aunt Judy pulled on a sweater. "I have to stop in and see Mrs. Yuen next door, she's recovering from having her veins stripped — you don't mind, do you, honey?" she said, her hand on the doorknob.

"Go ahead already," said Uncle Paul, waving a hand in her direction. Julia thought he sounded uncharacteristically gruff. She felt a twinge in her side.

As the door snicked shut behind her aunt, Julia turned and faced Uncle Paul. "Judy told me that birth certificate is for my sister," she blurted. Paul looked down at his feet, then looked up.

"That's right," he said.

Julia was stymied. For a moment she couldn't think of what to say next. Finally she said, "What does that mean?"

Paul frowned. "Well, that was your mother and father's first baby."

Julia's heart was thunking inside her. "What happened to her?"

"They gave it up for adoption."

Julia concentrated on breathing. "But why, Uncle Paul?"

Paul sighed. Finally he said, "Honey, it wasn't like now. It was an accident. They weren't married. They didn't let the family know they were living together. It was a *shonda*. They were ashamed."

"But they knew they were going to get married, didn't they? Why didn't they just keep her?"

Paul sighed again, looked at his knees. "They felt they were too young, I guess."

There was a silence. Julia didn't know why she cared. She didn't even know this person. In fact, once she thought about it, it occurred to her that given how crazy her mother was, Baby Goodman might well have been better off with her adoptive family. Julia smiled grimly. Maybe Baby was the lucky one.

"What happened to her?" she asked.

"They gave her up," Paul said.

"I know, but what happened to her? Doesn't anybody know where she went?"

Paul stared at her. "Honey, they don't tell you that."

"Do you know what she looked like?"

Paul shrugged. "Your mother never saw her in the flesh," he said. "Your mother was knocked out. They took the baby away while she was still asleep." He looked down again. Julia had the sense that a hidden door was opening. "It was very hard for her," he said quietly. Then he looked up at Julia again and smiled. "She was thrilled when she became pregnant with you, honey."

Julia felt her throat thicken, and she swallowed. She didn't want to cry in front of her Uncle Paul. She stood up. "Well," she said, and then stopped to clear her throat. "Thanks a lot, Uncle Paul." She leaned over to kiss him on the cheek and he held her to him, the angle awkward, hugging her hard. She knew he knew she was crying, but she didn't want to admit it, so she turned away and went straight to the door, picking up her purse from the telephone table. She opened the door and, still standing there, closed it again. She waited a minute for her voice to settle and then turned around. Paul stood in the doorway of the living room, leaning on his walker, watching her.

"Why didn't she tell me?" Julia asked. Paul shook his head.

"I don't know, dolly. I wish she had." He shrugged. "Maybe she couldn't get past that feeling of shame. And maybe ..." he shrugged again. "It was hard for her to talk about it. She always felt sorry about it. She felt she had lost a child. It was as if ..." he started. "As if the child had died, almost."

Julia nodded and waved goodbye. She didn't trust her voice. She walked outside and started up the sidewalk toward the bus stop, her stomach fermenting. Her mother had given away her sister. She suddenly became aware of a terrible weight bowing her back. *She was thrilled when she became pregnant with you, honey.* Her mother must have been waiting for her, Julia, to make up for the loss of that first child — waiting and waiting.

Julia stood by the bus stop, the rectangular blue and white sign above her head, the dusk settling around her. A group of young teenaged boys and one girl in a red skirt were playing soccer in the park across the street, shouting happily, sentences slipping easily between French, English, and Spanish. Julia smelled fresh-cut grass and car exhaust, and a subtle odour of rot spilling out of the fruit store behind her. The tears poured out of her, water running from a tap, spilling down her neck and onto the neckline of her cotton tank top. She wished Nicholas were standing here so she could burrow into his chest, have him hold her, have him be her rock. Just a temporary rock.

❦

IT'S TOO HUMID TO SLEEP. Julia doesn't know if it's the weather, or maybe the weight she feels in the air is the burden of the loss her mother suffered, which she, unknowing, has been carrying all her life. She sees herself as one of those children born with a miniature twin growing out of her chest, or a head growing on top of her head that cannot speak or eat but yawns and grimaces, the two skulls attached like fused-together coconuts. She is lying across her one big chair, her legs splayed over one of its fat upholstered arms, and she actually touches her head to reassure herself that it is singular, intact.

The streetlight radiates through the window into the dark room and her calves shine, silvered by the errant illumination. In this light they look smooth, sleek. She admires them and wishes Nicholas were here with her, stroking them. She would like to smell him, see the top of his head as he looks down at her body. He has a way of cocking his head. She would like to have a moment of deep quiet and strange peace with him, like this.

Somehow, no matter how calm they are together, she has not ever felt at peace with him. There is perpetual tension, if only at the looming prospect of their eventual leave-taking. Her underwear shaken out and slipped back on. Two wine-glasses soaped and rinsed and dried, the dishtowel spread to dry over the faucet's bent head.

In the spring she'd gone on vacation, a long weekend with Campbell in Nova Scotia. She'd sat by the edge of the ocean early every morning. With the hushhhh-hushhhh of the waves coming up the beach the only sound apart from the occasional melancholy cry of a gull, the diffuse light of dawn expanding the visible world before her, she'd felt bathed in tranquility. Back in Montreal, lying naked at Nicholas's side, her hand resting on the perfect gentle curve of his belly, she'd told him of that moment, of how she'd thought of him then. That she'd wanted to be somewhere like that with him, enveloped in serenity. He lay among the tousled sheets and stared up at the ceiling, making no reply. The silence between them grew until it elbowed her off the bed and herded her into her clothes. She'd gone into the kitchen and banged open the silverware drawer, clattered dried dishes into cupboards until Nicholas finally appeared, dressed, to say goodbye.

She thinks of this and in spite of the way the old unhappiness still sits undissolved, a dull ache low in her belly, she wants him to be beside her. She craves the dry warmth of his hands on her legs, which are stretched out before her. It is as if they are wasted without his fingers, his eyes. As if they don't fully exist if he is not there to offer tacit confirmation. Julia understands that her feelings are bitterly contradictory. At the same moment that she does not completely exist without her lover who does not love her, she exists in a burdensome multiplicity for her mother, who herself no longer exists.

She can laugh at this, but it burns.

❧

CAMPBELL PHONES AND THEY TALK for an hour and a half. He is one of the only people in Julia's life who knows about Nicholas, and now he becomes one of the only people who knows about Baby Goodman. He suggests that Julia come back to Nova Scotia. She can stay on the pullout couch and wander Halifax, buy saltwater taffy or browse through bookstores on Spring Garden Road, drink fairly traded coffee in the student cafés. Have a "thinking holiday," as he calls it. Julia knows better. She'd be haunted. She'd think of Nicholas and want him to be with her, to see what she sees, to smell the salt around the harbour and hear the noon cannon and feel the fog like dew on her skin. She'd think of Baby Goodman, wonder whether every fortyish woman might be her sister, examine every cheek for her own bones, every ass for the saddlebags her mother and her grandmother have shared with her. She'd wonder whether every brown-haired schoolchild or sullen teenager smoking outside of Harvey's might be carrying a part of her, one generation later. That is, it would be just like at home, only worse, because she would have no work, no grocery shopping, no bill-paying to distract her. She'd feel she couldn't relax because she ought to be doing something to find Baby Goodman, although she doesn't know what.

What else can Campbell offer? He gently reminds Julia that Baby Goodman may not want to be found. He agrees, endearingly, that Baby might have gotten the better bargain, handed off to some other family, one without crazy parents. Why would she want to know she came from a family like Julia's? No one wants to know how close an escape they had. It's a quirk of human psychology — the fate you didn't get frightens you. It casts a shadow over the good fortune you actually have.

Hanging up the phone, Julia knows it's true. She has no right to impose that knowledge on the person Baby Goodman has become. She sits in her fat chair and gazes absently out the window at the windswept street, stark, divided by the streetlights into zones of white glare and black dark. A cat weaves its way around the wheels of a parked car and sinuously disappears into a trough of shadow at the curb. You might not even have a name, she thinks, watching the place where the cat slipped out of sight. And maybe you don't care.

She can't stop herself from wanting to know what happened to her sister. Maybe she lives in one of those apartments there, Julia thinks. Maybe that's her cat. Maybe, Julia thinks to herself with a kind of inexplicable grief, that's Baby's cat, named Julia. She takes a sip of wine, as if the liquid has the power to convey knowledge. I'll have the Baby Goodman Chardonnay 2004, she thinks, a good year. Then it would only remain to drink the bottle, and she'd know. Maybe Baby is Campbell's next-door neighbour in Halifax, and she teaches grade-five kids with special needs. Or maybe she became a stripper at nineteen, working the small-town circuit in north- ern Ontario, her mutilated body found in a dumpster in 1984, result of a drug deal gone bad.

"Do I have the right to know anything? It's her life, after all," she'd said to Campbell.

Campbell had answered, "Good question."

"Maybe she's looking for her mother even as we speak, and she'd be thrilled to hear from me." Julia could hear the child in her voice, the plea. That tone that meant, tell me the world is not real. Tell me the truth I know is not true.

Campbell sighed. "Could be. But that would still be her journey to take." There was a silence. He probably knew Julia was swallowing, breathing. "Why do you want to know, sweetie? It won't change anything that's already happened."

Julia draws her legs up and hugs them. That's the prob- lem, she thinks. What she thought had really happened has changed. The past is not what she thought it was. Now she knows that she doesn't know what happened.

Why does she want to know? Julia thinks of the fate Baby escaped. It makes her stomach ache to realize that whatever has happened to Baby might be what would have happened to her, Julia, a series of events she avoided by being born sec- ond. Baby might be living out the good fortune she snatched from her younger self — or she might be dead. Or she could be living across the street, working at a garden store. In love with a man who is in Morocco sharing a meal of chicken stewed with prunes and olives with his recently-met travel companion, another Canadian named Nicholas.

The cat appears again from between two cars. It stops and looks both ways, then casually begins to cross the street, the light catching the tips of its shaggy fur. The pelt looks like wet sealskin, the way it's bathed in the streetlight. "Hello Julia," she whispers as the cat comes closer, disappears from her field of vision.

⚜

NICHOLAS HASN'T EMAILED SINCE HE left Spain. It's only been a couple of days, and not wholly unlike him. Internet access is less widespread in Morocco, of course, and Nicholas does get caught up in his work — or whatever he is doing, which may have as much to do with fruits of the vine and pleasures of the flesh as with scholarly pursuits. Julia knows he likes to portray himself both as monk-like scholar and *bon vivant*, and she has assumed each is, at times, true. She feels his absence much more when he doesn't send her a line.

Deepa O'Malley comes into the store. Julia can't help watching from the office. Deepa and Olivier stand to one side, discussing a contract they are both involved in, designing and furnishing a garden in Westmount. Julia waits until Olivier goes into the back to fetch the plans and then she goes out to the cash. She is planning to pretend to need something from the drawer, but hates how it makes her feel stupid and dishonest. So she just waves in Deepa O'Malley's direction. "Hi," she says, and smiles. "Julia," she says, pointing at her own chest. "We met a few weeks ago."

"Of course," says Deepa O'Malley, and it sounds like she really remembers. She steps forward and offers her hand. "Deepa." They shake. "I wondered whether I'd see you here." This makes Julia's breath come short, although she doesn't know why.

"I think I've met your husband," Julia says. She didn't want to say this, had planned not to say it, but it was so vivid in her mind she couldn't stop herself. Deepa smiles. Clearly, it is a common occurrence for her to meet people who have met her husband. "I took a course with him, at the CCA," Julia says.

"Oh yes," Deepa replies vaguely. Julia has the distinct impression this means nothing to her. Still, she is not dismissing Julia.

Julia sees Olivier approaching, the roll of plans under his arm. "Well anyway," she mutters, and withdraws toward the office with another short wave, another quick smile. Deepa waves back, smiles too.

"Nice to see you again," she says as she's turning back toward Olivier, her eyes already on the unrolling sheaf of paper.

Julia goes back to the pile of resumés she'd been reading. She looks at them, but cannot actually read any of them. She listens to the murmur of conversation between Olivier and Deepa. She can't hear what they're saying but she can hear the rise and fall of their voices. Then she hears the crackle of paper and the voices take on the rhythm of a conversation winding up, then there are footsteps. She's gone, Julia thinks. She tries again, but can't concentrate, and finally she rises from her desk. She has to pack up a shipment of decorative tiles that came in damaged. She'll go do that, occupy her hands. She emerges into the store and almost runs right into Deepa O'Malley, who is standing in front of a bin of miniature tulip bulbs, considering.

"Oh," Julia gasps. Deepa looks up and smiles. She has been fingering one of the little bulbs, its papery skin.

"Do these need a lot of sunlight?" she asks.

They talk about flowers for a few minutes, and Julia puts a handful of the bulbs in a paper bag and gives them to Deepa. "On the house," she says. She doesn't know why; she'll have to pay for them herself. Deepa is putting the folded bag in her purse and Julia says, "So, how is Nicholas?"

Deepa snaps her purse closed and looks up. "He's away," she says. "He's gone to Morocco to do some research." She smiles vaguely. "Actually, I'm a little worried. He usually calls me regularly, but I haven't heard from him since he left Spain." This was the day he sent Julia her last email, too. Deepa moves toward the door of the shop. "You know what it's like abroad," she says, "sometimes it's hard to get a phone line." She waves an open palm. "God knows where he even is, he's probably camped out in the desert so he can write about some buried temple." Then she smiles. She opens the door and the sun floods in, firing her beautiful hair with a ridge of pure light, one side of her face haloed. Julia lifts a hand. The musty bulbs suddenly smell like old people, something conversant with death.

≈⋆≈

BILL SOUNDS SURPRISED TO HEAR her voice. Julia is surprised too, actually — she'd decided not to call him, and then picked up the phone and dialed. He is not unfriendly, but they hardly know each other. They chat about Bill's new puppy. Julia has nothing to report about her own life. What can she say? Work is more or less the same every day. She's having an affair and her lover is halfway around the world, and he's not writing to her. She has found out she has a mystery sister and this drastically incomplete knowledge has unmoored her from the past she thought was hers. The small talk runs out. She takes a deep breath.

"Actually, Bill." There is another pause. "You know about this Baby Goodman thing," she began.

"Yeah," said Bill.

"You do?" Julia suddenly doubts herself.

"Yeah, my father told me before the funeral that he was giving you the birth certificate."

"Did you know about it before that?" Julia's heart is pounding. Now that she's asked she doesn't want to hear the answer, wants to suck the words back in and swallow them.

"Yeah," Bill says. Julia is suddenly furious with him, but says nothing.

"Yeah and ..." Julia prompts.

"Well, we knew there'd been this baby given up for adoption. But I never learned any of the details," Bill says. "I was young, just a kid. They didn't tell kids about that kind of stuff in those days." He sounds a little defensive. Suddenly Julia just feels tired.

"Do you remember anything else?" she asks, because now she is embarrassed for having called long distance to interrogate someone she will probably only ever see again at a couple of funerals. She is ready to say thank you and goodbye.

"Nothing, sorry," Bill says. "Except the thing about the private detective."

❧❀❧

"PALLADIO" CALLS JULIA AND ASKS her out to a movie. They meet for coffee first and end up skipping the film; they are so caught up in their conversation they keep gabbing. They finish their coffee and go off to have a beer, which becomes two beers. They talk about their lives. This is the conversation Julia thought she'd like to have with Andrea all those evenings when she got a ride home from Nicholas instead. She's happy about it.

She doesn't tell Andrea she's been seeing Nicholas, but they do end up talking about the seminar they both took. Andrea had done a year of architecture at McGill before switching to the Management Information Systems program. Now she designs information flows instead of buildings. "But I didn't stop being interested in buildings," she laughs. Julia is sheepish; she hasn't ever been interested in buildings. They talk about the other people in their seminar. "I see Michael the Romanian sometimes," Andrea says. "We go to movies. He's a huge film buff." She pauses to swallow some of her beer. "He used to watch lots of movies on TV in Romania, only he never got to see them whole, because the state TV network used pirated copies of these great films. They cut off the beginnings and endings because it made it harder for them to get caught." Now that he has settled in Canada, she adds, he is renting and re-watching the movies he's already seen. "Especially the beginnings and the endings!" Andrea laughs again. She's really animated; every time she laughs she looks totally alive.

Eventually the talk turns to Nicholas. How disorganized he was, how he never came to class with the readings planned for the following week, left books in his car and had to go outside in the rain to get them. They shake their heads.

"It's not like it was a whole semester of three-hour classes," Andrea says. "It was eight goddamn weeks, two hours a week!" His lectures were really good; he was passionate about his subject, Julia points out timidly. "Oh yeah, definitely," says Andrea. She's willing to give him his due. She tips her head back and drains her beer. A curlicue of foam coils at the corner of her lips. It looks to Julia like a tiny spate of ocean rolling unexpectedly onto the shore of Andrea's pale mouth. Andrea catches it with her tongue like a cat.

She leans in. "He was always flirting with me," she says. Julia smiles and nods. Is this true? "You must have seen it," Andrea says confidently, leaning back in her chair again, "he was doing it right in class. And he's married and everything."

It is true, Julia knows. Nicholas called on Andrea frequently. He nicknamed her "Palladio." Maybe he trained his liquid black eyes on her, too, and Julia was too dull to see it. But he didn't give Andrea a ride home every time, did he?

He liked to flirt. It's part of his *bon vivant* side. Maybe he was casting his net wide, willing to catch whatever fish it pulled in, his gutting knife at the ready. Julia's shoulders sag. She looks at her watch. Maybe she's had too much beer. The music in this place is loud and she's starting to feel terribly tired. She doesn't have the energy to revisit, revise, relive everything she thought she knew about her past, even so recent as this. What else has happened around her that she hasn't seen, or known about?

She puts her purse in her lap and smiles vaguely at Andrea. So sorry, but she has to go home and get to bed. Big day tomorrow. Andrea flashes a look at her own shapely wrist. Ah, it's later than she thought too. They walk out together. Julia sees Andrea's lovely jaw, her smooth pale face, her dancer's body. Andrea and Nicholas would be a beautiful machine if they ever made love together. In the dark, Julia shakes this thought from her head.

At home, she emails him. Baby, send me one word, she writes, one single word to let me know you're still alive. She hopes it comes across as wry, but later, lying awake in the dark, she worries that it sounds desperate.

She watches the fragmented arrows of light from passing headlights arc smoothly across her wall and disappear. The thought that Nicholas might have slept with Andrea while he was courting her makes Julia's stomach hurt. Maybe it was Andrea with whom Nicholas had been, as he put it, an unfaithful lover. For all Julia knew he could have left her house, stepped out onto the street, and walked himself down the many blocks to Andrea's cleverly arranged apartment, with its pottery bowls and well-chosen art. All those evenings Julia wanted to pull Nicholas to her bed and take him inside her, but was too shy to come out and say it, and he dallied at her table over his glass of wine, conversing idly until it was time for him to leave — maybe he was conserving his middle-aged erotic energy for Andrea's sylph-like charms. Julia cries a little. As much from embarrassment as from sorrow.

SUNDAY MORNING JULIA TUCKS HER feet up under her in the big chair, a huge mug of coffee resting on the fat arm, and pulls the phone close. The sticky remains of a couple of freezer waffles glisten on a plate on the floor, the closest she can come to a big Sunday breakfast these days. Doing anything seems like a lot of trouble recently.

She remembers Sunday mornings with Stewart. It was often their one really free day of the week. They would sleep late, nuzzling as they woke, reach groggily for each other and make love before setting foot on the floor, then get up together and cook. Stewart would mix pancake batter while Julia showered, then Julia would cook the pancakes while Stewart shaved. Or Julia would dip the bread for French toast and Stewart would fry it, the two of them standing so close their hips touched, Stewart burning his fingers grabbing golden bits of stray batter out of the pan for Julia who was impatient with hunger. Stewart usually made something extra, sauteed apples or sage-fried potatoes or, in summer, a bowl of sliced strawberries macerating in their own sweetened juice. Julia would have shopped the day before with this morning in mind, buying cream for the coffee instead of their usual 2% milk, or in spring, a can of the new season's maple syrup.

The parts of their relationship that seemed fullest when they were together are now the emptiest parts of her life. It was in these vacant moments, in the months following their breakup, that she still sometimes felt a flash of hatred for Stewart. Lately the hatred has eased off, slipped down a notch to resentment. She knows well that by the time Stewart left, it had been a couple of years since they had the kind of luxuriously blissful Sunday mornings she remembers. They rarely had sex anymore, and when they did it certainly wasn't the juicy coupling that used to be compulsive, starting the moment they woke and discovered each other. They no longer cooked together. If they had a big Sunday breakfast it was in preparation for a day spent apart, Stewart fuelling up for a hike in the country with friends, or Julia getting ready to go off to the noon-to-five shift at the store.

Now her Sunday mornings are lonely; the quiet that meant peace and intimacy with Stewart now means being alone in the world. She would like to get an email from Nicholas today — just one line. She knows better than to court disappointment by actually checking for it. There will be time enough for disappointment.

She pulls the phone over and sits with it on her bent thigh, her hands resting on it as if on the head of a child. She wants to call Campbell and tell him about her conversation with Bill, but she isn't sure she has enough energy to tell the whole story. To think about it. Holding the phone in place with one flat palm, she carefully picks up her heavy mug and sips. In the absence of loving company, she'll take the comfort of coffee. Maybe if she drinks it she will feel less tired, more motivated to call Campbell and talk. He is the one she's been able to talk to ever since they met in high school. They were boyfriend and girlfriend for six months in grade nine, holding hands, inseparable in school and out. They never kissed; theirs were intimacies of refuge. They both drooled over magazine photos of Deborah Harry of Blondie, and David Bowie; Julia laughed as Campbell pressed his lips to Bowie's rouged face and, watching him out of the corner of her eye, did the same with Debbie Harry's wide red mouth. Campbell taught Julia to apply makeup properly, before she gave up fussing with it. They giggled together, not knowing quite why, when their parents refused to let them sleep over at each other's houses, though all they wanted to do was stay up late together, eat popcorn and May Wests, listen to records. Julia sips her coffee again, smiles to herself. She will have Campbell forever, but at a remove. He has a life now and it takes place far to the east of where Julia's unfolds. Nicholas, on the other hand, is much farther away — east or west, it almost doesn't matter, he's so far. Of course, when he's home he's sometimes very far away from her, too.

She sometimes wishes she knew what Nicholas was thinking. For a second, a single flash. She looks at her watch. It is 10:20 a.m. Morocco is four hours ahead. That means it is 2:20 in the afternoon for Nicholas. Maybe he's having a siesta, out of the heat of the sun. If Julia could glimpse his thoughts, she might get the equivalent of TV snow, or perhaps a passing image from a dream — Deepa's golden eyes in a bowl of water, or the floating sound of the afternoon call to prayer echoing off the ancient walls of a public bath. Maybe he is not asleep. He could be sitting in a hotel bar drinking with some fellow foreigner. Or, Julia thinks, she might catch him in the middle of making love, admiring the face of the woman beneath him, or thinking of the way it feels to be pushing into her warmth, her moistness. She smiles to herself, a tight, passing expression. This is why it would be a bad idea to be able to read his thoughts. She wishes him all the pleasure he can squeeze out of life, but she doesn't want to see him squeezing it.

She heaves a sigh and dials Campbell. If it's 10:25 a.m. here in Montreal, it is 11:25 in Halifax. Campbell might be gone already, off to play tennis or have brunch or read in the library with his studious beau; he might still be asleep. Hard to tell. The phone rings twice and then Campbell answers. "Hi, Honey Pie," he says. Julia smiles. No wonder she calls Campbell when she's feeling low.

She tells him about her conversation with Bill; as she talks, her pulse begins to tap in her neck. She grips the phone, yells into it that he knew all this stuff and didn't think, didn't bother, to tell her. "Bill actually remembered hearing his father talking to my mother on the phone about the private detective. He remembers that they argued about it," Julia says. That was the time Julia and her mother left Julia's father, staying with Paul and his family for a couple of days before a series of hushed telephone calls brought Raphael to the door to take them back home. Bill didn't understand, as a teenager, what they were arguing about; they kept their terms deliberately vague. Now he thinks it must have been about Baby Goodman.

"Give him a break, Jules, he didn't know what the big deal was. He was only a kid," Campbell says.

Julia can't reply. She chews her lip, testing the way the pain feels.

"Who are you really mad at?" Campbell says.

Julia begins to answer, then stops. This question makes her feel terrible.

"Uncle Paul," she answers. She begins to cry. Campbell is silent, waiting for her to think it all out. "But it's so much easier for me to be mad at Bill!" she shouts. "I don't have to talk to him! I don't love him!" Campbell is still silent. "Not the way I love my uncle," Julia whispers.

"Your uncle was your mother's brother first," Campbell says.

"Shut up," says Julia.

Campbell laughs gently. If he were there with her, Julia imagines, he'd nudge her arm. Then he'd hug her, hooking his arm around her neck and pulling her toward him. Julia smiles. They've known each other for so long; she imagines that they'll have adjacent rocking chairs in the nursing home and he'll still be reaching over, liver-spotted hand shaking, to poke her slack old arm. If she ever has a slack old arm — it occurs to her that Carol died before age could pull her skin away from her flesh, river it into that wrinkled, papery soft-ness, leaving it to hang in bunches like old curtains. Perhaps disease did that job, eating the flesh out from the inside, a scavenging parasite. Julia imagines her emaciated mother lying on her white sheets, wired to an IV, a purple-yellow bruise blooming on her white arm where too many needles have broken the fragile blood vessels, sliding in and slipping out again, channels for fluids thick and thin, salt blood and sweet sustenance.

Julia wishes Carol had had someone like Campbell to sit by her bedside — then again, Carol wouldn't have wanted one. It wouldn't have occurred to Carol that a friend could offer the same love and support as a family member. Would she have wanted Julia? She would have wished for Raphael — there's the old egg basket again, Julia thinks. She wonders whether Carol ever questioned the wisdom of investing all of herself in her husband and child, whether she ever imagined that she might end up with no one. Maybe, Julia thinks, the time Carol tried to leave Raph. She must at least have thought about what it would be like to be alone.

Julia remembers. She lay in bed, suspended in a sort of half-awake state. The summer dusk had barely slipped over into night. She was in her usual going-to-sleep position, the pink doll (her only doll, but for some reason she'd always called it "the pink doll") on her chest. She twiddled the edge of its bonnet, thinking about the brush of the soft, twiddle-worn flannel against her thumb. Then her mother came into the room and started opening Julia's chest of drawers, stuffing articles of clothing into the worn diaper bag Julia was much too old to need now. She was about to start school, in one week. She hardly remembered the quilted, red-flowered diaper bag.

She'd sat up in bed, watching, holding the pink doll. Her mother was being very brisk, not her usual gentle, tiptoe-and-whisper nighttime self. At first Julia didn't think her mother saw her sitting there in bed, but then Carol turned and looked at her and said, "Get up." She tossed a pair of pants onto the sheet covering Julia's legs. "Put those on over your pyjamas." Carol wasn't mad, exactly. There was something exciting about her tone of voice, but strange too. Julia felt uncertain. Her mother finished with the drawers of Julia's bureau and pushed them closed, picked up the packed bag and turned to leave the room. "Come on," she said, motioning "up" with her arm, her voice sounding almost sad.

It all seemed like fun, but an unsettling kind of fun. Raphael stood, stiff, as Carol bustled out the door holding her own suitcase, the diaper bag over one shoulder, gripping Julia's small hand. Julia turned back to look at Raphael, and she remembers that there was a still moment. Carol stopped in the doorway. Julia was terribly confused. She didn't want to

leave her father, who could be counted on to smile with pleasure when he saw her. He smelled clean and spicy from the
aftershave he let her help him put on in the mornings because
he knew she loved to smell it on her own small hands afterward. "Is Daddy coming?" she asked, her eyes fixed on Raph's
face, knowing the answer before she finished uttering the
question. Her mother didn't answer except to step forward,
pulling Julia after her. Julia wanted to pull back, to resist; she
could already imagine the constant, wearing pressure of
Carol's scrutiny, her sharp, critical voice correcting Julia's
posture or her table manners. Around her mother, Julia felt
she had to be on guard; she knew she was a constant source of
small disappointments to Carol. When Raphael was around
he made her feel that someone loved her, in spite of her trailing shoelaces and dirty fingernails. Standing in the doorway,
he smiled at Julia. He lifted a hand in salutation then shoved
it deep into his pocket, as if to hide something.

They went in the car to Uncle Paul and Aunt Magda's house.
Julia now realizes she hasn't thought of her Aunt Magda,
Bill's mother, for years. A child, Julia didn't know her well.
Aunt Magda was Hungarian, and when she spoke, which
was rarely, it was with the kind of thick accent that as a child
Julia associated with old people. It occurs to her now that
Magda may have been self-conscious about her English, which
didn't improve beyond a certain point even after she'd lived
in Canada for decades. Julia remembers her best in her kitchen,
an apron over a crisp dress, sleeves rolled up into thick cuffs
that rode Aunt Magda's forearms below the elbows as she
bustled, stirred, poured things, chopped peppers with hard,
decisive movements of her big knife. She used to speak sharply

to Bill in Hungarian, Julia suddenly remembers — a word here, a phrase there. Bill, a big awkward teenager during much of Julia's childhood, obeyed silently, glanced at Julia out of the sides of his eyes, if at all.

When they arrived at Uncle Paul and Aunt Magda's, the street (what street was it? She was too young, she doesn't remember) was quiet, hung with a mist that seemed to glow from inside, lit by a low-slung yellow moon. Julia stepped out of the car, still hugging the pink doll close, and looked around. It couldn't have been very late if she hadn't quite been asleep yet at home, she knows, but she remembers this as if it all took place in the middle of the night, with all the surrounding houses sunk in an unmoving stillness. It was as if the neighbourhood were under a witch's curse, the quiet houses all filled with Sleeping Beauties, unable to awaken before the kiss of morning's first rays of sunlight.

Inside the house, all was hushed as well. Magda's kitchen was disconcertingly empty, gleaming, no pots on the stove or plates on the table. Bill emerged from a room at the back in jeans and a white sleeveless T-shirt and stood for a moment, wordless, in the doorway. Julia saw in his smooth face that she and her mother were an intrusion — even worse, that they were doing something that was not quite right. It was Bill's face, deliberately blank, that made her anxious where before she had been curious. She put the edge of the pink doll's bonnet in her mouth and sucked it for comfort, a habit she'd dropped years before. Her mother, head bent as she murmured to Uncle Paul, turned suddenly and, seeing her, stepped over to Julia and yanked the doll from her mouth. You're too old for this anyway, she'd said. Julia felt something burst inside her. Her face melted and she began to cry, the abject, hopeless weeping of a young child.

Sitting in her chair now, with Campbell patiently silent at the other end of the phone, the wire between them an empty channel, Julia feels her chest ache. She is amazed at how the sadness, the helplessness, can come back to her, its force unabated by the distance of years, as if she has been carrying it in a secret pocket in her body.

Uncle Paul picked her up and tried to soothe her against his warm shoulder, but Julia was mortified by the strings of viscous snot bubbling out of her nose and onto his shirt, and his solid flesh felt suddenly alien, animal. They put her to bed on a blue loveseat in the living room with a flowered cotton sheet tucked around her shoulders, and then the adults slipped through the doorway and turned off the light. Julia lay there, her face hot and swollen, sticky with half-dried tears, and looked at the strange configurations of light and shadow. She'd been in this room many times, but with the lights on; in the dark it was almost frightening. She heard the tense murmur of adult voices elsewhere in the house. She missed her father.

In the morning when she opened her eyes she found the pink doll standing next to her face, its feet tucked between the cushion and the arm of the love seat. She stumbled into the kitchen and found it bustling in the familiar way, full of the smells of food and coffee. Paul, dressed in a suit, saw her first and swept her into his lap with a hug, offering her a miniature glass of orange juice that sat beside his plate, its sides flecked with pulp. She sagged against him, allowing herself to be doted on, sucking the juice little by little across the rim of the glass. Well-groomed Aunt Magda, her hair tidy and her face made up, was busy cooking something. Julia's mother sat, erect in her bathrobe but with her hair uncombed, her face pasty and tired, turning her coffee cup between her fingers.

Uncle Paul's voice and his warm breath went right past Julia's ear. I'm not saying you don't have a right, he was saying. I'm just saying he's your husband and you owe it to him to discuss it. Make the decision together.

Julia could see her mother was almost crying, and it scared her. Carol's voice sounded like a child's, protesting to a parent. But he won't, she was saying, he said he wouldn't allow it. Her voice was hoarse, whiny. The cup between her hands scraped its saucer. Julia could feel Paul's body tense, his chest against her back filling up and emptying as he sighed; she remembered him saying, I don't know what to tell you, which surprised her because she still thought grown-ups knew everything. He gently pushed Julia and she slid off his lap; he stood up and pulled his chair closer to the table so Julia could sit in it. She knew, because of his suit, that he had to go to work. Julia could tell her mother was waiting for something, that something hung, unresolved, in the air of the kitchen. Paul stood in the middle of the floor for a few minutes and then, sighing again, stepped forward. He patted Carol's shoulder as he passed her but she shrugged his hand off, staring straight into her coffee cup.

I'll see you tonight, he said, turning in the doorway; Julia can still see him standing there, the words echoing, but she isn't sure whether he was talking to her mother or to Aunt Magda. Then, she remembers, he looked right at her and smiled and winked. You, he said, pointing at her, his voice cheerful, eat your breakfast! Aunt Magda slid a plate onto the table in front of her, a steaming hot apple pancake dusted with powdered sugar, the edges still crisply sizzling, the smell of butter and apples rising into her face. Julia still remembers how she gasped, and how her lit-up face had made Aunt Magda smile.

"Thanks," she says to Campbell. "I love you."

❧

ON MONDAY AFTERNOON CLAUDETTE PHONES. She's had a fender-bender and is up at the Montreal General Hospital getting X-rays. She insists she's fine, only bruised, but Olivier, his face flushed, rushes out of the store, patting his shirt front for his glasses, his pants pockets for his car keys. He phones Julia from the car ten minutes later. Could she look on his desk, there's a cardboard tube, revised specs, would she take it over to Deepa O'Malley? He had planned to drop them off on his way home, they have to be delivered by the end of the day. Julia should take money out of the cash and take a cab.

She waves a cab out of the thick stream of late-afternoon traffic rushing down St. Denis Street. In the back seat, with the plans across her lap, she watches the city pass from this unfamiliar vantage. She rarely rides in cars. The taxi threads south through downtown to the Autoroute Ville-Marie, the sunken concrete artery that, choked with cars and trucks, cuts an ugly, noisy trench into the southern edge of downtown. Julia frets as the taxi crawls through the canyon, pressed on both sides by suburb-bound commuters. To distract herself, she tries to make out the evening news issuing from the taxi's radio in Haitian Creole. She recognizes a few place names —

Port-au-Prince and Cap-Haitien — and understands when they talk about deposed president Aristide. She looks at the dark, close-cut back of the driver's head and realizes suddenly that she is sitting in this man's life. It occurs to her to feel fortunate to have had this unexpected glimpse, however narrow, into it.

Finally they turn off the autoroute and back onto city streets. They arrive at Deepa's brick row house and Julia offers a twenty across the back of the seat, waiting while the driver casually slips a receipt card from his sun visor and scrawls the date and amount on it, taking his time as if he were alone at his desk at home. Once out of the cab, Julia stands on the sidewalk and looks at the house, extremely self-conscious. She reminds herself that Deepa knows nothing about her and Nicholas, and anyway, she's only here to drop off the specs. She'll push the cardboard tube into Deepa's hands and leave.

It must have rained earlier; along the whole street the tiny front yards glisten green, the overgrown flowers still bright in the belated end-of-September warmth. Children play on the sidewalks. Little boys play with toy guns. Girls wearing small versions of grown-up women's clothes, narrow midriffs bare, puckered little belly buttons peeking out, hang around the gates of the houses, argumentative. No one gives Julia a glance.

There is a wooden sign at the top of a worked-iron archway beside the house. "Workshop." Julia walks tentatively through the narrow space between the wall of Deepa's house and the wall of the house next door. The concrete path is damp and the air smells of wet brick. Then Julia gets a whiff of something chemical. Varnish, or lacquer. The workshop is a new, modern construction attached to the house but with its own entrance, taking up most of the small back yard, its pine walls and broad glass windows all clean angles. Deepa O'Malley sits in the open double doorway, her legs spread wide, a tall chair leaning back against her shoulder like a cello. She is painting something on it with a tiny brush, her face caught in a frown of concentration. Julia hears children screeching happily, the bottled sound of a woman's voice shouting in some other house nearby. She approaches, timid.

Deepa looks up and peers at her, squinting against the late afternoon sun. She points with her brush. "Julia." Julia smiles, relieved, and waves the tube.

"Yes, hi, sorry to bother you, I .... Olivier was called away. He asked me to drop these off for you."

Deepa pushes the chair forward onto its own four legs and wipes her hands on a rag. "Just give me a minute, okay?" she says, and disappears into the workshop with her brush and palette. A moment later her hands emerge from the door, grasp the chair, and pull it inside.

When she comes out, she has removed her canvas apron and loosened her hair. She pulls the doors shut behind her. "Come inside," she says, motioning toward the house. Julia's confidence drains away. She doesn't want to see the inside of the house. This is the scene of Nicholas's life. She feels that if she sees it, she'll somehow be betraying him — and Deepa as well.

"I'm just here to drop these off," she says, waving the tube without moving from the end of the concrete path.

Deepa laughs. "Come on in," she says, her voice bubbling with good humour. She disappears into the house without giving Julia a chance to answer.

Inside, Deepa sits down at the big wooden table in the dining room, pushes a pile of books and papers out of the way, and takes the tube from Julia. Julia stands, ill at ease, the old-paper and waxy polish odour of the house mixed with other scents from the nearby kitchen — cooked meat from previous dinners, vanilla and lemon — her hands on the back of a simple wooden chair. The walls are painted a deep, plastery ochre, and black-framed prints of old farmhouses, their stone walls and thatched roofs rendered in pale watercolours, hang here and there. Deepa studies the plans for a few minutes, then looks up at Julia, her expression serious. "Anything else you need to tell me about this?"

Julia shakes her head. Efficiently, Deepa re-rolls the work and slides it back into the tube.

"Thanks for bringing this. I'm supposed to cost the materials tomorrow." She shakes her head, her smile rueful. "It's going to be nice once it's done, Mackintosh-style benches and espaliered fruit trees against a dry-stone wall, the whole nine yards. They're bringing a mason in from Yorkshire! But Jesus, could they be more anal." She sighs tiredly and stands up. "I'm about to have a glass of wine, can I convince you to join me?"

Julia wants desperately not to be here, but she wants more desperately to stay and talk to Deepa O'Malley. So they sit in the backyard and sip their wine, the pale, almost greenish liquid throwing circular yellow sprays of light against the insides of their glasses. Julia tries to picture Nicholas and Deepa sitting at either end of the long dining-room table, entertaining a roomful of boisterous, witty friends. She tries to see them there alone, sitting one at each side of a corner, close enough to feel each other's body heat. Deepa is pointing out the rows

of overblown cabbages and leggy tomato plants tucked between the far side of the workshop building and the brick of
their neighbour's house. "I start out every summer with good
intentions, but, I mean, who has time, really?" she says cheerfully. "The truth is, Nick usually picks up my slack, but this
summer he was busier than usual himself."

Julia is shocked, hearing him called Nick. She wouldn't
have imagined anyone calling him something so casual — he
has far too much gravity. To her, he is only Nicholas. She is
so far outside his life, she realizes. Suddenly their intimacy,
the brush of skin against skin, the flutter of eyelashes against
the tiny hairs lying along a shoulder, a collarbone, seem trivial.
What does it matter, after all, that he has been inside her
body, if his mind was really elsewhere? She sips a mouthful
of wine and warms it in the hollow of her mouth before
letting it slide down her throat. Insects buzz somewhere
close. The sun is hot on her face.

"So what is it, exactly, that you do at the store, Julia?"
Deepa asks.

Julia shrugs. "Bit of everything, I guess," she says. "On the
retail side. I don't usually have much to do with the design
stuff. I schedule the staff. Order product. Keep the place clean.
Budget, banking."

"Olivier must really have confidence in you if he entrusts
you with all that."

Julia picks at a shred of fingernail. She and Stewart had
once planned to open a business together. Stewart's father
had owned a small chain of stationery stores where Stewart
worked all through childhood and high school. Stewart had

finished university and begun law school at his father's suggestion, as preparation for a future role in the family business, but while he was still in his first year his father had a bout of colon cancer and suddenly decided to sell the chain. Stewart never got over his disappointment.

He clung to the idea of having his own business, and when he and Julia moved in together she left her position managing a small theatre company and took the job at Le Jardinier to get some retail experience. She'd loved the idea of having a business with Stewart, of spending every day with him. Handling sleek expensive pens and clean stacks of writing pads, rolls of gift wrap in gorgeous new colours marking the start of each new season. Stewart stayed on at the little law office to save some capital, and Julia walked down to meet him after work. They went for a beer, dazed with tiredness and hunger, and giggled as they imagined their apartment decorated with tissue-paper pumpkins or strings of plastic chili-pepper fairy lights chosen from the stock of their store.

Some time during the years they were together Stewart lost his focus. He sank into his routine at the office while Julia kept going to work every day at Le Jardinier, waiting for him to feel the time was right to start planning their project in earnest. Julia sees now, in retrospect, that by the time Stewart finally admitted he'd lost his drive to open something of their own, their relationship had begun to slide too, and she never mustered the energy to begin something else for herself. She wonders whether they would have stayed together if they'd had a business to build together. Or if Stewart's abandoning their plan was a symptom of his gradual loss of interest in their relationship. Maybe he was responding to a kind of general dry rot that was spreading between them. So many possibilities she hadn't seen before.

"I've been there a long time," she says to Deepa, and smiles wryly. "I've absorbed it all just by breathing the air." She looks down. A line of ants is carrying crumbs past her feet, some of the bits bigger than their shiny black heads. She admires their determination. She swallows the last of her wine and sets the glass carefully on the ground.

"I guess I should be on my way, then," she says.

Deepa smiles. "Well, thanks for keeping me company." She picks up Julia's glass and her own, and stands. "It's awfully quiet around here these days."

Julia's mouth feels dry and she swallows. "Any news from Nicholas?" she asks.

Deepa shakes her head. "If he doesn't turn up soon I'm going to have to send out a search party," she says, and she smiles with her mouth, but the rest of her face is grave.

"Really?" Julia asks.

Deepa shrugs. "Yeah, actually," she says. "He didn't arrive at his hotel in Casablanca. Of course, travel can be disrupted, and he could have changed plans. But if he doesn't show up tonight and I don't hear from him, I'm going to start asking around."

Julia realizes she's gawking, her head thrust forward like a chicken's, her mouth hanging open.

Deepa laughs shortly. "I'm sure he's fine," she says, opening the screen door to her house. "He's probably completely lost himself in his research. He'll step out into the sunlight some time next week, blinking like a turtle."

Julia takes a step toward her. She has the strangest urge: to console her lover's wife. Deepa lets the door swing shut again and steps over to Julia and they hug.

"Thanks for coming," Deepa says.

"Thanks for the wine," Julia stammers, and turns into the shadow of the walkway.

❦

BEHIND HER EYES JULIA'S MIND begins to stir, like a mouse sniffing behind wainscotting. It is a strange and yet ordinary sensation, this coming to consciousness. At the moment that she becomes aware of being awake she has the unhappy suspicion that it is not yet morning. She opens her eyes and yes, it's dark; she looks over at her bedside clock and her heart sinks. She was only asleep for an hour. This is becoming her unfortunate pattern: if she manages to fall asleep when she first goes to bed, she wakes up after an hour and remains awake for ages.

She looks around, follows with her eyes the bars of light coming in from the street, dividing the walls and ceiling. Upon waking, usually she thinks of Nicholas first, but tonight Deepa comes to her mind. The colour of the wine in the glass, like young straw, with rings of sunlight playing in it. Deepa's rough, strong hands and her shiny hair, a black-brown curtain with the first sneaky strands of grey hiding among the chestnut highlights. Julia wonders what those hands would smell like, if she brought them up to her nose. Those fine, dry fingers, the subtle veins running like rivers between the knuckles. Fascinating, generative hands.

Julia lies in the dark and thinks of how familiar Nicholas's skin must be to those hands; how many times, over their years together, she's had the pleasure of cupping his testicles, precious eggs hanging in fragile nests; of running her fingertips along his inner thighs. How many times he slipped his own long-fingered hands around her from behind to hold her soft breasts, his wrists against her ribs. For the first time since she began to love Nicholas, Julia thinks, *Why can't I have someone of my own?* Then she remembers that she did, once.

She wonders, with a small thump of anxiety in her chest, where Nicholas is now. She glances at her clock again. She calculates quickly — she is getting good at it, the result of frequent practise. If it is 12:41 a.m. in Montreal, it must be 4:41 a.m. in Morocco. She hopes he is asleep in a dark, clean hotel room, the window open to a soft breeze. His research notes — which so absorbed him that he forgot to tell his wife he'd changed his travel plans — encoded in the metal and plastic of his computer, the lid carefully closed, on the desk. She sees his face, lost in dreams. She wonders what he ate earlier in the evening. She imagines for him that the people in the hotel have come to understand what he likes, and send him to restaurants only the locals know. As she imagines it, she feels the urge to touch his sleeping face; the desire is so strong it is a taste in her mouth.

She wonders if Deepa misses him. She is used to his being away, but then so is Julia, and Julia misses him at every moment. Deepa is surrounded by him, lives in his house, has his bed to sleep in. She can pull out a drawer and look at his underwear; open a closet and see his jackets hanging, empty of him; slip her hands inside the pockets where his fingers have nested. Julia sees her own hand slide into Nicholas's pocket on top of Deepa's pale-cinnamon one.

Well, she thinks, one thing's for sure: Deepa is not Baby Goodman. Too old, and definitely not the child of Julia's parents. She laughs to herself. All this time she's been thinking of who in the world could be her sister. Now she thinks of all the people who could not be her sister. None of the men, no one who isn't forty-two, no one who isn't white, with a Semitic air. That leaves out an awful lot of people. Thought of this way, her search for "Baby Goodman" is effectively narrowed down. Of course, a forty-two-year-old can look thirty-two or sixty, depending on the life she's led, her draw in the genetic lottery. Maybe Baby had Tay-Sachs disease and plateaued at three, growing backwards from there toward death. Arriving at the end of her life before baby Julia had begun to walk.

After talking to Campbell on the phone, Julia had screwed up her courage and called her Uncle Paul. He answered, and she thought she detected a sigh of resignation when he heard her voice. She felt sorry for him then, left holding the memory bag for her mother. If only Carol had understood how hard it would be for everyone around her to be left with this fragmented secret, would she have told Julia about it before she died? Julia frowns in the dark. Not bloody likely. If Carol had been thinking of anyone but herself she'd have told years ago.

Julia asked Uncle Paul whether he knew if Carol had considered telling her. He sighed. "After the thing with the private detective, when she had such a big fight with your father, she couldn't talk about it with him anymore. So she got in the habit of not talking about it at all." Julia could hear Paul's lungs rattling as he breathed. It seemed he'd gotten old very quickly in the brief time since her mother's death. Is he sick? Has he been sick all along?

"I don't think she meant to keep it from you, dolly. She just didn't talk about it."

"But my father's been dead for twenty years," Julia said. "In twenty years it didn't occur to her to mention it?" She could hear her voice rising in anger and tried to calm down.

Uncle Paul didn't say anything; Julia imagined he was shrugging, sitting on his beige couch, the handset of his cordless phone clutched in his swollen fingers. She felt guilty; she didn't want to punish Paul for having had the decency to give her the birth certificate after the funeral. He could have thrown it in the garbage. Or worse — tucked it away to be found only after his own death, when no one who remembered what happened would have been left.

Now Julia lifts herself tiredly out of bed and goes to sit in the big chair by the living-room window. The street is empty, the streetlights shining white on the asphalt of the road, all the windows opposite blank with darkness. She wonders why she doesn't want Paul to have thrown the birth certificate in the trash. It would have been easier for him. It would certainly have been easier for her. She rests her head on her open palm. What is it that she wants from this?

A movement in the street outside catches her eye. She looks, and sees a cat — the same cat? — walk out from between the curb and a parked Toyota, and slip underneath the front fender of the next car. Julia smiles. This cat has a particular attitude, almost a swagger, as if it believes it owns the street. Why not, Julia thinks, it owns the street as much as I do. More.

How many sisters do you have? she asks the cat silently. You know less than I do.

Uncle Paul's face was tense as he handed the envelope to her in the car. She hadn't really been aware of it at the time; the fuss and stress of the funeral seemed a good enough explanation for everyone's various moods. "I think you should have it," he'd said. And so she should. But why? Many times since the funeral she's thought that Baby Goodman actually has nothing to do with her.

In fact she knows that's not true. Her whole life has been lived, unknowing, in the shadow of her precedent. Under the dim shape of her mother's grief, and perhaps her father's. It must have been worse for her mother. How is it possible to carry a person inside you, grow it from the cells of your body, feed it with your blood — and then have it removed like a tumour and carried away while you lie unconscious, sleeping a chemically induced sleep? Julia can't begin to think her way into that.

She had surgery once as a child, to correct a minor deformity of her left foot. She awoke briefly in the recovery room, lying one in a row of bodies on gurneys, all covered with white sheets like corpses; she was sobbing wildly without knowing why. Desperately she struggled to sit up and look around, but she couldn't lift her head. It was terrifying. Afterward she understood that the crying and the partial paralysis were side effects of the anaesthetic, which hadn't completely worn off yet. But at the time it was like waking up half-dead among the dead, wrapped and bound by a grief no less wrenching for its obscurity. This is how she imagines it must have been for her mother, waking to find her baby gone. Simply removed.

The months leading to the birth must have been immeasurably harder for her mother too. Alone in a strange city, trying to make a home on too little money, working in isolation in her cramped apartment. Oscillating between the anxiety of living a forbidden closeness, deceiving both families, and the euphoria of being with the man she loved, the joy of all the small, ordinary intimacies. Biding time until she could marry him and begin her real life. Raph, on the other hand, was out all day, surrounded by people, doing stimulating work and respected for it. His life had already begun; he was living it. Then, Julia thought, for her mother to find herself pregnant and know her family would be ashamed of her, when it was only love that had made this child — and, even more, when she ardently desired to have children, and knew that her family would, after her marriage, expect it of her. To carry it every moment, from room to room, up and down the stairs, onto the toilet where, burgeoning, it would sit in her lap; into the bath, where water would pool against her rounded outer shell, where fluid buoyed her ball of life on the inside. Knowing it would be given away. Julia is astounded by how much courage it must have taken for her mother to get up and live through every day, alone in her sweltering apartment, the child accumulating inside her. Courage — or a kind of dull, stubborn resignation that would have required its own effort of will.

This is an aspect of her mother Julia never imagined. Sorrow unexpectedly floods her as she realizes how much of her mother she didn't even know existed. So much of Carol's personality lay shut away from the only daughter she ever really had. How much more bitter, then, that they were estranged for so many years. In a way they'd been separated by this secret since before Julia was born.

She thinks of her mother lying in her hospital bed, a dying husk, grieving for the child she'd given up so many years before — and also for Julia, the child she'd thought she'd keep. Tears flow down Julia's face, run down her chin, make her neck itch. She stares fixedly out the window. All her life she has been consumed by her anger at her mother. Now she wonders, sobbing, whether her mother was angry at her too — for not giving her what she wanted from Baby while being Julia too. Or for not healing the festering absence that oozed in her where Baby once curled, limbs accruing, baby heart blooming with the passage of the weeks.

Or was Carol angry with Julia for not being able to get past the snarl of bitterness that made Carol so difficult, that dammed up the love with which she should have been able to nourish Julia? Julia didn't know Carol had to swallow over that sharp knot in her throat with every swallow, breathe past it with every breath. If only Carol could have untied the knot, opened the channel and let her love for Julia flow, soothing her wounds on the way out (for Julia now thinks there must have been some love in there somewhere, roiling and liquid inside Carol's body like sick diarrhea seething in her gut). Snot is running down her upper lip and into her mouth, salty and slick. She is glad it is the middle of the night, no one walking the sidewalk to peer in at her white face, shining wet through the glass.

Julia wipes her face with the hem of her T-shirt; she feels puffy and hot, but she is calming down. Then, for the first time since her mother's funeral she thinks to be angry with her father too. He kept this secret also — in fact, in a way, it seems he made it the secret it became, refusing to discuss it with Carol until it became undiscussable. Now Julia is furious again, collapsed on the fat soft arm of the chair, crying again, the sound of it embarrassingly loud as if the inside of her head were as big as the room. Her father was supposed to be her good parent. The funny, impulsive, tickling parent. The parent whose love and pride in Julia suffused his face whenever he looked at her. She was supposed to be able to love him wholeheartedly, without complications.

※※※

HAVING LOST SO MUCH SLEEP in the middle of the night, Julia doesn't wake up until after eleven, and then she is groggy, weighed down by a thickness, as if recovering from some kind of illness. She feels only slightly better after a hot shower. She stands at the kitchen counter, holding herself up with two hands splayed at the counter's edge while she waits for the coffee to drip through. The machine gurgles at her like an old man trying to draw breath through failing lungs, air crackling through phlegm. She thinks of her Uncle Paul on the phone. He sounds weaker all the time; she doesn't know whether this is normal aging or whether he is really failing. She is afraid to ask Aunt Judy.

She regrets harassing Paul with questions — but how else can she find out? It's not as if of this is written down; she can't look it up somewhere. Her head hurts. It occurs to her that if Paul died tomorrow her only source of information would be completely gone. She presses her cool palm against her forehead and closes her eyes.

She has only taken a first sip of her bitter, restorative drug when the phone rings. She almost doesn't answer; she feels unequal to the prospect of having a conversation with anyone. She forces herself to stand — there are only so many people who could be calling. Clutching her mug, she walks over to the phone. Her voice comes out still rough with sleep and exhaustion.

There is a hesitation at the other end, and then she hears a voice like a drop of warm caramel. "Julia?"

Julia exhales. She summons all the self-possession at her disposal, aided by another furtive sip of coffee. "Good morning, Deepa," she says. She feels afraid, guilty.

"Hi." Deepa hesitates again, then laughs, a clear, gentle sound. "Have I woken you up?"

"No," says Julia, embarrassed. "I was up. I — I'm tired. I didn't sleep well last night."

"Oh, I'm sorry." Deepa says, and Julia believes that she is. This eases her tension, a hurt she hadn't realized she was feeling that has nothing to do with Deepa. There is a pause, and Julia begins to suspect that Deepa is shy. This puzzles her.

Deepa clears her throat. "I'm sorry to bother you, but ... you asked about Nick. Yesterday. How did you know him again?"

Julia feels struck in the chest; slowly the seizing fear subsides. Deepa's voice doesn't sound suspicious, accusing; it's open, curious — a little bashful. Julia breathes. "I took that seminar with him at the CCA. The architecture centre. 'Architecture for Non-architects'," she says. She sips coffee. "We kept in touch ... a bit ... after that."

"Oh, that's what I was wondering," Deepa says in a rush.

"I'm probably overreacting, but he never showed up at his hotel in Casablanca, and I thought I would try to find out if he'd been in touch with anyone else, maybe his plans changed or something. He can be absent-minded, especially when he's working. I tried his publisher, his colleagues at the CCA, his brother. Then I remembered you, and I thought, maybe ..." She trails off and Julia hears the hope sifting through her fingers and blowing away like desert sand. Her own throat is tight. Nicholas.

"No," she begins, "I haven't heard from him lately." Then she thinks, don't hide anything, what if you could help him be found? "Well, I got an email from him a couple days ago — I guess the day before he left Spain. Just saying hi," she says, and then she can't control her voice, her breath anymore. If Deepa hadn't happened to come into the store that first day, if Claudette hadn't been clipped by a taxi yesterday afternoon, if, if, if ... She might not even know Nicholas was missing, much less ever hear what happens to him. Tears spring to her eyes; she chokes on them, trying to push them back. She succeeds in not sobbing aloud, but takes an audible, gasping breath. She is mortified.

"Oh Julia, I've upset you," Deepa says in a low soothing voice. "I'm sure he's fine, don't worry, honey."

Julia coughs and then gives a bark of laughter. Deepa is comforting her. How embarrassing. "Sorry, sorry," Julia says, "You caught me by surprise, that's all. I didn't realize ... I didn't know he was seriously missing." She pauses. "This must be very hard for you," she says.

Deepa sighs. "Well, I'm sure he's fine, you know, but I ..." There is another pause. Julia imagines Deepa wringing her hands in her lap, the phone wedged between her shoulder and her bent head. "I'm used to his not being here, but usually it's still like he's here with me because I know he's going to come home. But now, thinking that maybe he won't actually come home ... anymore ..." Julia hears her draw a long, ragged breath, clear her throat. "I just wanted to cover all the bases," Deepa says, brisk, businesslike once more. "What did he say in his email anyway?"

Julia closes her eyes. "That he was in Spain, leaving for Morocco. He'd ... been in a walled garden the day before." Somehow that sounds to her like a terribly intimate detail. "He knows I work at Le Jardinier," she says. "I suppose he thought I'd be interested." How ironic — she wasn't, not really. Or anyway not interested because it was a garden, but rather because it was him. She'd pictured him running his beautiful hands, browned by the Spanish sun, across the mosaic walls, touching the intricate pattern someone had painstakingly created centuries before. Standing in the glow of lush greenery, the smell of flowers carried to him on a breeze, hard little green lemons waving over his head, the sound of traffic muted beyond the thick stone.

Julia imagines the garden, seen from above: a perfect, gentle enclosure in which to keep a treasure. She sees a tiny Nicholas moving around inside this magical box, suspended in time, secure in his isolation, kept there by Julia's wish that he be safe. In fact, Julia is the isolated one: Nicholas is anything but. He moves swiftly through life, making his way through throngs of people, books under his arm, his graceful strong hands holding boxes of slides like thin, brilliantly translucent slices of the world slotted into their cardboard compartments according to some meaningful order his quick mind has devised. Wherever he goes he brushes other lives — sometimes briefly, almost imperceptibly; sometimes more slowly, luxuriously, leaving lines of electricity in his wake. Inevitably — Julia is coming to see — on a path that, however it winds, ultimately leads back to the narrow street in the Verdun neighbourhood of narrow houses. There, Deepa, behind their own brick facade, bends her head in concentration, her hands filled with the fragrant vegetable spice of new wood — or perhaps the soft, nearly odourless fabric of one of Nicholas's cotton shirts, the plastic buttons cool circular nubs against her roughened palms.

Deepa is silent. Julia is wondering if Deepa can hear what she hears in her own voice. Longing. Desire. The fear of grief to come.

"Did he say where the garden was, or who he was with?"

Julia shakes her head although she knows Deepa can't see her. "No, sorry. Not that I remember. I'll look in my trash and see if I still have it, maybe there's a detail I forgot. But I don't think so," she says. She is hoping there will be something. She wants to find Nicholas, for herself and for Deepa.

Deepa sighs. "Well, thanks. Thanks anyway." She pauses. "It was nice having that glass of wine. Maybe we can do it again sometime." Julia's heart swells.

"I'd like that," she says hoarsely.

Later that afternoon, folding her laundry, Julia replays the conversation in her head. She can't remember exactly how Deepa's voice sounded when she asked how Julia knew Nicholas, what Nicholas said in his email. She feels a shiver of fear at the thought that Deepa might suspect after all —

how likely is it that Nicholas would have maintained a casually friendly email correspondence with some ex-student from an eight-week seminar? She shakes her head. Nicholas probably emailed all kinds of women, all the time. All kinds of people. He must have hundreds of ex-students. Anyway there was nothing in Deepa's manner to suggest anything other than open curiosity, a plain and pressing desire to find her husband. Julia's sure.

⋘⋙

UNCLE PAUL'S FACE IS LINED and pale, the texture of his skin coarsening as he sinks deeper into ill health. Aunt Judy flutters around him, bringing tea with a wedge of lemon, a little tray holding six pills of different colours and sizes laid out like soldiers, a glass of water. She offers him a pillow, stuffs it down behind him when he leans forward to swallow one of his pills. He turns around and shouts at her — "Enough!" — with real force, his face turning briefly red. He gasps. Shouting used up all the air he had, and he must now recover his breath, wait for his blood pressure to subside. Aunt Judy has stepped back, standing behind the chair where he can't see her, hands clasped tightly at her chest. Uncle Paul sits and breathes, looking down at his lap. Tension vibrates between them. Julia waits.

She considers leaving; she doesn't want to cause her uncle more aggravation. But since it occurred to her that he might die without having told her everything he knows, it has become urgent that she question him. She berates herself mentally. Why did she not get all this information from him before? She doesn't even know what all this is. It's not as if he could give her a box with the whole story in it. The story doesn't exist until she thinks it. The facts of her mother's life, of Baby Goodman's birth and adoption, of her parents' marriage — these are not one story, but many stories, all interwoven. It's up to Julia to tease out the information she needs. "Get out of here," Uncle Paul barks without lifting his head. Julia is startled, but then she sees that he means Aunt Judy. Judy knows it too; Julia understands that this scene has been played out before, has been repeated many times since Uncle Paul got so sick. Aunt Judy takes a half-step forward, then steps back again. She shoots a look at Julia, beseeching, then rattles off to hide herself in the kitchen. Julia isn't sure what Aunt Judy was asking her for.

(Later, standing before the gas stove where the kettle heats for yet another round of tea, she'll whisper to Julia. "He doesn't mean it, dolly. Don't worry. You know that's not him." Julia will embrace her aunt, the old woman's frail body hardly capable of holding any warmth, the wiry tendons Julia feels under her outspread palms tying the old, fragile bones together under the soft, slack skin.)

Alone in the living room, Julia and Paul sit silent for a while. One by one, he takes his pills, obediently sipping from the water glass after each one, gasping after each swallow. When he's finished, he lifts the teacup, squeezes the lemon over it, then takes a series of rapid little sips. He sets the cup down and sits back, adjusting the pillow behind his back. Then he lifts his head and looks at Julia.

"Ask," he says. He sounds tired. Resigned.

Julia bites her lip. "Tell me about the private detective," she says. He nods.

"When you were a little girl," he begins. He tips his head back and closes his eyes, then opens them. "Let's see, it must have been about 1970. Yes, it was the year of the October Crisis. You wouldn't remember this, but they brought the army in."

"I remember the army," Julia says, "although I didn't understand why they were there. In any case we learned about it later, in school."

Paul nods again, puffy hands braced on his thighs. "Everyone was very frightened," he continues. He says it with emphasis, as if it is crucial that Julia understand the depth of this experience. She is touched, and grateful to him. For the first time she thinks that maybe it is good for him to have the opportunity, as he stands so close to death, to reconstruct these pieces of his life. She wonders whether Carol had the chance to tell her life to someone. If she did, which stories did she tell — and which did she keep hidden, folded in her throat, tucked behind her ribs, stuck away in all the secret places like knots of dirty string too old and tight to unpick?

"One night we were discussing how frightening it all was, and your mother said, 'I hope she's living somewhere else,' and your father gave her a look like death. He knew who she meant, and that was really the last time I ever heard it mentioned." He picks up his teacup again and lifts it to his lips but doesn't sip; it's as if the gesture helps him think.

"I know you loved your father very much," he says, looking at Julia. "He was a good person. But he could be ... hard on your mother. He had a certain sternness, which ... maybe he got from his own father." Paul turns his gaze back to his teacup, but Julia has the sense that he is actually still watching her, waiting for her reaction.

Julia has only the vaguest memories of her paternal grand-father; to her, he was a mild, almost befuddled old man with a beard. But she has seen photographs of him, a forbidding expression on his face. She interpreted that as piety; her grand-father was always spoken of as having had a certain religious authority, although he had allowed many of the habits of religious life to lapse. Now Julia can see that his seriousness could have been a kind of authoritarianism, a brewing thun-der. She remembers the deference, bordering on timidity, with which her father treated Zaide Goodman. As a small child Julia didn't question that, attributed it to her grandfather's advanced age. Now she sees that it was a kind of exaggerated respect, even fear, in her father. This is a new aspect of him for her. She thinks again of her grandfather, of his brooding darkness. Seeing that, she can easily call it up in the similarly-made face of her father.

She smiles ruefully and shrugs. "I know," she says, think-ing that she probably doesn't know, really. All her life she has thought of her mother as the difficult one to be with, but she is beginning to understand that the power her mother wielded within the family was simply more visible to her than her father's.

Paul nods slightly and continues. "Sometime that spring, your mother was walking with you on St. Catherine Street, and she saw a little girl walking hand in hand with a pretty woman. They were both wearing white gloves. The child looked very much like you, your mother said, but a little older." Uncle Paul looks over at Julia, his eyes crinkling as he smiles. His voice warms. "You were a beautiful little girl, Julia. You had golden curly hair and green eyes. You were the girl who was always smiling. You had little dimples," he puts his teacup back on the table next to his chair and pokes a finger into his own cheek on each side of his mouth, "right here."

He grins, sheepish, flaps a hand. "Well," he says. "You know what you looked like."

Julia's heart hurts. She wonders when she stopped being "the girl who was always smiling." She doesn't remember that girl. Instead, she remembers running toward Uncle Paul, her arms wide, expecting to crash into his warm legs and glue herself to him in a full-body hug — and having her mother grab her by the arm in mid-flight and wrench her back, leaning over her to say, through gritted teeth, "Young ladies don't run." The hot shame that made her face burn. She'd forgotten this. This must have been the beginning of her forgetting that she loved her Uncle Paul. Julia's chest hurts. She is ashamed again.

Paul sighs, lays his swollen fingers over his knees. "In any case. Your mother saw this child." For a second Julia thinks he means her, her child self; then she remembers that he is telling her about her lost, her ghost sister.

He looks up at Julia again. "I suppose she couldn't keep herself from looking all the time, whether she meant to or not. She saw this woman and child go into Eaton's, and she pulled you in after them. It seems she became a little hysterical. She ran around the store, looking in the children's department, in the restaurant, in the ladies' room, but she didn't find them. When she got home she told your father about it and I gather he was very angry. 'Don't open up that can of worms,' he told her."

Julia is astonished. She has no memory of this at all. At five, surely she would have been old enough to remember such a strange event? She feels anxious. What else does she not remember?

"In those days adoptions were ... sealed, they called it. Once it was done, it was finished. *Finito*. End of story. They were worried that children would come back and bring shame on families. Or that parents would have second thoughts and take back their babies. You weren't supposed to want to find your child again."

"Why was my father so angry?" Julia asks.

Uncle Paul shrugs. "I suppose he felt it wasn't fair on the baby and the people who took her in. And maybe ..." Uncle Paul hesitates. "To tell the truth, I think he was ashamed." Julia hears the Baby Ben clock ticking on top of the TV. It echoes in the room, unaccountably loud. Uncle Paul seems to be remembering things he's not telling her. "You know, his parents never knew about the baby. His father was very strict, very traditional. He studied to be a rabbi, although I don't think he finished. He wouldn't have accepted a baby conceived out of wedlock, even if your parents had married before it was born. Your father was afraid of disappointing his father."

Julia hasn't heard this before. She barely remembers the man; her father's parents moved to Florida the year she turned nine. "Maidalah," he used to call her, stroking her cheek with his dry fingers. He would pull a thick roll of cash from his baggy pants pocket and slowly, with great ceremony, peel a green one-dollar bill off it for Julia. A whole dollar. So much money!

"Our parents weren't so religious, but they wouldn't have been happy about it either. My mother was very conscious of her position in the community. She did a lot of community work, raised money for the library, the workman's circle. That kind of thing. She worried about how well she was dressed, whether she had the right shoes and hat. And they didn't have a lot of money, so she felt she was at a disadvantage." He shrugs. "She cared about that type of thing."

Julia remembers Carol's parents from pictures. They were older than Raph's parents, and died when she was very young; Carol had a battered hatbox filled with photographs of her family. Posed photographs, faded and yellowed, of Carol's own grandparents in the Ukraine. Stiff in their old-fashioned clothes, their faces grave, her grandfather's beard divided into two points where it lay on his chest. Carol and Paul as children, wearing funny clothes too, standing on the steps of their various childhood homes. In one series each of them is holding the reins of a pony they got to ride on somewhere in the country, the patient animal standing, head down, its child-sized saddle gaily painted. Photos of Carol's mother and father, mostly from fancy dinners where, Carol had explained to her, a photographer came to their table and they paid him to take their picture. Julia's bubbe in shiny satin or lace, sometimes with long wrinkly gloves that covered up her elbows, and funny cat's eye glasses, black plastic with rhinestones set into the frames. Everyone at the table would be in the picture, all leaning in toward the middle, smiling at the camera.

Paul lifts his teacup again. This time he sips from it. "Your mother sometimes felt that your father blamed her for getting pregnant. It was always ... it remained a problem between them." Julia is shocked. Her father was the warm, loving one. The patient one. Her mother was the rigid, critical parent, ready at any moment to find fault with Julia, to criticize her for some mistake or inadequacy. When uncoordinated Lillian Peperzak accidentally ran into Julia and knocked her down in the hallway at school and Julia's retainer was irreparably bent, her father laughed at the story. Carol was furious and yelled at Julia for not being more careful — didn't she know how much it was costing them to fix her teeth? Julia is starting to see that her parents' relationship with each other was very different from their relationships with her. She is beginning — just beginning — to understand how they became the people they were.

They have strayed far from the private detective, and into territory Julia didn't know existed. She is sad for her mother, and ashamed of her father; this is unexpected. She presses the heel of a hand into her side. The image of the mother and daughter disappearing into Eaton's returns to her mind's eye. Had she been within calling distance of her big sister on St. Catherine Street in the summer of 1970?

❦

JULIA IS TENSE ALL DAY at work. She spills a small vase full of water on the cash desk, the slippery glass disappearing from her fingers before she can stop it. Marie-Soleil puts the wrong prices on a shipment of expensive gardening gloves and Olivier notices only after they've sold several pairs. The store has lost almost twenty dollars, and Olivier is upset. He throws the remaining armful of gloves on the desk in front of Julia's face with a curt "Fix this." When he's gone out to the bank, Julia tosses them at Marie-Soleil, icily telling her how careless she was. As she's speaking she is sick in her stomach; she turns her head so she doesn't have to look at Marie-Soleil's stricken face.

Olivier returns and finds Marie-Soleil red-eyed and sniffing at the cash; he glances at the pile of gardening gloves on the counter next to her and comes charging into the office where Julia is sitting at the desk, picking at the corner of the weekly schedule with her fingernails. "Did I tell you to fix those price tags?" he says, standing over her.

"It wasn't me who made the mistake, it was her —"

"*Franchement*, Julia!" Olivier growls. He takes a breath, points a finger at her. "It was up to you to supervise her. You are responsible. Now," he steps back to the cash and grabs the gloves, dropping them on the desk in front of Julia again, "now you do the job I told you to do." Olivier stalks out of the office. Julia's face is steaming like the bottom of an iron.

She feels ashamed of herself, but also hard done by. Yesterday Marie-Soleil made a more costly mistake at the cash and Olivier didn't yell at her. Julia looks out the office door at the golden Marie-Soleil. She is wearing clingy low-rise lululemon pants that allow her hipbones to arch up into view, her perfect bum sloping down to perfectly rounded, smoothly muscular thighs. The little fleur-de-lys that dangles from her pierced navel draws the eye to the plane of her flat belly; her ready smile is so open it's as if she has no idea how gorgeous she is. Julia knows it's useless to compare herself with a woman twenty years younger. When she is forty, Marie-Soleil may still be ravishing, but she will probably be comparing herself with twenty-year-olds too.

Julia turns back to the gloves and begins to strip off the incorrect price tags. In the first blush of her affair with Nicholas, she'd felt juicy and sweet as ripe fruit, constantly hot and damply slick at the thought of him. She would meet him at the Romolo or the Casa del Popolo and see him watching her as she walked in; he would pass through the door of her apartment and his hands would fly to her body as if of their own volition. They both attended a lecture at the CCA one evening and she'd looked up to find him observing her from across the room, his face rapt, desire plain on his unguarded features. For these few months Julia had felt beautiful, richly desirable, in a way she never had before in her life — and, she worries, never will again. The feeling has faded along with their attachment to each other, marred by their arguments, their constant cross-purposes. Now she mourns the passing of this moment; she wonders if, had she been braver, clearer, smarter — whatever it took — would their relationship have declined this way? Would she still be the object of such intense desire?

In any case, the magical feeling of ripeness is gone. Now Julia sees herself standing at the edge of creeping decrepitude, looking back over her shoulder at firm, careless youth. Nicholas caught her at the cusp of age, as she was tipping over into middle-aged slackness; now she tracks the progress of the drying, the withering, the loosening. She finds the traces on her skin with every shower, under her eyes after every sleepless night.

From now on, she supposes, whatever dismissal or disrespect is due to unattractiveness and age will come to her more and more regularly. She is ashamed to be getting old and slack;

if she were more diligent perhaps she could at least delay the decay. Olivier passes the door of the office and looks in at her, his face stone blank. Julia feels it as an almost parental rebuke.

She stifles her sniffling, embarrassed to be so sorry for herself. It is as if the desk is suddenly much too big for her, the chair so high that her feet swing in the air, well clear of the floor. Julia smells a familiar smell — a combination of clean cotton, cooked meat, and cool skin that makes her gorge rise a little, her heart clutch inside her — and she finds herself turning her head, sharply, expecting to see her mother standing behind her. Julia swallows a little sob, shaking her head, smiling painfully at herself. Her dead mother. She closes her eyes and lets the tightness of revulsion subside in her chest, a stray tear dry to stickiness on her cheeks.

Julia breathes deeply and wonders at herself. Is her mother standing behind her, still? The desk is slowly shrinking back to its normal size; the soles of her feet touch the wooden floorboards. She remembers the shelves of Steinberg's, rising high above her head. Her mother is glowering down at her. On the floor, a spill of glittering white sugar fanning out from the ragged split in the paper Redpath bag. The nauseating lump of shame is so far up Julia's throat that she has to concentrate to keep from gagging. Carol's eyes flash hard. She's in a hurry, heels clacking on the tiled floor of the grocery store, trying to get the shopping finished in time to get home and make supper. Julia swallows. For Raph, and someone from his work. Carol scans the shelves, muttering the name of each item from her list as she searches for it. "Sugar, sugar," Carol murmurs. Julia sees it, the row of squat white bags with their blue stripe and red lettering, and she darts ahead and pulls one down, proud of herself for helping, until the heavy bag doesn't stop in her little arms but keeps falling and then smacks the floor with a sickening tearing sound. Carol cries out and then grits her teeth; Julia knows she is controlling herself because they are in public. She grabs a handful of the shoulder of Julia's dress and pulls Julia painfully upwards, hissing into her ear. "Why, why are you such a bad girl?" Then, a deep breath, Carol's voice almost on the edge of breaking, "I should have had a good girl."

Now Julia is like a black hole, a ball of compressed matter — invisibly small but unbearably heavy, unable to move one muscle in her chair. Breathing is a terrible effort. She has a picture in her mind of her mother marching her into an aisle of the store where the shelves are lined with little girls. Carol scans the children until she finds the one she wants — the good one — and removes her, pushing Julia up onto the shelf in her place. Julia stands, arms rigid at her sides, feet aligned, and watches as her mother walks away down the aisle with the daughter she was supposed to have. She knows Carol has made the right choice: she is not good enough.

A cool breeze passes across Julia's face; she hears the little bell as the door of the shop swings closed. She sees the bulletin board over her desk, the invoice on which they were short-shipped a dozen hyacinth greeting cards, stuck there with a yellow pushpin. She remembers the feeling of Nicholas's finger stroking the skin on the back of her leg, pulling gently on the edge of the hole in her pantyhose, the way the thrill ran up her leg and collected in her stomach, how at the same time her tongue felt as thick in her mouth as a rolled-up Ace bandage and her head swam with shame, the shame of being stupid. She'd wondered then how long it would take Nicholas to realize she was not good enough for him. How long it would take for him to stop sending the magic out of his fingertips and into her nerves, her marrow. She looks up, focuses on the yellow pushpin. She takes a deep breath, exhales. Better remember to follow up on those greeting cards.

She pulls the calligraphy pen and the bag of clean price tags out of the side drawer, but before beginning to write the new prices she pulls a tissue from the box at the side of the desk and quickly blows her nose, dabs her eyes dry. She'll pull herself together.

Julia looks up and is abashed to see Marie-Soleil watching her from her post at the cash, through the open office door. Marie-Soleil smiles tentatively and Julia smiles back, thinking, if my sister had a child at eighteen, Marie-Soleil could be that child. The good daughter of the good daughter. Then: no, no one in my family was ever this beautiful. Julia wonders whether her sister could have ended up in a Québécois family. Speaking French, going to mass on Sundays — or not going to mass, but playing hockey in the park with a tangle of brothers. Tracing her lineage (not knowing it wasn't her lineage at all) back through generations to some original pair of Norman peasants willing to risk the desolation of this snowbound vastness in order to escape the persistent agony of hunger. Julia has a vague idea that they would have tried to place a Jewish baby with a Jewish family. The thought that she will not only never know her sister, but will also never know her sister's children, or their children, suddenly makes her terribly sad again. She won't have the chance to sit and talk with a niece as her Uncle Paul has sat and talked with her.

She doesn't know why she is feeling the loss of something she didn't expect to have, didn't want. Bill has a son and she's never been particularly interested in him. She begins to inscribe prices on the clean white tags, tries to concentrate on something useful. Something outside of herself.

She follows the strokes of her pen with her eyes. The black ink flows into figures. While she has been sitting here feeling so pitiful, Nicholas may be dead or dying. Maybe he is half-covered with sand in the blazing sun, his throat painfully dry, unable to raise himself to his feet to stumble any farther. Or maybe he is lying on the tiled floor of a hotel bathroom, wracked with dysentery. He could have been mugged in an alleyway and left to bleed his life away, his laptop with its notes on Moorish architecture already miles away, being exchanged for a handful of some foreign currency. Julia puts aside the price tags and turns on the computer to check her email. There is nothing from Nicholas. Her chest aches with missing him, but also with sorrow for Deepa. She sees Deepa's lovely face, looking as tired as Deepa sounded on the phone. Nicholas is important to Julia, but he is in the very walls of Deepa's home, in her drawers and her cupboards. His clothes, his shoes, his aftershave lotion. The jar of roasted artichoke hearts he bought for a pasta dish he didn't get to make. Julia can't imagine a loss on this scale.

There is an email from Campbell, saying hi, and one from Lauren inviting Julia to go for a drink tonight after work. Julia replies, accepting. It will be good for her to be in company, to be forced to act like a normal person.

⊹✦⊱

"SHE COULDN'T GET THE IDEA out of her head," Paul says. He is drinking a fresh cup of tea which Aunt Judy has slipped into his hand without speaking, the already-squeezed wedge of lemon lying on the saucer. Julia smells the sweet-bitter oil from the lemon rind. Aunt Judy reappears from the kitchen and, still wordless in an effort to avoid irritating Uncle Paul, hands Julia a cup too. Julia's saucer has three little round gingerbread cookies, like coins from some country of children, arranged around the edge. Paul looks over. "Give me one of those," he says, hooking his forefinger as if he could magically attract a cookie with this gesture, make it float up off the white porcelain. He's diabetic and therefore not supposed to eat anything made with sugar, but Julia can't bear to refuse him this tiny pleasure. She hands him a little gingerbread coin and Paul bites it with the side of his mouth, as if testing to see if it's real. As he chews, crumbs fall across his chin and into his teacup. He chews that tiny bite of cookie for a long time, his dentures jarring, apparently unaware that his chin is scattered with brown specks of cookie.

"Mom?" Julia prompts. Paul nods, pushing the rest of the cookie into his mouth. She wonders if he is stalling. It occurs to her that he may feel he is betraying some sort of confidence. She gets angry at the thought. Fuck that, she thinks. Carol's dead. I'm alive. I win.

"She couldn't stop thinking about that little girl. She was kind of" — Paul raises an eyebrow, taps his temple — "*meshuggenah*. Obsessed, almost. At that time, she had a pair of gold earrings that your father's parents had given her as a wedding present. They made her ears swell up." Paul leans in, lowers his voice. "I suppose they weren't very high quality gold," he says. Julia wants to smile, but she doesn't; there must have been tension between the two families, something she wasn't aware of during her childhood. It would be fascinating, if there weren't so many painful little secrets stuck in the cracks of this new knowledge. Paul sits up straight again, his breath harsh in his throat. "She never wore them. So she took them to a jeweller and sold them, and used the money to hire a private detective to find your sister."

Julia hadn't known about the earrings, but she'd more or less expected that this was what the private detective was about. Yet her heart is pounding so hard she can barely hear Paul. "Oh, what *tsuris*!" he says, batting the air with a swollen paw as if to wave away the trouble. "When your father found out about the detective, he was mad. But when he found out about the earrings, he was furious. Furious!"

"'I just want to know she's okay,' your mother said. 'That's what you say now,' he said. 'You'll find out she lives in such and such a place, then you'll "just" want to know about the family. Then you'll "just" want to see her. It'll never end, and it'll only cause grief.' He forbade her even to hear what the detective found out. Oh, how your mother cried."

Julia racks her brain. How could she not remember such a fracas in her family? They must have done all this arguing at night, behind the closed door of their bedroom.

"In a way that was worse than anything, because then she imagined this detective had some information, which she had already paid for, and it killed her to think she was so close to knowing something, yet so far."

Julia is standing by her mother's bedside and her father is trying to pull her away. "Mommy's sick today," he's saying. "We have to let her rest." Julia is wearing her favourite dress of that summer, pink gingham with a shirred bodice and puffy short sleeves; she is also wearing white ankle socks and her dress-up Mary Janes. When her father suggested she wear her pink dress she'd been thrilled, because now she and the pink doll would match. Why is she dressed up? She sees her mother, eyes swollen and red, her face looking utterly leached of any vitality. She knew, Julia realizes, that her mother wasn't sick in the normal way. At the time she had no idea what was actually wrong. Now she sees her mother's deadened eyes.

"I went to Daddy's office one day," Julia says slowly.

Paul nods. "That's right, dolly, you remember that? I think it was a few days. Your mother was in no shape to take care of you. Your father had forbidden her ever to contact the detective. In fact, I think he contacted the man himself and told him not to call the house. I think so."

Julia remembers sitting on the floor of Raph's office, colouring with a brand new box of crayons and a fresh colouring book. She has recently learned from a girl at school how to make outlines with dark crayon, then fill them in with the same colour in a lighter shade. She loves how it makes the pictures look. She works very hard at it. At lunchtime Raph takes her to the cafeteria and buys her a hot chicken sandwich, a silky, salty brown square with a pile of soft fibrous green beans on the side of the plate. She can't bear the sticky feeling of the wet bread in her mouth, and she understands that her father is embarrassed when she tries to pull the chicken slices out and eat them by themselves. So she leaves them and eats the beans instead, one at a time, spearing them with her big fork and dabbing them in the gravy and then chewing, chewing until she can swallow them. He makes her drink a glass of milk, which she hates. Her mother, two generations removed from the last housewife in her family to keep kosher, doesn't serve milk with a meat meal, and it tastes terrible to Julia.

She had forgotten this critical, nervous father, this out-of-the-ordinary day. That evening, her father dropped her off at Uncle Paul and Aunt Magda's at suppertime, and she'd eaten pot roast and carrots with them. Aunt Magda promised her a special dessert if she ate enough supper, so she tried her best. Finally, it was enough: after clearing the plates, Magda told her to close her eyes, and when she opened them, there in front of her was a luscious cupcake, golden, with swirly pink frosting and two cherries on top. Julia bites her lip. Magda must have given her an extra cherry. Why didn't she remember how nice Aunt Magda was?

"When did Magda die?" Julia asks suddenly.

Uncle Paul nods his head. "1975." He pauses. "Bill was only twenty," he says softly.

"Like me with Dad," Julia says. Funny, it hadn't occurred to her that she and Bill had this in common.

"Yeah," says Uncle Paul. "You remember the funeral?" he asks. Julia has only a fragmentary vision of the graveside ceremony. Carol took her out of school for the day so she could attend. Bill stood at the head of the rectangular hole, face tight. He must have been back from college for the funeral. Carol's face was strikingly pale under the big round black sunglasses she wore in spite of the greyness of the afternoon; her hand was clenched around a crumpled handkerchief. Julia remembers that she wore her shiny black dress-up shoes, and they got smeared with gritty grey mud from the mound next to the grave. She sees herself take the shovel from her mother, feels the strain of it in her shoulder as she levers a clot of mud off the top of the grainy pile.

"I shovelled some dirt in by myself," she says. Paul smiles gently to himself, nods again.

"She was really nice to me," Julia says. She's embarrassed not to have recalled this before.

Uncle Paul turns to her. "She was really nice," he says quietly.

They're silent together. Julia thinks she hears rustling from the direction of the kitchen and feels a little guilty, as if she is being disloyal to Aunt Judy. "I'm sorry I didn't know Magda when I was older," she says.

Paul sighs. "She was born in '33, in Europe. She never remembered a time without war, or after that, in the DP camp. It wasn't a normal life. So it was very important to her to make a good life for us, especially for Bill." He stops, raises his cup. "But it also meant she could be very hard on us. On herself. Especially on Bill." Paul takes a sip of tea again, then looks at Julia. "You know, dolly, when you have a child you don't think of them as a person who starts from scratch. You think of them as a chance to make good, someone who could avoid your mistakes, your miseries. You have good intentions, but ..." He looks at his hands. "It's the hardest thing to let your child be someone else."

Julia is struck with pity for Magda, her aspirations for her son coming between him and her love for him. She feels sorry for Bill too. She sees his face again, his teenaged, studied blankness as she and her mother came into the kitchen that night. At fifteen, he was already very good at closing himself off. This amazes her. Bill — dull, quiet Bill — has a past that shaped him, made him the way he is. Julia almost laughs; somehow she'd imagined her boring cousin was born boring.

Paul lifts his head and smiles at Julia. "Lightning's not supposed to strike twice," he says cheerfully, "but I got lucky twice." He jerks his thumb toward the kitchen. "She's nice too," he says, happily, and Julia is so glad for him, and then without feeling the transition she is breathless with pain, loss tearing through her like shrapnel. She thinks she won't get the chance to say that about someone she loves, and she bends her mouth in a smile for Uncle Paul while she watches Nicholas emerge from the ragged wound in her chest and disappear like a creature of mist. She sips at her tea as she mentally works at shutting off the flow of tears before it starts. No need to juggle two griefs at the same time. Do the family right now, she thinks. Plenty of time for the rest later.

She sips more tea and feels her throat relax. "So," she says. "Do you know whether Mom ever did hear from the detective?"

"No," Paul says firmly. "No, I'm sure she didn't. She couldn't have. Your father really laid down the law. And after she got over her ... sickness" — he peers at Julia — "her breakdown, is what it was, she seemed better. And it didn't come up again."

Julia feels caught. What if the detective had found something? She sees her mother again on her deathbed, a desiccated bundle of bones laid among institutional sheets. Julia wonders whether Carol regretted not disobeying her husband, not calling the detective back. She thinks of her mother looking around her hospital room, seeing the three other shrivelled old women lying in their beds, tubes attached to them with white tape or with needles inserted into the backs of their blue-veined hands, daughters or sons or grandchildren sitting quietly by their beds. As she smelled the metal and the medicines and the disinfectant they swabbed on the floors, did Carol imagine that if she had found her first child she wouldn't be dying there alone? Julia reminds herself to unclench her fists, to breathe. Carol gave up her right to have Baby Goodman by her side, released Baby from that particular obligation. Baby probably has some other mother to accompany through that last passage. Julia clenches again. Carol died alone not because she had no daughters, but because she couldn't love the one she had. The one who would have loved her.

❧

JULIA SLEEPS ALMOST THE WHOLE night, awaking from an unhappy dream shortly after six. It is similar in mood to dreams she has often had. During her last year of living with Stewart, he was in them; before and after that period, this sort of dream usually featured her mother. Stewart or Carol would be an authority figure, disapproving, absent, or unresponsive. The actual events in the dreams were often ridiculous — Julia would be craving a bowl of cereal, say, and Stewart would be berating her for it, forbidding the consumption of cereal — but he was like a thunderhead, dark and looming, and Julia invariably woke up feeling terrible. Guilty, angry, ashamed.

This time, Nicholas is in the dream. He is standing in obscurity, in a doorway between rooms, in an unfamiliar house. Julia assumes he will come forward to greet her, but he doesn't, only stands and peers out at her from inside his shadows. She begins to feel that it was presumptuous of her to think that he wanted to see her. Still she watches him and he is silent. She sees that she should doubt whether he ever actually liked her. The house is getting darker and there are no lights; she can barely see him now. She starts to realize, to her horror, that she can't rely on basic social conventions in their interactions. She feels ashamed for having made such a misjudgment, for having expected of him an affection he clearly does not feel. Now it has become dark in the house, and although she senses that he is still there, she can no longer see him at all. Somehow it is her fault that she cannot see him. The dark begins to feel dangerous.

She checks the clock. It is almost light out. She doesn't have to get up, but she feels really awake. 6:17 a.m. That means it is 10:17 a.m. in Morocco. She thinks of Nicholas sitting at the desk in his hotel room, the night's sweat recently sluiced off him in a cool shower. The smell of coffee lingering in the air, him reading a book. A novel someone has given him, she decides. *A Complicated Kindness*, perhaps. Without looking, she reaches down and touches the cover of her own copy, lying where she put it before turning off the light last night. The smooth cover is cool, almost glassy beneath her fingertips. She fervently wishes for Nicholas to return, to be able to read this book when he has come home safe. Julia decides that she will buy him a copy. Lying there, her pillow hard, compacted from six or seven hours under the weight of her head, she thinks, I can buy a copy for Deepa and she can read it until he gets back.

❦

THE UNEXPECTEDLY SUMMERY WEATHER CONTINUES into the first days of October. Julia sits in Jeanne-Mance Park with, it seems, half the city, absorbing the sun's radiance into her upturned face. An avenue of tall old trees that extends the line of Rachel Street along a wide asphalted path, right up through the centre of the park, offers a weaving margin of shade to those who stroll beneath its extended branches. The grass is still green, still doing service to impromptu soccer players, wobbly toddlers and dogs of all shapes and sizes. Lauren lent Julia her paperback copy of *A Complicated Kindness* — actually, in typical Lauren fashion, she wouldn't allow Julia to leave her house without taking it. Lauren's a cop, and although she has a desk job now she spent years on the beat, and has a practised and effective commanding tone of voice. The book sits in Julia's lap, but the sun is so bright she can't focus on the page. An extended Latin American family has congregated around one of the nearby picnic tables. They are grilling some sort of meat, and the smoke gusts past Julia every time the wind shifts. The grand, towering old trees are confused; their leaves are not exactly turning colours, but they don't look fresh anymore. They are pale, worn. Brown, dried bundles of seed pods — the helicopters of spring — hang like strips of dried tea-soaked paper, rattling in the warm wind.

Julia watches the family as they tell each other stories, feed their children, kick around a soccer ball. None of them are her sister. Three men are standing a little apart, talking earnestly, apparently with good humour. One of them cocks his head, listening to the others, and Julia experiences an arrested moment; the gesture is so like one Nicholas makes that she suddenly sees how much the man resembles Nicholas — his hair is the same, so is his way of standing. She thinks, he could be back and I wouldn't know it. She knows this man isn't Nicholas and yet she sits up — her spine suspended by tension like a marionette's, pulled from above — waiting to see. Then the man turns, and his face is round and youthful, he is probably only twenty-five, he has dark hair running up his forearms like a wave of shadow. He is wearing a mesh T-shirt. Nicholas would never wear a mesh T-shirt. Julia laughs at herself, a little wistful.

Once this has happened she can't sit peacefully anymore. She tucks the book under her arm and starts to walk. She'd really like to go home and sit in her fat armchair with a glass of ice water and keep reading this book, but she can't bring herself to "waste" the day. A precious extra day of warmth — Julia unconsciously believes that if she doesn't stay outside and enjoy this now, the coming winter will last a day longer. Thus do Montrealers worship the god of summer, submit to its power, adore its caprices. She skirts the park, walking the asphalt sidewalk along de l'Esplanade, avoiding cyclists and dog walkers as she passes under another row of big trees.

She wishes she could wander, aimless, but she is not that kind of person. She needs a destination. On impulse, she stops at a pay phone and looks up Deepa's number. She almost hangs up after the first ring, stops herself. Deepa said they should have a drink together again sometime; Julia tells herself it is reasonable and normal for her to phone and say let's have a drink, even if only a day has passed. Call answer clicks on. She shrugs, leaves no message. Hangs up.

She decides to just do what she wants, and begins to walk home. She feels a little emptier than usual. She suffers from guilt, for not being entirely self-sufficient. "People are supposed to live with other people," she'd shouted at Stewart once during an argument. She believes that. She also senses that the culture around her teaches an expectation that people can, alternatively, live happily by themselves, that it is a mark of maturity to be able to live alone without loneliness. In fact, she has lived alone since Stewart left, and is fine much of the time. Yet when she is not she feels it as an inadequacy on her part. Like now.

She sees people sitting together in cafés. They issue from the doors of the big Provigo in pairs, white plastic bags of groceries stretching from their wrists, the shapes of cans and boxes, the yellow arcs of bananas visible inside the thin skins of plastic. Paper-collared brown nubs of bread stick out at angles as if to look around. Those people are going home to eat that bread together, she thinks. She shakes her head. Only yesterday she and Lauren and two other friends ate bread together, bread and cheese and olives, peaches in wine. Cups of dark coffee, chocolate seeded with dried cherries. Then why so gloomy? *Because I want Nicholas*, she answers herself. Standing at a crosswalk waiting for the light to turn, she closes her eyes, concentrates on the heat of the sun on her delicate lids, and tries to see him. It's about three in Montreal, so it's seven in the evening in Morocco. She pushes away her fears for him, tells herself everyone is probably overreacting. He hasn't called because he couldn't get a line. He didn't like the look of the hotel, so he stepped across the street, chose another. He's probably eating dinner, she thinks, and then, satisfied, he'll go back to his room. He'll shower away the day's heat and dust, throw open the shutters on his window as the sky darkens and the noise of the city wanes. Maybe he'll climb into bed naked, wind the sheet around his waist, read over his day's notes by the warm yellow light of the bedside lamp. Then he'll close his laptop, fold his reading glasses, lie back among the clean sheets. Julia sees him drop off, his graceful arm warm brown against the white linen, his face so peaceful that decades of life drop away from his expression. The picture of his skin fills her with a fierce craving; her lips tingle and her mouth actually waters at the thought of pressing her face to his smooth side, inhaling the subtle fragrance of his narrow waist.

Julia opens her eyes and begins to cross the street. She would make him safe by wishing it, if only she could. Let him sleep, give him purple flowers in a glass on the table next to the bed so he'll see them when he opens his eyes. She feels the core of her body pressing the wish forward, like an eager dog pulling on a leash. But it all fades, because she cannot know, cannot see, cannot make anything happen just by wanting. He's a smart guy, has a certain terrier quality — doggedness, she thinks — he looks out for himself. He must be fine.

She imagines the surface of the world. Its vast unendingness, its great constant curve, its long, wide, round, outspreading surface-ness. Wherever he is, whatever has happened to him, they are connected by this thin skin of dirt, rock, and water. They are held by gravity's great open palm to the topmost layer of this ball. If she could keep walking without end — step, step, step — she could eventually get to him, no matter where he is. Elsewhere on this ball might be her sister. She thinks: if she could pinpoint their locations, the three of them, the area in between would form a triangle. A shape that would be one way to define her life. A geography of love, a geometry of errors. All other ways of saying history.

She opens her door and throws her keys on the little table. She falls into the big chair and pulls her knees up to her chest. Somewhere else, relatively close, Deepa O'Malley is doing some Sunday thing. If she added Deepa to her life-shape it would be a trapezoid. Julia bobs her foot, looks at her dirty toenails, the dusty bump of bone where her big toe connects to other foot bones under the skin. Maybe Deepa is eating croissants with a cabinetmaker friend. Or trailing hand-painted silk scarves across the insides of her small, open palms in a boutique in Old Montreal, trying to decide which one to buy. Or standing by her dining-room window holding the phone to her ear, the repeated robotic tones of the overseas connection bouncing off her auditory nerve, her other arm crossed over her chest like half a hug, holding her heart and lungs inside her until she gets some news and can afford to stop thinking about whether each pump of blood will take place, whether each breath of air will enter and exit as it should.

Julia grabs her phone and calls information and gets Deepa's number again and dials it. The thought of Deepa standing cloaked in grief, her pulse hammering with anxiety, fills Julia with pity and a sort of strange desperation. The phone rings.

There is a click and Julia sighs because it will be call answer again, but then Deepa's voice fills her ear. She sounds tired, but the keyed-up kind of tired. There is a poignant edge of hope to her voice.

"Deepa," Julia says.

There is a pause. She imagines Deepa cycling through a series of thoughts: it's not Nicholas. It's not anyone with news of Nicholas. There's no good news. Well, at least it's not bad news. It's Julia. "Julia," Deepa says.

"How are you?" Julia asks. Deepa sighs and Julia thinks she can hear water in it, that fraying of breath through which tears seep.

"Oh, same as usual," she says. "Just trying to clean the garden up a bit before winter. I told Nick I'd do some of that before he got home." There is another pause, more thoughts. "Want some last tomatoes? They're ugly, but they taste good."

Julia almost says no thank you by reflex, but catches herself. "Yeah, I'd love a few." Deepa pauses again and Julia thinks, if I didn't know she was so anxious I'd admire her confidence, not needing to rush to fill any quiet space with the next remark, however thoughtless. Having thought that, Julia can't resist the silence herself, her own social anxiety creeping up her neck. "Can I make you supper?" she blurts.

"Sure," Deepa says, "thanks," and through the flatness of her voice Julia imagines she hears a small smile.

⁂

JULIA WALKS SOUTH ACROSS THE flank of Jeanne-Mance Park, past the volleyball players in their sandpits, then dips into the built environment again. The towers of La Cité, with their various middlebrow merchants — the health club, the grocery store, the Asian/gourmet store facing the Thai fast food — guard the corner of Prince Arthur Street and the suddenly parkless Park Avenue. She realizes, passing the walls of nubbly calamine-coloured brick, that she can't remember what was on that corner before La Cité was built, before the church up the street was turned into condos. Her vision of the urban past is slipping away, increasingly irretrievable; she wonders how much of her personal past is gone too, so gone she doesn't remember it once existed.

She drifts through the narrow streets of the McGill ghetto, old stone houses cheek by jowl with newer, less graceful apartment blocks, so gentrified it no longer deserves its name. She passes doorways that now open onto expensive condos, but which once led Julia into ramshackle student apartments where beer was drunk and The Clash clashed, apartheid was decried and silver-ringed young women displayed the first, most daring tattoos. She laughs a little, wistfully; gazing upon the dark swirls inked along the pale flatness below sweet clavicles, none of them could have imagined the ubiquity, the current total lack of shock value of this form of adornment. How old am I, Julia thinks.

Milton Street. As a student she'd fancied, very romantically, that it was named for the poet. Julia ducks into The Word. The fairy-tale tiny, picturesquely-crammed second-hand bookstore has been so long entrenched in its miniature house that Julia imagines its very walls are now, for all intents and purposes, actually constructed of the books that fill every corner. She makes her way among the browsers, mutterers and hangers-on who stand squeezed between the floor-to-ceiling shelving on the walls and the centre tables piled with thematic drifts of books; histories of Wales over here, F.R. Leavis giving way to structuralism, old buff-covered Barthes and stacks of Foucault over there. The little old building smells moistly, pleasantly of dust and decomposing paper.

Running her finger along the alphabetically-filed fiction shelf, Julia locates a single paperback copy of *A Complicated Kindness* to give to Deepa at dinner. She knows it's completely irrational, but ever since she thought of it this morning she has been firmly decided. Then she goes home, stopping along St. Lawrence Boulevard, changeable spine of the city, for wine and other necessaries for the meal.

Once home, she is jittery. She is trying to make a salad but continually has to interrupt herself — she notices a fuzzy coat of dust on the shelf where she keeps her cookbooks and has to go wipe it clean; there is a miniature carpet of crumbs under the toaster. She goes to pee and can't believe she didn't clean the yellow-stained toilet bowl before now; she must scrub it, and then her hands, before she can go back to the food. Eventually she stands before the kitchen sink, hands immersed in cold water among a litter of pale, cupped lettuce leaves, and closes her eyes. She sees Deepa's dining room, warm mustardy walls, motes of dust floating in the sunlight that washes in through the big window. It's okay, she tells herself. Everybody has dust. Deepa won't stop wanting to be my friend if everything isn't spotless. She opens her eyes and turns the stopper to let the water drain. Nicholas might, she thinks, smiling ruefully. She shrugs, spins the lettuce dry, cracks the brainy, convoluted leaves into smaller pieces and tosses them in the bowl.

Deepa arrives. She wasn't kidding when she said the tomatoes were ugly. Happily, the unsightliness turns out to be only
skin-deep. Julia cuts away the scarred parts, the splits, the
tiny round brown depressions where rot has made its first
entry into the overblown late-season fruit; firm meat, almost
the colour of human flesh, is revealed. Deepa sits nursing a
glass of beer, her upper lip dipping into the foamy head, her
tongue passing over it leaving it clean and moist. Julia watches,
glancing up from her preparations. She flashes Deepa a smile.
The back of her neck prickles; she can almost see Nicholas
sitting, as he has so many times before, in the chair where
Deepa sits now. He has run his fingers along the cool glass
that Deepa's fingers hold. Julia can hardly believe that Deepa
doesn't feel the ghost of Nicholas's past presence here, his
palimpsest on the air, the molecules of his smell, his skin
floating into her nose. She sees Deepa look around the room
with a considering gaze.

Julia's cheeks feel hot; she bends her head to her work.
This secret weighs on her like a heavy blanket, stifling and
scratchy. She sees the blade of her knife flash silver as it cuts
through the red curve of a tomato's skin, and thinks of her
mother's hands, preparing meal after meal, bearing her own
deception. How did she live with that, day after day over the
course of a lifetime? For a moment Julia wishes she could
have helped her mother free herself from this burden, but she
can't think how she could have. She is weak and helpless.

Deepa rolls her beer glass back and forth along the table
between two open palms. "So there's no Canadian consulate
in Casablanca, or anywhere except Rabat," she is saying. "I
spoke to them just before I came here. They referred me to

the British High Commission. They, apparently, have an office in Casablanca." She sips again, seems to be concentrating on the bitter sweetness of the beer on her tongue. She shakes her head and laughs a little. "That time difference is a bitch."

Julia is sipping wine and it makes her almost giddy. She is slicing fresh basil into tiny ribbons for crostini and it releases its green perfume between them. It's been a while since she bothered to cut fresh herbs into anything.

They sit at Julia's little table and eat, exchanging bits of conversation like chess pieces. Move one square to the right. Move two squares diagonally. Capture a pawn. Julia pours Deepa another beer and they divide the last raggedy bits of salad between them, the accumulated juice from the tomatoes pooling on their plates. Deepa doesn't pick up her fork again; instead she raises her glass to her lips, her dark hair falling forward in a thin cascade to cover her eyes, and she sips steadily until half the glass is emptied. Then she puts it down with a loud clack of glass against wood.

"I almost felt like they were suggesting that I was foolish to try to find Nick," she says, her voice tight. She waves a hand. "Not that he was ever anything but polite. Very professional. Monsieur Lang*lois*," she says, an edge of bitterness turning the corners of her mouth as she pronounces the name. "But it was that missing persons thing, you know, there's the unspoken suggestion that the person is ... missing on purpose." She breathes in sharply, exhales. She takes another drink, then looks up, shaking her hair out of her face as she looks straight at Julia. "Nick's much too honest to take off like that. If he didn't want to be with me anymore he'd just say it. It wouldn't occur to him not to."

Julia's heart is thumping at her. She's absolutely sure there are plenty of things Nicholas hasn't told Deepa. Below the surface of the table, she presses the heel of her hand into her side where an ache has begun. Deepa isn't looking at her. She seems to be staring at her plate, although Julia's pretty certain she isn't seeing the little pile of lettuce leaves flecked with dark snips of chive that lie scattered across the white circle, glistening. Julia can't believe that she has actually invited Nicholas's wife to have dinner at her house. What was she thinking?

"At our wedding," Deepa says slowly, "we wrote our own vows, and one of them was, 'Because being together should be better than being alone, I promise not to stay when I ought to go.' Another one was, 'Because being together should make us each more than we would be apart, I promise not to let it make me less.'" She looks up at Julia and laughs quietly. "Does that sound stupid? We were really idealistic."

Julia is twisted up inside, but she knows the only way to get through this is to get through it. She smiles and forks a piece of lettuce into her mouth, feels the vinegar bite her tongue. "It doesn't sound stupid to me. Who would ever get married if they weren't idealistic?"

Deepa laughs, really laughs this time. "You got that right!" she says, and shakes her head. For the first time since she arrived she seems to have relaxed a bit. Her eyes flick up and meet Julia's; they are a luminous brown with a suggestion of gold behind it. Julia thinks: how extraordinary, they both have amazing eyes.

Deepa picks up a piece of crisp-toasted baguette spread with goat cheese, basil shreds, and flakes of sun-dried red pepper, and takes a firm bite, scattering crumbs across her chest. She leans over and brushes the debris down over her breasts and onto her plate, then lifts her eyes and smiles at Julia. Julia smiles back, but her cheeks are hot again. She was paying good attention to the way Deepa's small, strong hands turned across her gentle cleavage like the wings of a pigeon settling on a perch. Deepa hasn't noticed — or doesn't mind. They devote themselves to eating for a little while.

Julia asks Deepa how she began to make her famous furniture, and Deepa begins to talk. Her father was a cabinetmaker, although he worked for other people, not on his own account. She didn't learn any specific skills from him; he taught her younger brother, who chose to become a car mechanic instead, and now sells insurance in Etobicoke. She went to art school. Three years at Concordia, then off to the Rhode Island School of Design.

"It was a crazy scene," she says. "All of us maladjusted art students packed into this little New England town. When I think of it, I think of ..." She leans her head back and closes her eyes, as if she can see the past better that way. She counts her memories on her fingers. "Cigarettes and pizza, beer and hair dye, the smell of photo developing fluid."

She opens her eyes again. "And these intense brownies they used to sell in this café that was in what used to be a little clapboard house, painted light blue — what do they call them? — a saltbox. Plus I think I drank more coffee in that one year than in my entire life since. There were people there doing knitting projects, there was a guy who made a copy of his dental impressions out of paper he chewed — you name it, we'd do it if we thought we were pushing the envelope."

"No way!" Julia says, leaning forward. Deepa's smiling to herself, and Julia sees a little indentation, distinct but too small to be a dimple, at one corner of her perfectly shaped mouth — only one. "My high school boyfriend went to RISD. He was a bit older than I was; I spent a lot of time visiting him there. Early eighties." She pauses, then raises both her eyebrows. "In retrospect, it's a fucking miracle my mother let me go."

"Maybe we passed each other in the halls," Deepa says mischievously.

"Maybe," Julia says eagerly. It makes her feel happy to find even this tenuous connection with Deepa, circumventing their fraught link through Nicholas. "I wouldn't remember, though. All I really recall from those days, besides the terrible sex, was everyone gathering in Todd's dorm room to listen to the Talking Heads' 'Psycho Killer.' Hunched around the record player, smoking. They played it over and over again, and they were absolutely reverent." Deepa is nodding her head and they're both laughing. "It was like, 'They're from here.' For Todd and his friends it was almost proof that art school was good for something."

"I remember that, when that record came out. It was kind of thrilling!" Deepa says. Julia gets up to make coffee and then changes her mind. She's out of beer but divides the remaining wine between two glasses; they are quite full. She sips from her own and sets the other one by Deepa's elbow. Deepa takes a long drink then sits quietly for a few minutes, rolling the round belly of the glass between her fingers.

"After a while I got exhausted," Deepa says. "I realized I didn't want to make art, capital *A*, as in grand conceptual statements. I really just wanted to make more beauty in the world. But, beautiful things people could live with. I came back home and moved in with my parents temporarily and started helping my dad on the job, to make a bit of cash so I could move out. And the rest is history," she says abruptly, tossing off the rest of her wine.

Julia watches as Deepa throws her head back and gulps, the muscles of her throat moving as she swallows. *The rest is history*. What a funny expression — as if it isn't all history. All constantly lost, sometimes found, filtered and fragmented, and misunderstood, claimed and reclaimed and reconstituted. She and Deepa are now history, their present slipping away into an overlapping past like the track disappearing behind the train. She gazes at Deepa's fine-boned face. Julia's side hurts less now.

She sets a single round little chocolate mousse on the table between them. She unwinds its stiff plastic collar and hands Deepa a fork, and they eat it together, both concentrating on the rich dark sweet, their forks dipping in and out like birds feeding on the surface of a lake. When they're finished Deepa sticks her tongue out and presses the back of the fork against it, licking off the last of the dessert; Julia watches as the soft stippled pink flesh of Deepa's tongue pillows out between the silver tines. She is charmed. She loves to eat with people who also love to eat, especially if they are unselfconscious about it.

⚜

THE TABLE CLEARED, THE DISHES washed, the marinated mushrooms and olive-stuffed bocconcini put away, the wine bottle rinsed and lying in the green box across the weekend's newspaper, Julia brushes the alcohol fumes off her teeth and washes her face. She climbs into bed with a large glass of anti-hangover water and picks up her book. She remembered to give Deepa her copy as she was stepping out the door, car keys dangling from her hand. Deepa had looked surprised. Julia was anxious, bottled up, because she could not, of course, tell Deepa the book was really ultimately for Nicholas. Instead she said, "For you to read while you're at home alone," and then immediately regretted it, as if she'd spoken of something forbidden. "While you're waiting for news. By the time you're finished with it you'll have some," she'd added stupidly, and then mentally cursed herself for making things worse.

A crease of pain had crossed Deepa's forehead and then melted away. She lifted herself on tiptoes and hugged Julia and kissed her, once, on the cheek. "In that case," she'd said, smiling softly, "I'll read the whole thing tonight."

Now Julia sits in her bed in the small cloud of yellow light cast by her bedside lamp, and feels the glossy surface of the book's cover cool against her open palms. She thinks of Deepa, sitting in her own bed holding the same book. Julia has a cartoonish image of herself and Deepa like the cans at either end of a child's play telephone, with a string pulled taut between them across the lap of the city. She imagines Deepa sitting with the book in the bed she shares with Nicholas — not reading it, but thinking of him. Of Nicholas's beautiful long body lying warm and vivid next to hers, the duvet (Julia imagines a duvet for them, covered in a light blue cotton cover, with matching sheets and pillowcases) puffing up on either side of his pale brown length, his chest sprinkled with dark hairs just starting to be threaded with secret grey, his legs and arms and torso soft to the touch but gently muscular under the skin. She imagines Deepa imagining Nicholas raising his face, eyes almost dissolving with love, to kiss her.

Julia's stomach aches dully. She turns over, holding herself around the waist and squeezing her legs together as she pulls them up to her chest. She wanted Nicholas's attention but she conceded the primacy of his marriage in his life. Now that she knows Deepa, however, it is impossible to ignore the pull of Deepa's desires — for Nicholas's love and for the life they have made together. Now Julia can imagine what Deepa might want, and it matters to her. She feels protective. At the same time she misses Nicholas, all the more because she is not sure she can see him again when he returns. She doesn't know whether she will be able to continue to be friends with Deepa either. When it was only Nicholas, it seemed so simple. Now the plain, smooth little ball of their self-contained passion has sprouted Hydra heads, waving in all directions, growing and lengthening and catching in unexpected tangles. It is getting too hard. For the first time in her life, Julia feels orphaned. It lodges like a stone in her chest and she breathes painfully around it, her lungs heaving.

She finally falls asleep with the light on, head still buried in her tear-damp, snotty pillow. In the morning, she feels the stiffness on her face pull apart as she yawns.

⚶

SUMMER FINALLY TURNS ITS BACK and disappears all at once. The day is cool and rainy. She and Marie-Soleil are shivering in the store, but they keep the door propped open anyway, out of some wistful loyalty to the season that has just passed. Olivier is happy; sales have been slow and he thinks the cool weather will help. People will be reminded that it is the time to plant their fall bulbs, to get their gardens in order for the dormancy of cold and the spring that will follow. Julia likes this about working at Le Jardinier — the coming spring is implicit in everything they do every fall. It adds an element of hope to the dying season.

But nobody is shopping in the rain, or the heavy grey damp that hangs low to the ground between the periods of hard rainfall. Julia finds herself distractedly standing in the doorway, listening to the wild honking of geese as they fly over in disorderly multiple Vs. Having waited so long to get their cue from the turn of the weather, now the birds are all leaving in a hurry. Today. She doesn't know why, but she loves hearing the sound of the geese as they fly away in the fall or return in the spring; she always has. As a child she would run outside without her coat as soon as the faint beeping sound penetrated her consciousness — wherever she was in the house, whatever she was doing — and stand, shivering, to watch the black specks move through the sky in their asymmetrical carets. Now she leans in the doorway of the shop, her black sweater pulled tight as she holds her cold hands under her arms, and wonders why the birds honk as they fly. Perhaps they are like a squad of marines, the big bird at the head of the V honking orders to the others, who reply. Yes, sir! But no, the sound is too scattered. Maybe they are a collective, using consensus decision-making to arrive at a route? Julia watches them as they pass through the undifferentiated grey above. Most of all they look like a group of toddlers holding onto a rope so they won't wander off and get lost. Julia wonders what beauty is, for this ephemeral passage of black flecks against an overcast sky to be so imbued with it.

Somehow this evidence of the quick, tardy change of the season makes Nicholas seem very far away. Before, they were both marinating in the damp closeness of summer, their skins filmed with sweat and the grime sweat attracts, though they were on opposite sides of the earth, the big water ball. Now Montreal's weather has abruptly slipped from relentless heat to bone-damp chill; now something more separates Nicholas's days in sunny Morocco — or wherever he is — from Julia's cold hands. While Nicholas sips chilled beer in an effort to cool himself, Julia pulls her sweater around her, tosses under an extra blanket in bed at night. Julia feels the damp against the exposed skin of her face and gazes into the expanse of grey sky. Nicholas is that much farther away.

She sighs, and turns back to the empty store. She goes to the computer and, once more, fruitlessly checks her email. What if he doesn't come back? She breathes. Squeezes her eyes shut, and when she opens them, blinks. There, tears staved off. She goes out into the store and tidies the bushel baskets of bulbs, the artful mounds of large and miniature decorative gourds, their deep yellows and variegated greens cheerful under the pot lights. Deepa told her Nicholas's brother was planning to fly to Casablanca tomorrow if no news came. Julia's emotions are curiously divided over this. It emphasizes her outsider status — she doesn't know Nicholas's brother, never will; she is not part of Nicholas's family, and has no role in this search. At the same time she feels a secret and

guilty relief that her distance allows her to escape any responsibility — if Nicholas is not found, it will not be her fault.
(What if Baby Goodman isn't found? Has this responsibility
devolved onto Julia? Is it hers to choose to accept?) She
watches herself sorting these things out and knows it is strange
to be having all these thoughts on one level, while deeper in
she suffers her constant ache of longing, now admixed with
fear. Laid lightly on top of all that, a desire for Deepa's company. It's all painfully complicated.

Marie-Soleil has a new boyfriend, a nice guy with long
sandy dreads pulled back from his face and massed against
his back. He works on an organic farm outside the city, and
drops into the store when he comes to town to make vegetable
deliveries. Julia watches him standing easily against the cash
desk, his muscles and bones comfortably loose, Marie-Soleil
animated and flushed with pleasure under his gaze. Julia feels
a tug of affectionate envy for their youthful grace and for the
long road of potential ahead of them. She goes into the back
to fill a watering can, and also to allow them a moment of
privacy. She can see Olivier outside on the patio, stacking the
supplies they store out there — bags of cedar mulch, sacks of
little red stones and white pebbles; once it snows they probably won't go outside again until spring. Although he is only
a couple of feet from her, the wall and window keep any sound
from passing between them. He moves in silence on the other
side of the glass and it makes him seem far away, as if he is
in another dimension. He is in good shape, a nice-looking
man of the well-fed bourgeois type. His jaw and neck have
accumulated a layer of dense flesh in the last few years; his

Quebec-made Kanuk windbreaker, the ubiquitous owl logo on the collar, pulls tight over his belly. He is passing into later middle age.

Julia thinks of her mother, dead at sixty-five. Some people's roads are shorter than they expected. Perhaps hers will be too. Maybe, she thinks, turning off the faucet and standing at the big metal sink, balancing the water-heavy plastic jug on the curled steel edge, there is a lump of cells growing, uncontrolled and menacing, in one of her breasts right now. Plenty of women her age get cancer. She sends her mind into her chest. Maybe there, in the right one, above the aureole and to the side. Or it could be on her cervix, that strange sea creature, that blind pink round of flesh that flinches away from the pinch of metal when the doctor takes a tiny flap for testing. Why is it that she imagines cancer striking her female parts — are they somehow more vulnerable than the others?

She emerges into the front of the store, watering potted plants as she perambulates, just in time to see Marie-Soleil pull her head away from Émile's, lips damp and curved upward in an involuntary smile, eyes lowered. Julia smiles to herself and turns to the hyacinths trapped in waisted glass, bright green spears thrusting up from split bulbs, their hairy white roots proliferating in the water below, bathed in light. When she turns Émile has gone. Marie-Soleil holds up a long, heavy stalk studded with little green balls. Smiling, she waves it like a flag.

"*Choux de Bruxelles*!" she cries. "Biological — I mean, organic. You like them? We can share." She lays it down across the glass cash desk and begins to snap the individual sprouts off the thick, cudgel-like stem. Émile often brings Marie-Soleil an offering from the farm, although as far as Julia can tell, Marie-Soleil lives largely on Diet Coke; she's not a big vegetable girl. She bravely tries whatever Émile brings her, but she often shares with Julia so she won't have to eat it all. Julia scoops her Brussels sprouts into a plastic Le Jardinier bag and then hears another round of distant honking. She takes Marie-Soleil by the hand and draws her around the cash counter to the open doorway. They stand pressed against one other for warmth and watch as the geese come into view over their heads, sprinkling the sky above the rows of hundred-year-old greystones that line St. Denis Street. It is a big, four-tier V, the geese flying close to each other, honking shrilly. Julia wonders whether each flying group is a family. If she were a goose, who would be flying with her? Was Baby Goodman flying south now, from somewhere else, surrounded by geese of her own?

❦

SHE CALLS LAUREN AND THEY agree to meet for a drink. Julia steams her organic Brussels sprouts and pulls the leftovers from her dinner with Deepa from the fridge. She never willingly ate a Brussels sprout in her life before she lived with Stewart. She learned to eat a lot of vegetables from him. As a child she'd hated vegetables, but she didn't understand until she moved in with Stewart that it was her mother's cooking that was bad, not the spinach and broccoli. She sweeps the litter of outer leaves and stem cuttings into the garbage and pulls a plate down from the cupboard. Stewart taught her to buy fresh vegetables and to prepare them without leaching the taste from them with overcooking. This, she knows, is one of the gifts she retains from her time with him. She rolls a couple of olives onto the edge of her plate and pops one into her mouth. She smiles slightly to herself. She is getting soft on old Stewart. She pours herself a glass of water. She'd like to think that if she hadn't learned to cook vegetables properly from Stewart she'd have picked it up elsewhere. She certainly wouldn't have gone on eating the food she grew up with.

The meals of her childhood were unpleasant, conflict-ridden events where her child's ineffective resistance was invariably pitted against her mother's inflexibility, her powerful impulse to control. Carol would hector her into eating whatever over-boiled frozen vegetable was heaped on her plate, stacked next to "a protein and a starch." None of it sounded good to Julia. Little of it tasted good. There was no appealing to her father, who sat as quiet as possible, methodically forking the food into his mouth. Julia sees now that his silence was a form of acquiescence — or, worse, a kind of passive reinforcement of her mother's will, allowing him to avoid discord with Carol while also not being the bad guy in Julia's eyes. She doesn't know whether this was a deliberate or even a conscious policy on his part, but it strikes her now, as she drains the steaming water from her Brussels sprouts, their stems almost neon-green from the heat, as bordering on dishonest. He wasn't as good a guy as he'd allowed her to think. As she'd wanted to think. Her mother shouldn't have had to be the bad cop, when by his silence he was supporting her behaviour.

Julia sits at her table and cuts a Brussels sprout in half with the side of her fork. Its intricate layers, ruffled and complex, the leaves coming off the sides of the tiny central stem in imitation of the way the whole sprouts stuck out from their long stalk, strikes Julia as a lovely kind of order, charmingly baroque without being excessive. What if her father had borne his share of the laying-down of rules? Would it have allowed her mother to be a lighter, friendlier mom? Or maybe Carol's rigidity was permanent, guarding not against Julia but against a bubble of grief Carol held inside herself, a shame that could contaminate everything. It's too hard for Julia to tease out her parents' several levels of responsibility; it is all too deeply interwoven. She can't shake the sense that between the three of them — her mother, her father, and herself — was a long history of opportunities lost. Chances that slipped away, unused, the love evaporating through the cracks in their bonds with each other. She puts her fork down, swallows with difficulty the chewed Brussels sprout in her throat.

⁂

SHE MEETS LAUREN AT THE Sergeant-Recruteur. Since it moved up St. Lawrence Boulevard to the corner of Villeneuve it is non-smoking, which both she and Lauren prefer. There are rumours that the city will disallow smoking in all bars and restaurants, but that seems too good to be true — in Montreal, unlikely.

Julia normally chooses wine over beer, but since they make their own at this bar she often drinks their special beer of the week. This time it is a pumpkin-and-spice-flavoured beer. It sounds kind of awful but the waiter assures Julia that it's good, so she agrees to try a half-pint. She folds her red trench coat, lining zipped in, over the back of her chair and settles in to wait for Lauren, who is usually a little late. The mid-week crowd is thin but lively. Julia thinks of Nicholas's favourite bar, dense with smoke and music so loud it bounced off the walls. Nicholas complained about the smoke and the noise every time, but kept going there anyway. It was far from the house he shared with Deepa, south of downtown in Verdun, which Julia figured was part of its appeal — it let him be the man he wanted to be while he was away from his wife. People can put up with anything once it becomes part of their idea of themselves, she thinks.

The young waiter brings her beer and she sips it. Not bad. The pumpkin and spice flavours are almost undetectable; instead, the beer tastes full, without the bitter echo Julia doesn't like. So what became part of her mother's idea of herself after she had her forbidden baby? Did she see herself as shameful? Or perhaps as the martyr mother, suffering a great loss for the sake of her child. Then, having her second child, which as far as the world and her family were concerned was her first, she expected to reap all the rewards of her martyrdom — only, paradoxically, she didn't, because she couldn't get credit for a sacrifice made in secret.

What became part of her father's idea of himself? Who did he imagine he was, leaving Carol to bear the stigma for something he was equally responsible for? Blaming her? Julia is ashamed of the unthinking adoration she felt for her father as a child. She can see his young face from below, the way it looked when she crawled into his lap and sat there in the crook of his arm, warm and safe, gazing up at him. Then it is as if an elevator drops inside her. She is terribly sad at the thought of losing her memories of the unquestioning love she felt for him. She feels guilty for having loved him so much when he, unbeknownst to her, had behaved so badly toward her mother. Selfish. Cowardly.

Lauren slides into the seat across from Julia, her coat rustling. She reaches over and tips Julia's face up and peers at her. "What's up, Tiger Lily?" she says. "You look dejected."

Julia is startled; she'd hardly been aware that her thoughts might be visible to anyone else. "Just thinking," she says, and pushes her beer across the table. "Here, try this, it's pumpkin flavoured."

Lauren takes a generous gulp. "Beer of the week?"

"Yeah."

"I'll try it, what the hell." Lauren waves at the waiter, smiles, points at Julia's glass. She peels her coat off, smooths her hair, pulls up her tights. She's incredibly busy. The waiter brings her beer. "So, what's up?"

Lauren doesn't know about Julia's relationship with Nicholas, but Julia has mentioned him as the leader of her architecture seminar. During the intense beginning of their affair she couldn't help talking about him. Now she tells Lauren about meeting Deepa in the store, having dinner with her.

"Is she hot?" Lauren asks, grinning.

Julia is shocked. "God, Laur, she's straight. And she's *married*."

Lauren smirks. "Well, first of all, so what, she could still be hot, and second of all, so what, she could still be available for a little extracurricular —" and Lauren winks exaggeratedly, comically; mimes a nudge of the elbow.

Julia feels herself stiffen. She knows she has a rigid side, which she hates, but she can't help it. "Yeah." She hesitates. "Yeah, she's hot." Julia thinks. "She is. But I don't know if she is the extracurricular type." As she says this, she wonders why. She doesn't actually know anything about Deepa's personal life. Except that she is married to Nicholas, who is definitely "the extracurricular type." Maybe they both are. Something in the cool, even tone of Deepa's low, rich voice echoes in Julia's mind.

"Anyway, her husband is missing in Morocco, so she might not be up for a lot of fun right at the moment." Julia hears her own voice. She's trying to sound airy, as if it doesn't matter to her, but it comes out constricted, and she can feel a fragile ball of tears in her throat. She swallows carefully so the ball doesn't break and spill out.

Lauren looks concerned. "Honey, I'm so sorry. That's awful," she says, covering Julia's hand with her own. Julia shrugs.

"Yeah, terrible, huh? I guess the upside of being single is you can't be hit by that particular kind of misfortune." She is continuing to speak as if she is unaffected, but Lauren squeezes her hand.

"So," Lauren says, drawing her hand away, "speaking of being single, Annika's coming back to town in November. They just acquired a piece of hers at the contemporary art museum."

The stained-glass artist from New York. "Well, by then it'll have been so long I might have forgotten how to have sex entirely," Julia says sourly.

"You can't forget," Lauren mumbles around the rim of her glass. "It's like riding a bike." A dribble of beer begins to roll down Lauren's chin and she licks it up with one swipe of her tongue. "And fuck" — Lauren slaps her open palms on the table, leaning in toward Julia with a grin — "am I up for a bike ride!" Julia smiles. Lauren has a great capacity for enjoyment; it's one of the things that attracted Julia when they had their fling. Lauren throws herself into the moment and whatever unique pleasures, sensual or social, it has to offer. Julia can see that Lauren is really tasting her beer, enjoying the flow of it down her throat, opening like a flower in the convivial noise of the bar. Julia warms toward her friend. Two more half-pints later, she lets Lauren josh her into walking her back to her apartment for a couple of tequila shots and a bowl of corn chips. When they've wiped the last of the salt from the bottom of the green plastic corn-chip bowl with their fingers, and washed it from their tongues with the last of Lauren's Mexican-vacation tequila, Lauren stands and holds her hand out to Julia.

"Come on," she says lazily, "we can't let you forget completely. You don't want to embarrass yourself when Annika hits town." Julia stands up and, despite the fog in her head, walks steadily behind Lauren into the bedroom. They undress each other, kissing sloppily, drunkenly, breathing noisily through their noses. Julia knows that at a certain point she decided to let herself get this drunk so she could let herself have this sex; she also knows Lauren knows it. Julia tastes the dry tang of lime inside Lauren's lips and breathes the haze of digesting alcohol from her warm, open mouth. They lie on Lauren's bed with their hands between each other's legs and Julia closes her eyes, dividing her mind between Lauren's soft damp warmth, the gentle resistance of her flesh, and a series of indistinct images of Nicholas and Deepa that pass through her like the pictures thrown by a revolving paper lantern, colours and shapes distorting against her mind's eye, elongating as they disappear. She falls asleep with her head pillowed against Lauren's warm breasts, one of Lauren's legs hooked around hers. Her last thought is that she is drooling a little onto Lauren's bare skin, and how nice it is that Lauren wouldn't mind, if she noticed.

⁂

THE MUG OF COFFEE IS steaming on the little table and Julia takes a moment to appreciate the wonderful, richly bitter smell. She loves, loves, *loves* coffee. This is something else she learned from Stewart. His first birthday gift to her was a coffee grinder and a bag of high-quality beans. She wonders if she should call him some time, say hello.

Right now, however, she is calling Bill. It is a grey Sunday and so dim outside that she has turned the light on even though she is sitting right in front of the window. She balances the phone on her thigh and waits while it rings. It rings for a long time; Julia is getting ready to be grumpy that Bill is not there. She doesn't actually know anything about him. Maybe he works on Sundays, or is out ... birdwatching, or something ... with his kid, maybe. Whatever. There's a rattle as if someone has picked up the receiver and then let it fall back down, then his voice. "Hello?"

"Hi, Bill, it's Julia," she says.

"Oh hi," he says. His voice is pleasant, low-key.

"I ..." She can't think exactly why she called. She is embarrassed. "I just thought I'd call and say hi."

"Oh," Bill says. "Hi." He sounds friendly enough.

"I um ... I was talking to your dad a while ago, and I suddenly realized we have something in common. Both of us had a parent die when we were twenty," Julia says, and even as the words are rolling out of her mouth she can't believe she is saying them. So much for "just saying hi."

Bill takes a breath, then gives a short laugh. "Well. Yeah. We do have that in common."

"I didn't really realize it before," Julia says.

There is a short silence, then Bill says, "Yeah. Actually I tried to talk to you a bit after your dad's funeral, but you were really upset. You didn't seem to want to talk much."

Julia is dismayed. She doesn't remember that. How could she not remember that? She racks her brain. She has always thought she remembered every agonizing detail of her father's funeral; at the time it felt as if each sound, every individual sight had a cutting edge, and they were slicing her into bloody strips.

Her father had a heart attack in his office. She arrived at the hospital from a dress rehearsal at Concordia — a secretary had interrupted the run-through of a student play with an emergency message from Uncle Paul. She was still dressed in her costume, her features grotesquely exaggerated by makeup, her dress artfully ragged and amplifying her cleavage, the skirt slit at the sides to expose her thighs. She took the metro two stops to McGill and then stomped up the steep incline of University Street, her heart thumping with the effort and the anxiety. At the Royal Victoria Hospital, perched on the side of the mountain, she rushed through the maze-like corridors searching for her father's room. Finally finding it, she was about to burst through the door when her mother stepped out and grabbed her arm in a viselike hold. "You are not going in there looking like that!" Carol hissed, her fingers digging into Julia's arm. In tears, Julia had retreated to a public washroom and wiped savagely at her face with paper towels, smearing away the oily makeup, hating Carol, even as she saw the distress that had drawn her mother's features into a pale mask.

When she got back to her father's room, her mother's borrowed cardigan buttoned up to her throat, her arms and neck and chest itching from the wool, she found him deep in a drugged sleep. He never woke again, slipping from life sometime during the night several days later. Julia spent the intervening days curled in a chair by his bedside, refusing to speak to her mother who sat on the opposite side of the bed. She was like a Pharaonic guardian statue, back straight, her purse upright in her lap, a crumpled paper tissue screwed tight in each hand. At the time it was as if the wall of hateful resentment Julia projected at her mother were necessary to keep the space between her and her father clear; if she let Carol leak in between them, Carol's fear and grief might overwhelm her. Julia stared at his grey face, the salt-and-pepper stubble pushing through the skin of his cheeks and chin making him look even more fragile, the white-sheeted mound of his body lying still, arms at the sides, his hands empty. Julia steadfastly ignored her conscious parent, willing her mother to remain outside of her field of vision.

Uncle Paul came every day after work, his appearance breaking the painful tension in the room. He guided Carol out the door, taking her to get something to eat, his hand chivalrously cupped under her elbow. Julia could finally relax when her mother was gone. She would unfold her aching muscles and walk around, the flat medicine-and-disinfectant smell of the hospital in her nostrils. She leaned over the bed, holding whichever of her father's hands had no IV needle sticking out of its bony back, murmuring to him until she dissolved in tears. Eventually her uncle and her mother would return and Paul would take Julia out. In the coffee shop he'd sit quietly while Julia picked at her food.

"I know this is very hard for you, dolly," Uncle Paul said, every time. Julia nodded, her mouth trembling. "It's very hard for your mother too," he said. Julia nodded again. "You could help each other," he'd suggest, and Julia would shake her head, putting her fork down on the table and straightening it, meticulously placing and re-placing it on the paper napkin while Paul continued, gently trying to convince her. She pitied him, stuck with the thankless role of peacemaker.

At the funeral Julia was dull, jittery. She'd cried herself out over the previous day and night, and her head was heavy, stuffed, every movement of her eyes in their sockets sending twinges of pain through her temples. At the reception afterward, at her parents' house, Julia watched and despised her mother, who sat like a queen in an upright chair in the middle of the living room, receiving condolences. Julia haunted the room, a shadow. She'd been sternly instructed by her uncle — on her mother's behalf, she assumed — not to leave, which was what she really wanted to do; she'd have given anything to be alone. Instead she sat numbly in a corner, the rank smell of chopped liver threatening to turn her stomach. From time to time she escaped to the relative quiet of the kitchen, pulling the saran wrap off another platter of cookies or refilling the saucer of lemon slices.

Thinking of it now, she is amazed that she had no sense of her obligation toward the people around her. She'd been too sunk in her own mourning as if it were a pool of quicksand, the heavy wetness of it immobilizing her limbs. It pressed down on her shoulders and around her neck, pushing in at her windpipe. She was afraid that if she stopped concentrating on her own pain for even a second she'd sink another inch in and begin to drown.

She knows that those last few days in the hospital must have been hell for her mother, watching her husband die while her sullen daughter radiated hatred and contempt across his failing body. She knew at the time that she was making it harder for Carol; but then, that was what she'd wanted. She was losing the parent who loved her. She knew it wasn't Carol's fault that Raph was dying, but it was her fault that his death would leave Julia loveless.

"I was pretty upset," she says. "Sorry if I was a bitch to you."

She can almost hear Bill shrug. "I understand. It was a hard time. I guess you didn't get along with your mother that well, eh?"

Julia is trying to remember Bill being there, at the funeral or the reception. She sees Uncle Paul, dressed in a dark blue suit with a light blue yarmulke askew on his thinning hair, his face lined with fatigue. Her mother, wearing a grey dress with a black jacket, the turned-up cuffs and lapels the same dove grey as the dress. She remembers wondering, ridiculously, when her mother had bought that, whether she'd been planning for Raph's death.

"I'm sorry," she says, "I don't remember you from the funeral."

"That's good," Bill says, and laughs a little, "because I got my cookies all over your dress." As soon as he says it Julia remembers. She was sitting on the bottom step of the staircase leading upstairs when Bill approached. He wore a dark blue suit like his father, a diagonally striped tie visible between the lapels.

"Hi, Julia," he'd said, "I'm very sorry about your dad." She looked up at him and thought, he's a grown-up now. His face had begun to mature, his body beginning the shift from lanky young manhood. His cheeks smoothly shaven.

"Thanks," she muttered, looking down at her hands twisting in her lap.

"I haven't seen you for a while. What are you doing these days?"

She hated him for making small talk, although she sees now that he might really have been interested in hearing about her. That he was trying to make a connection with her — probably for her sake. She's sure he didn't need her company for himself.

But his question made her think of the play she'd been in, the only activity she'd been passionate about at university that fall. The play she'd had to drop out of the week before opening so she could sit with her father, watching him fade away inside his stricken body. The thought made her sick with grief, and she stood up suddenly, intending to seek refuge in the bathroom. Standing, she accidentally knocked the little plate of cookies out of Bill's hand and the cookies fell onto the front of her dress and left it streaked with sugar and chocolate. Since it happened, she has remembered it as if

Bill was clumsy and dropped the cookies on her, but she was the one who knocked them onto herself. He was gracefully apologetic, kneeling to pick up the broken pieces while Julia stomped upstairs to clean herself off, grateful to have a legitimate excuse to leave the gathering.

"Oh yeah," she says, "now I remember. Actually, I think it was my fault. Sorry again." Her hand is curled around her hot coffee mug and she is glad for the warmth passing through her skin from the cup. She feels small and cold right now.

"So what made you think of all this now?" Bill asks, and Julia is impressed that he would wonder that.

"Oh, all this adopted baby stuff is stirring up a lot of old shit," she says.

"Oh," Bill says. "Yeah, my dad told me you were asking him about the private detective. Me and my big mouth."

"No," Julia says hastily, "not at all. I was so glad you mentioned that. Otherwise I wouldn't have known about it."

"So you're glad you know?" he asks.

Julia hesitates. "Well ... now that I know, it's better than not knowing."

Bill grunts.

"It's still kind of insane, though," Julia says. "I mean, that private detective could have had all this information about my sister just sitting in his files, and my mother wasn't allowed to go get it. That would have driven me crazy if it'd been me."

"Oh yeah, me too," Bill says. "I remember at the time, my father saying to your mother, 'Forget about it.' And your mother saying, 'I can't forget about it. I pass his office every week on the way to Steinberg's. Arthur Lemberg, Private Detective. I have to look at it every week!' I think for a couple of weeks my mother drove their Dodge Dart over to your mother's house and took her grocery shopping in the car so she wouldn't have to go past the place."

Julia throat is blocked by something. She coughs. "What?" she says.

"My mother took your mother shopping in the car," Bill says. "You probably remember this more than I do, but I think she normally used to walk to the store for her groceries. She had one of those wire grocery carts on wheels that all the old ladies use, right?"

"No," Julia says, speaking carefully, controlling her exasperation. "I mean, did you just say you know the name of the private detective?"

"Oh yeah," Bill says, "I guess so. I think that was it. 'Arthur Lemberg, Private Detective.' Limberg maybe. Limburger. Something like that."

"Office on the way to Steinberg's," Julia repeats, her voice trailing away.

⚜

JULIA IS PREOCCUPIED. SHE WAKES up thinking of Nicholas, and every thought of Nicholas leads to a thought of Deepa. When she showers she wonders when he might last have showered — and thinks of Deepa at home in her own shower, water spraying over her fine shoulders, wondering the same thing. Julia goes straight home from work so she can watch the BBC World News at six, hoping for some mention of Morocco, or Spain; she riffles through Olivier's *La Presse*, thinking they are more likely than the English newspapers to cover events in Morocco, with its partly francophone history and culture. She checks her email on every break, picks up the phone receiver to make sure she hasn't missed a message from Deepa.

In the morning before work, as she eats her cereal, she wonders whether her sister is eating cereal. She tells herself she'll google Arthur Lemberg after work, look him up in the phone book. Wouldn't it be ironic, she thinks, if they hire a private detective to find Nicholas.

Finally she can't stand waiting anymore. The fact that no one would think to tell her if there was any news about Nicholas increases her anxiety. She thinks of Deepa, imagines that she wakes with Nicholas in her mind every morning too. Julia is wistful; if only she and Deepa could share their worries. She is sorry this secret lies between them, although she can't see how it could be otherwise. Telling Deepa would accomplish nothing besides destroying their friendship and making Nicholas angry with her. Anyway, even if she were to tell Deepa about her affair with Nicholas (and, for all she knows, Deepa wouldn't care — is that possible?) now is not the time. Now, when Nicholas is missing, maybe ill or injured, maybe gone forever. Maybe dead.

The next afternoon, on her break at work, she waits until Olivier steps out and Marie-Soleil is kneeling in the display window, her head completely invisible behind a bird bath filled with bunches of varicoloured corn, and then she phones. Deepa answers, her voice low and tired.

"It's Julia. I was wondering ... how you're holding up."

Deepa sighs. "I'm okay. I have a lot of work. Someone I deal with here is doing some stuff for free for a museum in New Orleans, replacing some pieces that were destroyed by the flood. I agreed to help. I lie in bed at night and I can't stop smelling the paint and chemicals on my hands," she says wearily. Julia waits.

"And how are you?" Deepa asks.

"I'm okay." Julia reins in her impatience. "Any news?"

Deepa sighs again, deeply, and Julia wonders whether she'd been trying to avoid thinking about this subject. She feels a little guilty bringing it up, but is nevertheless eager for Deepa's response. Hopeful.

"No news," Deepa says. "Nick's brother, Allen, is there. He says the people at the British High Commission know a lot. Hopefully he can dislodge something."

"Oh. Well, I really hope so." She hears the tremor in her voice; she hopes Deepa is too wrapped up in her own concerns to notice. Julia feels like a vampire, feeding off Deepa's vulnerability. She tells herself the support she offers Deepa is real, but there's a hard little knot in her side, made up of a strand of guilt tied up with a strand of anxiety for Nicholas's safety, bound with a third strand of simple desire. These threads are too tangled to undo. The pause in their conversation begins to lengthen dangerously. Julia feels foolish for having called; evidently she and Deepa don't actually have anything to talk about. She is trying to think of a polite way to say goodbye when Deepa speaks.

"Any interesting plans for the rest of the week?"

"No." Julia almost laughs. She rarely has plans. She doesn't count finding Arthur Lemberg, which she continues to put off. "Just gonna finish reading my book."

"What are you reading?"

"*Complicated Kindness*. Same as you."

"Oh, yeah," Deepa says, her voice suddenly lively. "I'm halfway through, it's great! Thanks a lot for giving me that. It's been a while since someone gave me a really good book."

Julia thinks of how Lauren passed it to her, what a nice gesture that was. When she gave the book to Deepa she was caught up in her ulterior motives, and didn't think of it as replicating that friendly generosity. "A friend gave it to me and I had the same feeling, so I'm glad you're enjoying it," Julia says, the knot of guilt in her side loosening slightly.

"Look," Deepa says. "I think I owe you a dinner. Why don't you come over tomorrow night? We can eat, maybe rent a video if we feel like it. Talk a bit. I'd like to see you again. And the house is a little empty right now ..."

Julia's chest is warm, her eyes are closed and she is smiling. It seems crazy to add more wrinkles to her complicated relationship with Deepa, but for the moment she doesn't care. "That sounds great," she says.

She goes to bed early and reads almost to the end of *A Complicated Kindness*; she tells herself one of her tasks for the morrow will be to finish the last bit so she and Deepa can talk about it. She puts the book on the floor next to the bed and turns off her light. She is looking at the illuminated patterns thrown onto the wall of her bedroom by the streetlights, thinking of Nicholas coming home on an airplane and being safe in his house. She sees him tan and healthy, his dark eyes vibrant with experience, simmering with whatever he went through during this strange gap in his existence. It makes her want him. Her hand is between her legs but she is distracted by the thought of him returning to Deepa's waiting arms. Julia's fingers fall still and instead she traces with her eyes the bars of yellow light and the bars of darkness in between them until she falls asleep.

❧

THE LIST SITS ON THE little table next to Julia's crumb-strewn plate and empty coffee mug, a brown ring drying around the inside of the cup. She has the day off, and has made a list of various tasks to do, but she can't seem to get up and do any of them. She has started to fill the page with doodles; she is grumpy and isn't sure why. Finally, when curlicues and stars and little crosshatched boxes threaten to overwhelm the actual written items on her list, she pushes herself away from the table with a heavy sigh and clears her dirty dishes. She should wash them before she starts her tasks. Then she thinks she should clean the sink and the counters. When that's all done, she picks up her list and decides that rather than do things in the order in which they're written, she ought to start with her laundry. She does some ironing, some grocery shopping, runs over to the SAQ on the corner of Duluth and St. Denis to pick up a bottle of wine for tonight's dinner. The portly man who frequents the sidewalk outside the liquor store shakes his upturned baseball cap at her as she mounts the steps, barely pausing in his conversation with another beggar, the skinny fellow who usually stands on the opposite side of St. Denis, jerkily practising his trade on the drivers of cars that stop at the red light. For a moment, Julia envies their fraternal ease with each other, their air of belonging to that busy corner — the way the stones of the restaurants, the streetlight posts, and the concrete curbs belong there. Lonely much? she thinks, shaking her head at herself.

She strolls around the liquor store looking at shelves of products she wouldn't want to buy — passion fruit-flavoured wine coolers and ground-cherry liqueur. Why would people make liqueur out of ground cherries? She supposes people will make alcohol out of anything. She might buy the vodka made from icebergs, she thinks. Eventually, she is walking up St. Denis toward Mt-Royal metro to go to Deepa's place, and has to admit that she let herself run out of time before she could get around to task number one: look in the phone book for Arthur Lemberg, private detective.

Without her being conscious of it, that prospect has been making Julia depressed all day. Now that she is walking toward something good, she is not sure why it affected her so much. For that matter, she isn't sure why she's trying to find this guy. She has no idea what she'll do if she does track him down. What would her mother have thought if she knew that Julia was trying to follow in her footsteps on this particular path? Perhaps if Carol had told Julia about Baby Goodman before their relationship became unsalvageable, they could have looked for her together. Perhaps if she had confided in Julia, their relationship wouldn't have been a lost cause in the first place.

Julia tries to picture Carol with her own parents, but they died when Julia was still so young. She remembers a Seder early in her childhood, a year when chocolate-covered matzoh were hidden for the children, a marvellous, unheard-of surprise. She must have been a toddler; she remembers having to stand on unsteady tiptoes to see over the dining-room table. That means her mother must have been very young too — much younger than Julia is now. Carol and her mother stood in the kitchen; Carol's fists were at her sides, tightly closed and white, while Julia's bubbe rearranged Carol's Seder plate. Julia remembers the older woman's loose-skinned hands grasping the lamb shank, and a fleck of dun horseradish, dislodged in passing, falling to stick on the shiny blue fabric of her hem. Julia reached for her mother's hand but Carol moved it away, then looked down at Julia, her face closed, a sheet of rock. Julia stood there, small and helpless — absolutely, frighteningly alone in the humid, noisy bustle of the holiday-crowded house. An aloneness that impressed itself so deeply upon her in that moment that she has never been able to shake it since. Unconsciously, Julia presses her fist against the hollow pain in her chest. Was Carol deliberately walling her out with that stone face — or was it simply the exterior of the barrier that kept Carol walled in?

Julia's fist relaxes, her fingers begin to unfold. She breathes, her chest opening, expanding as she walks this wind-scoured street. For a moment she feels free, walking alone here in the cool air. Well, maybe too cool. Julia hunches into her coat, turning the collar up against the wind. A scrap of newspaper rattles across the sidewalk in front of her until it catches under the wheel of a parked car. A number 30 bus roars past, exuding a cloud of sour exhaust that she can't help breathing. She has the sensation that the city is colonizing her body, that she is turning into an ambulatory fragment of Montreal, inside and out. The very particles of the place are settling in the pink linings of her lungs, nestling in the pores of her skin, sinking into her intestines — and once they are assimilated by her blood and her bones, the chemicals, the metals will be inextricably part of her, folded into her cells by digestion, respiration, all the processes meant to support life — developed over millennia when people lived with loam and salt and bark, not sulphur dioxide. She thinks of the little cells that might be thrown off their normal growth patterns, might be seeded with the out-of-control rush to reproduce themselves that could eventually cause her death.

Yet there is something almost comforting about being so intimately part of the place where she lives. About belonging somewhere, on the cellular level. This concrete, she thinks, this metal lamppost, this traffic light, this car might be my distant family. More than that woman there with her shopping in its white plastic sack, waiting to cross the street. Or maybe, she thinks, as the woman turns and Julia sees a face roughly the same shape as her own, hair more or less the same colour, maybe that's my sister.

She walks on, her hands deep in her pockets, the wine in its long maroon bag swinging against her hip. Arthur Lemberg could be dead, or at least retired. The chances that he still has the records of his investigation of her sister are low. Julia considers. If he is findable, and if he still has the information — if there was any information to be had in the first place — will he turn the information over to her? It's already paid for, she reminds herself. She shakes her head. Better to leave this train of thought on a spur for a while. She doesn't want to ruin the pleasant evening ahead by blurting out her over-wrought family history. She closes her eyes for a moment, feeling the echoing smack of her soles on the concrete sidewalk, and pictures Deepa's shiny dark hair and gentle golden eyes. Yes, think on this, Julia tells herself.

When she arrives, she's glad she did. Deepa's house smells wonderful — garlic and ginger and something else, maybe simmering tomatoes. Maybe those ugly tomatoes from the garden out back. It's the first time Julia has entered through the front door and she feels oddly formal, stepping over the threshold. In the small entrance hall is a simple but elegant wooden bench, big enough for one person to sit on while pulling her boots off. Underneath it, but visible, is a pretty, woven-bark basket filled with hats and gloves. Julia wonders which of the hats has cupped Nicholas's dark hair, which Deepa's; if the brown gloves have hugged Deepa's small hands, or Nicholas's fine ones. She is embarrassed to be probing their private life this way; briefly, she wishes she hadn't come. She doesn't want to know what Deepa and Nicholas's life together looks like. But it's too late to avoid that, especially if she is not willing to give up Deepa's friendship. With difficulty she returns her attention to her own coat, which her hands have been automatically unbuttoning.

Attached to the wall above, another simple piece of wood-work, a plank smoothed to a silky finish and stained a warm dark brown, with wrought iron hooks affixed to it. A single red scarf hangs from the centre hook. Deepa stands in the inner doorway, brightness from the warmly lit house glowing around the edges behind her. Julia hangs her coat on one of the hooks and puts her shoes neatly on the all-weather carpeting. She looks up and finds Deepa's eyes sliding over her, appraising; the moment passes so fast that for a second she doubts that it happened. Deepa turns, beckons Julia inside. Julia takes a long breath and steps forward.

They walk through to the kitchen and Julia sits on a stool next to the counter, sips a glass of the red wine she brought. It pulses like blood around the edges where the light catches it. Julia imagines lying on grass and looking up through her fingers, sunlight illuminating her own blood under her skin.

She has offered to chop something so Deepa sets her up with a thick fistful of cilantro and a cutting board. Deepa herself stands by the stove at an angle, stirring a bubbling pot with one hand, holding her own glass of wine with the other, looking alternately down at the pot then up at Julia as she talks about Allen's trip. He works for Foreign Affairs — as an IT manager, but still, he is as close as anyone in their family comes to having any useful connections. Deepa thinks that maybe with Allen standing in front of him in the flesh, Monsieur Langlois, or his British counterpart, will be motivated to try harder to find Nicholas. There are things the consulate doesn't have the staff to do — for example, take Nicholas's photo to hotels and train stations and car rental places where he might have been seen. They have assured her that they have checked with all the hospitals and police stations, and he is not known to be dead, injured, or arrested. Deepa lists these possibilities dully; she doesn't sound reassured.

She drops the wooden spoon she's been using into the sink and leans against the counter, her hands clutching the edge. Julia can see the tendons on her neck standing out, curved like flying buttresses on the exterior of a medieval church. It makes her neck look solid. Julia remembers the first day she met Deepa in the store, how relaxed she looked, how soft and beautiful. How her life has changed her since then, because of a single absence. Julia considers the way her own life was shaped from before her birth by another single absence. How our ties to other people pull us out of shape, she thinks. Or into the shapes that become ours.

The pot on the stove is boiling hard, spitting tiny drops of hot liquid into the air, onto the stove top, the pale-tiled backsplash. Julia slides off her stool and turns the heat down; then, without thinking, steps over behind Deepa and puts her arms around Deepa's waist. Deepa's back, shoulders, arms are all rigid. Julia holds her and feels her begin to melt, relaxing against the warmth of Julia's body. Deepa sinks back, lets go of the counter, lets herself be held, her eyes closed. She wraps her arms around Julia's, clinging with her small, strong hands to the flesh of Julia's upper arms. It feels as if they are, for the moment, one complex, intricate creature. Julia lays her head against the back of Deepa's neck, smells the warmth of her hair and skin. Her smell is nearly sweet, almost fruity. Julia sees that there is a very small, perfectly round red burn on the back of Deepa's hand near the wrist, a drop of sauce dried in the centre of it. She closes her eyes.

Julia wishes she could draw all of Deepa's pain away into her own body. She fantasizes taking it into herself, enveloping it like a protruding starfish stomach around a mollusk. For that matter, she would take in whatever Nicholas is suffering right now, if he is suffering. If he is not forking up a late breakfast on a hotel patio somewhere, strong mint tea and fresh bread perhaps. If he is not dead. She inhales Deepa's smell. She can hear Deepa's breathing, can tell Deepa is crying silently, tears of tension and exhaustion seeping from her closed eyes. This kind of crying is not agony, it is relief; it is being able to let go, just for a moment, because someone else is holding on. Julia is grateful to be able to hold on for Deepa.

When they finally pull apart, the kitchen is layered with silence like a deep snowfall. Deepa gives Julia's arm a quick squeeze and then, wordless, not looking back, picks her spoon from the sink, moves to the stove and slowly begins to stir. Julia returns to her stool, takes a big sip of wine and rolls it around inside her mouth as she begins to chop the cilantro. The rhythmic pounding of the heel of the knife on the wooden cutting board sounds profane in the still kitchen. This thunking will open up the silence, make room for one of them to speak. Finally Deepa lays the spoon across the top of the pot and turns, her hands falling, open, before her.

"You're like the sister I don't have," Deepa says, smiling gently. "A sister without baggage."

Julia smiles back, painfully. If only Deepa knew how much baggage Julia has dragged into her home. In her mind's eye, Julia sees herself bent like a Victorian railway porter under a roped-together pile of trunks, valises, and hat boxes. She can almost feel her vertebrae cracking under the load. Nicholas-baggage, Baby Goodman-baggage, mother-and-father-baggage, Stewart-baggage. It's all wearing on her, stacked along her back higher than her head. She rolls her shoulders to loosen them. She looks down. This cilantro could stand a little more mincing. She picks a light green stem out of the litter of leaf fragments and puts it aside, then reapplies herself to her task.

That night in her own bed she lies in the dark, wide awake. She relives the heat of Deepa's neck against her cheek, the smell of Deepa's body rising into her nostrils, the melting of Deepa's rigid muscles into her arms. She feels Deepa's pain and stress evaporate into the air around them, dispersing like the fragrant steam issuing from the bubbling pot of food they later ate. Julia squashes a pillow between her legs and turns to push herself against it, her hard-clenched fist keeping it in place. She is lonely, yet somehow, her melancholy has a sweet depth. She comes with the side of her face pressed into her pillow, and falls asleep.

⚜

SALWA, WHO IS SUPPOSED TO open Le Jardinier today, calls Julia at ten. Something is wrong with her key, she can't get the door open. She waited until the last minute to call, thinking she'd manage if she kept trying, but the store is supposed to be opening right now. Julia is still in her pyjamas. She's been sipping coffee, leafing lazily through her cookbooks; she wasn't supposed to go in today. Cursing, she stumbles around pulling on her tights and a sweater. This is one of the drawbacks of being manager.

They open the store with Julia's keys and Julia brings the cash out and turns on the lights while Salwa goes out to find a hardware store to get a new set cut for herself. There's a Rona up on Rachel Street a few blocks east of St. Denis; it'll take her twenty minutes or half an hour. Julia must stay until Salwa returns, so she sits at the cash browsing through garden-themed giftware catalogues while she waits. Olivier has circled products he plans to order. Frog-shaped floating candles; wall sconces made to look like tulips, with long, gracefully drooping leaves. A couple of prosperous-looking women enter the store and begin to browse. Julia pegs them as shoppers-for-entertainment — there's nothing they need, but they can afford to buy whatever they want, so they might end up spending a lot of money. She greets them, then retreats. She monitors their progress around the store with half her attention while she continues to page through the catalogues. Gardening gloves that moisturize as you dig in the dirt; herb-and-flower scented soaps.

The women are murmuring between themselves; a single phrase comes clearly to Julia's ear. "... wants to find her birth mother." Julia's tingling all over. She looks up into the middle distance, the better to eavesdrop.

"I told her," the woman with the wheat-blond hair says, "don't open that can of worms." Julia's stomach goes sickly cold, as if it's full of chilled oil sloshing gently from side to side. The women pause; each one picks up a blue-and-white ceramic cachepot. They examine the pots, turning them around in their well-manicured hands. "Is this the same blue as my dining-room curtains? Or are my curtains more peacock?" the wheat-blond woman asks. Her companion appears to be considering the answer.

Don't open up that can of worms. Julia hears it in her father's voice, the way she imagined it when Uncle Paul told her Raph said it to Carol. What an awful way to think of a person, a person and that person's life. A can of worms. Julia sees it, a tin can turning under the opener, the ruffle-edged top still attached on one side, starting to pop up on the other side. The silvery circle of the lid is pulled away and the inside of the can is revealed, filled with a writhing mass of night-crawlers. Their moist, segmented bodies the pale brown of earth-dwellers, their blind heads rising into the sudden light and air, probing blindly over the edge of the can, waving with a disgusting languor. An image comes to Julia of the body of the woman Baby Goodman might have become, disintegrated into a pile of earthworms pouring out of the can. It's like that episode of *The X-Files*, a missing woman who can't be found because she dissolves into a heap of worms whenever Mulder gets too close. How could her father have thought of his own child as worms?

The women are fingering an expensive arrangement of pink kalanchoe and mosses in a twig basket. Julia pulls her wringing hands apart, smooths her palm down over her stomach to calm it. She knows her father didn't really imagine his lost baby as worms in a tin can; it was only a figure of speech — but that's almost worse. Maybe he didn't really think of Baby Goodman at all. Julia is filled with pity for the baby her sister once was, sent away into the world without a single real thought from her father. Or anyway, she thinks, without a thought he could bear to acknowledge.

Wheat-blond approaches the cash register with the twig basket. She puts her credit card on the counter and turns back to her friend without so much as a glance at Julia. "It's all moot anyway," she says, catching a strand of her hair between long fingernails and carefully replacing it on her head, "because there are no records left, everything was destroyed in the bombings — and chances are, so was her birth mother." The machine spits up the credit-card slip and Julia rips it off and presents it to the customer. She looks at the woman as she signs her name. Julia wonders what country, what war she might mean. It could be any one of many places, nearly any year in the last lifetime. In any case, it's not her sister they're discussing. She wraps the basket against the inclement weather and lifts it across the cash desk into the customer's arms. When the women open the door to leave, a wave of cold, damp air rolls in. Julia feels it on her face as a relief. She hadn't realized how hot she was, how flushed her cheeks and forehead had become.

The ringing of the bell on the door dies away and Julia is left anchored in stillness. She is sad for the person the two women were talking about, but feels she herself has somehow been let off. She has the inexplicable sense of having narrowly missed a catastrophe. The cold oil feeling in her belly is draining away; she's steadier now. Compared with so many, Baby Goodman's story is simple, maybe even happy.

Julia begins to dust the display in the front window. There are small hand-thrown clay pots of brilliant African violets in a jungly cluster; next to them, glass bowls filled with smooth dark stones, narcissus bulbs rooting among them, their green heads stretching up from their papery shells. The long white filaments snake out of the bottoms of the bulbs and creep between the stones, seeking. Julia is a narcissus, her roots visible, blunt and ugly. Perhaps Baby Goodman is a beautiful, delicate-petalled violet, her roots invisible in the rich embrace of earth.

⁂

WHEN SALWA RETURNS, JULIA DECIDES to take herself out for a coffee before heading home. She walks down St. Denis Street, looking for a place to go, but every café she sees is too crowded, or smoky, or the tables are full of dirty cups and plates. She eventually finds herself nearing the Sherbrooke metro station. She dawdles on the sidewalk under the trees at the edge of Carré St.-Louis, as if considering entering the park to sit beside the high-splashing fountain among the drunks and junkies. This park is an anomaly, colonized by petty criminals, homeless people, young punks with dogs and guitars, though it is faced on all sides by expensive old greystone houses filled with actors, writers, and artists — the cream of the Québécois crop. Most famously, Michel Tremblay. Whenever Julia strolls beneath these trees she thinks of the man's avuncular bearded visage; unknowing, he inhabits her personal geography.

Finally, without quite admitting to herself that she has any particular intention, she crosses the street and passes into the glass-walled metro station, walking across the wide, tiled floor to the escalator, and descends. She stands on the platform in a daze; when the friendly blue metro pulls into the station, sighing on its rubber wheels, she gets into one of the half-empty cars and sits, staring out the window into the blackness of the passing tunnel.

When she gets off at Côte-Ste-Catherine station she emerges to a greyed sky and a newly cold, damp wind. She pulls her jacket closer and looks around. She hasn't been here for a long time; the street has changed. The little Jewish bakeries of her childhood have been hedged in by Indian groceries, Filipino hair-and-nail salons, printing services advertising in

English, French, and Arabic. It's alienating, but in a satisfying way — the world has been moving on without her, as it should. Different from the way she felt alienated when she lived here among those Jewish bakeries that were like her parents' assumptions about the world made solid, full of familiar objects, with sights and smells that reinforced hard-won certainties, recreated afresh from humble flour and water every day.

She knows the Steinberg's is long gone but she remembers where it was. She walks until she is standing in front of her parents' old house — her old house. She feels nothing except a residual distaste. She turns and begins to retrace her steps. This will be quick — a ten-minute walk. Her breath eases in and out of her chest. She tries to see everything as she passes, afraid that she might look in the wrong direction at the wrong moment and miss Arthur Lemberg's name on a door or on a window, rendered in faded gold paint.

She knows it is crazy to be doing this; his office could have been inside an apartment building, where she wouldn't be able to see his name from the street. He could have retired and moved to Florida by the time she started kindergarten. Looking off to the side, Julia almost walks right into a woman wearing an open nylon parka over a green sari with a gold border; the gold threads catch the flat light as the woman shifts on her feet before a sidewalk vegetable display, weighing the relative merits of two large cabbages. Julia swerves to avoid the collision and trips over her own toes, catching herself before she actually falls. It's ridiculous, but the jarring halt almost make her cry. As she continues down the street, still peering at windows and doorways, searching for signs announcing Arthur Lemberg's private eye business, Julia angrily wishes her mother had had a third child. A sister Julia could have kept, a companion who could be here with her now, helping her search for their older sibling, sharing the strange anxiety of it. Someone who would love Julia. Who could have deflected, or absorbed, some of the resentment and bitterness that Carol aimed at her only easy target. Who could hold on for her the way she held on for Deepa last night, so she could let go of this aching — if just for a moment.

If her mother had wanted another child so badly, why didn't she have one? A first raindrop falls cool against Julia's cheek. She supposes that her mother didn't want just any child, but the one she'd already made, carried in her body, had had removed from herself while she slept the deep, smothering artificial sleep. Julia slows, stepping closer to make out the name on a white plastic sign visible in a second-storey window, her pulse racing. ANTON MARBERG — she holds her breath — DENTIST. She exhales.

She knows she went through the stage most kids go through, wanting a sister or brother. That must have been a treat for her mother, Julia thinks, having her ask for a sibling. Her mother standing rigid in front of the kitchen counter, a half-cooked chicken laid out in a roasting pan. The plastic baster gripped in one white hand. Raph in the doorway, his briefcase dangling, his coat open, arriving home from work. They look tall, the kitchen counters above Julia's eye level, so she must have been quite young still. She asks her mother why she can't have a sister or a brother. Her mother's apron is cream-coloured, with tiny dark and light blue flowers all over it; Julia remembers she used to stand up close and hold a corner of that apron and look at those beautiful blue flowers.

This day she is not standing that close; she is afraid she might get hit, and backs up until she is standing with the edge of the kitchen table pressing across her back. "Ask your father," her mother says to her, and Julia doesn't know why, but she knows not to. Her mother is really speaking to Raphael, not to her, and her father's face is white, frozen, his mouth a funny shape. He sets his briefcase down deliberately in the doorway and turns around. They hear the front door open and close.

When the chicken is cooked, Carol serves Julia a drumstick with a roasted potato from the pan and some cooked carrots. The potato is reddish-gold from the paprika until Julia cuts it with her fork, and then the two halves fall away to reveal grainy white flesh inside. The round carrot slices are dark orange with yellow circles around the centres, like a pile of soft miniature sunsets on one side of the plate. Julia tries to cut the chicken leg properly, but it slides around the plate and pushes some carrot slices onto the table. She expects to be reprimanded by her mother for making a mess, but Carol sits, wordless, at her own empty place, watching Julia absently until she's choked down every mouthful.

Julia shakes the images out of her head and looks around. There is a large community garden here for seniors, the plots jury-rigged with old broom handles, string, and overturned buckets. Julia stands at the chain-link fence for a few minutes and considers a clump of overblown rhubarb, an abandoned rubber boot, a plot that has already been dug over for winter, its dirt mounded like a grave. There are probably vegetables being grown here now that her grandmother never heard of.

Bitter melon, cilantro. She continues down the street. She can no longer remember what it looked like when she lived here, but she knows it didn't look like this. There is a fish store connected to a restaurant — Yanni's — which definitely wasn't here before. She is peering at the windows above the street-level storefronts. On the second floors: boutiques, a psychic, a Vietnamese driving school.

She comes up on the corner and sees, to the left, the shopping centre. There's an IGA where the Steinberg's used to be. Julia waits for the traffic light. Fat, lackadaisical drops of rain fall against her face, the wind making the wet spots intensely cold. She looks at the generic strip mall that used to be part of her world. A year and a half ago, she would have thought: my mother might be inside the Pharmaprix, and she would have been tense, alert, ready to slip away to avoid having to talk to Carol. Now there is not even that. Now the drugstore means less than nothing to her. It is merely ugly.

Suddenly she becomes aware of how cold her hands and face are, almost numb. She wants to go home to her own warm apartment. She treks down into the Plamondon metro. The escalator is long, the station dug in deep under the city. She feels like an urban Persephone, descending into an underworld that looks more like the set of a cheap *Logan's Run* remake than anything the ancients could have imagined. Although in her case her mother pined not for Julia but for a different daughter, a child she sought but did not find. Carol never came after me, Julia thinks grimly, and she certainly won't now. She holds her jacket tight against herself all the way around the loop of nearly deserted stations. In spite of the close heat. She feels weirdly empty. The transformed neighbourhood, with the tiny possible link to her sister effaced among its weathered bricks, windows, doorways, leaves her adrift. It is as if her past no longer exists, dislodged by the onward rush of the burgeoning present; displaced by the ambitions, the strivings, the daily breaths and pumping blood and small accumulated actions of various peoples of the earth, all converging on Victoria Avenue to live in some kind of security, some hope of prosperity, as her grandparents did a hundred years before. Julia realizes that, as obscure as her mother's life is to her, the world her grandparents lived in is further from her reach. She thinks again of Carol standing white-fisted in her own kitchen while her own mother rearranged the Seder plate. What sorrows salted the love that should have nourished Carol? What losses did she bear for the generation that bore her?

Then Julia thinks to wonder what pains, what rages her young bubbe carried, stitched into the seams of the clothing she carried on her back from the packed-earth main street of some tiny shtetl, dirty and dangerous but familiar, across a continent and an ocean. What sadness was forever tucked away like red-hot pebbles in the chambers of her heart? Something must have burned there, Julia thinks, to drive her from the only life she knew, the only family she had, into a future so far removed that she had no reason to think she would ever be able to look back. Julia feels the weight, the subtle but inexorable moulding pressure of generations. A wall of time, building itself across her back.

Out of the metro at the other end, the rain has shifted in quality; it blows now in tiny, atomized drops, almost a mist, and Julia pushes her hair back off her forehead, the better to feel the coolness on her face. She is sheepish; twenty years ago, shaking the dust of her Snowdon neighbourhood from her heels, she would have welcomed this displacement. All she'd wanted from life was to be removed from her context, allowed to move off into the world without the past she loathed. It's not that she would wish the neighbourhood to be otherwise now — only, it is the latest in a series of small shocks that have progressively unmoored her from her idea of herself as coming out of a particular past. She is now drifting, in a fog. She knows there are other boats out here, other people in them; she can hear the slap of water against gunwales. She just doesn't know how to make contact, how to locate herself in her new position.

⚹⚹⚹

JULIA WANDERS THROUGH THE DRIZZLE, erring east instead of west toward home, thinking vaguely of buying bread or fruit. She traverses the familiar litany of names that once belonged to the families that owned these plots, when they were narrow strips of farm outside the borders of the very young city — Mentana, Boyer. Under the black pavement, now increasingly plastered with yellowed and brilliant red-green leaves, Julia has seen the antique brick arches that still serve as conduits for water and sewage. She loves to think of those, their beautiful Victorian forms evidence of the work of individual hands long passed from existence.

Her Plateau neighbourhood, planted on the hard skirt of rock that spreads under the surface from the city's eponymous hill, is still romantically fresh and lovely to her, an object of Julia's affection. She never felt that way about Snowdon, the quarter she grew up in, the neighbourhood that has forever, for Julia, looked and smelled like the home and family she only ever remembers wanting to flee. For her, the graceless square apartment buildings, the cramped storefronts, the very air extended the disapproving surveillance of her mother's gaze and the inference it provoked that Julia was somehow, inescapably, essentially lacking. Julia realizes that her fingernails are digging into the soft inner flesh of her hands. She relaxes her cramped fists and turns toward home.

⚜

THERE IS A MESSAGE WAITING for Julia. Andrea "Palladio" has invited her for dinner. Julia is happy Andrea called. They've tried to get together a couple of times, unsuccessfully. She would like to have another friend, and the image of Andrea trails an aura of sexual energy left over from the seminar, which adds appeal — but now she is fidgeting. Andrea makes her think of Nicholas, and his absence weighs on Julia. Seeing Deepa suffering so much yesterday makes Nicholas's potential peril all the more real in Julia's mind. It is likely that at some point during the evening she and Andrea will speak of him, and speaking of him feels risky, as if it might attract the attention of malevolent fate. This is, clearly, baseless superstition, but Julia can't shake it.

Andrea lays a table with dishes of food and they dip into them in a leisurely fashion, moving from one to the other like pigeons pecking among a selection of high-quality crumbs in the park. Andrea asks Julia whether she's continued doing any reading on architecture since their course. Julia has read the occasional article or book brought to her attention by Nicholas, mostly with the idea that it could help her understand what interests him about his subject. Andrea brings out a recent general-interest magazine that features an article by Nicholas, on gardens to visit while travelling in Europe. Julia feels a jolt, seeing this; she hadn't known about it, and although he must have written it well before leaving on his trip, it still feels creepy, a strangely impersonal message from the unknown. She pushes the last of a piece of bread and cheese into her mouth and wipes her fingers on the napkin in her lap, then picks up the magazine and pages through the article. There is a photograph of a garden in the Alhambra, and as Julia looks at it she imagines the figure of Nicholas, his sleeves rolled halfway up his sleek, delicately veined forearms, standing on the gravelled path. It makes her throat ache. At the end of the text, next to his name and the little biographical note, is a tiny head shot. A smudgy Nicholas looks up at Julia, his face grave, eyes dark.

"I met his wife," Julia says, immediately regretting having said it.

"Oh yeah?" Andrea says, carefully bisecting a stuffed tomato. The vegetable falls open on her plate and the vivid pale yellow-green of the avocado filling, edged by the red oval of the tomato, glows in the lamplight like an exotic jewel. Julia fixes her eyes on it. It's really beautiful.

"Yeah," Julia says. She is trying to think of some other subject to bring up.

"What's she like?" Andrea asks, and Julia hears the subtle prurient edge to her voice. She thinks, this is a tribute to the power of Nicholas's personality. If he weren't so magnetic, Andrea wouldn't care what his wife was like — nor would

Julia have. This also comes from the same source as the erotic charge that Andrea contributed to the atmosphere of the architecture seminar. It's what makes her personality crackle, for both good and ill. Julia is attracted and repelled at the same time, her pulse ticking in her neck. Nicholas hangs over the room, invisible but present.

Julia shrugs, over-casually. She helps herself to an avocado-stuffed tomato too, and starts to slice it. She hopes that reproducing the lovely moment of colour on her own plate will be soothing, ease her deepening tension, her ache. "She's nice, I guess," she says. In her peripheral vision she sees Andrea look acutely up at her.

"He's missing," Julia breathes. She hadn't meant to say that either. Andrea is peering at her now. Julia pushes her chair back a little, hoping to pull her face out of the pool of lamplight, reduce the effectiveness of Andrea's scrutiny. Andrea doesn't say anything, keeps looking at her. Julia feels compelled to speak. "Apparently," she begins, deliberately steadying her voice, "he went to Morocco on a research trip and hasn't called home or shown up where he was expected. His wife is really worried." As she speaks she hears it in her own tone: this is no longer just about Nicholas. This is about Deepa also. This is about Deepa now.

Andrea has heard it too. "What, are you friends with her now?"

Julia shakes her head. "She came into the store, she's doing some work with my boss. The subject of Nicholas came up. We talked a bit." The familiar pain is blooming in her side, a tiny, tight, pinching flower. She lays her fork and knife down by the side of her plate. She has a strong impulse to leave, to rush home and call Deepa. She can imagine Deepa sitting alone in her house, all the lights off except one, the base of a forgotten, half-finished glass of wine making a ring on the cover of a book on the side table. Her small hands knotted in her lap. Her face drawn.

Julia glances at her watch. 9:13 p.m. She looks straight at Andrea, not really seeing her while she calculates. That means it is after one in the morning in Morocco. If Nicholas is all right he could be lying in bed now, pleasantly digesting a late dinner while ruminating on the next day's plans, or perhaps already asleep in a wash of moonlight. If he is not all right ... it may not matter what time it is. Julia looks at Andrea's face, the graceful lines of her jaw, her lovely mouth, lips bowed like a well-crafted canoe. Her hair. For the first time she wonders whether Nicholas has in fact simply taken off. Perhaps he has slipped into a different life, sitting in the kitchen of some woman's house, staring at a different jaw, desiring a different mouth, his fingers entwined in some other woman's fragrant hair. Julia smiles wryly to herself. If so, she will be angry with him. On her own behalf, and on Deepa's.

Andrea stands, pulls her plate off the table, grabs the cruet of vinaigrette and the empty bottle of Merlot by their necks. "Dessert?" she asks. Julia hears a glinting in her voice; she isn't sure whether it's actually there.

＊＊＊

THE CLOCK SAYS 4:28. A minute ago it said 4:27. Julia stares at the robotic red LED display, hating it. Her temples throb with pressure. Her pillowcase is wrinkled; the pillow itself feels flat and hard. She tosses herself horizontally across the bed, pulling at the duvet so she is at least partly covered. "The sister I don't have," Deepa had said. If she'd known what those words could mean to Julia, who actually has a sister she doesn't have.

Well, she corrects herself, depending on what you mean by "have." If "having" a sister is living with that sister, forming a united front against unreasonable curfews and fighting over the last piece of pizza, knowing exactly what she's thinking when her eyelid twitches — then Julia does not now and never has had a sister. But if "having" is the sister taking a place in Julia's life and in her history, she has one, although until recently her existence was felt as a deforming force, not an individual presence. Carol's ability to love Julia, to accept her as herself and not expect her to be some kind of compensation, was foreshortened by loss — that was Julia "having" a sister. Insofar as Carol was unable to love Julia freely and let her be unashamed, she "had" a sister. As those flaws made Julia into a person who has difficulty believing she is loved and yet who craves loving with a ferocity that has been like a malign third entity in her relationships, has slipped like a bad shadow between her and her lovers, she has always "had" a sister.

She sees Deepa in her kitchen, small and drawn into herself to keep the pain from breaking inside her. "The sister I don't have," she said. Julia sees her mouth moving, her dark golden eyes warm, sunk into her face like a pair of sweets lying in dark water. She thinks of Deepa's Indian mother. She wonders whether Deepa has ever worn a sari, and smiles to herself as she pictures Deepa in the green-and-gold sari the woman on the street was wearing outside the Snowdon greengrocer's. Deepa would look radiant in such jewel-like colours. Julia thinks of her in her usual clothes, paint-pocked jeans and a T-shirt; black, white, and tan Peruvian sweaters; hiking boots. Julia's mouth moistens. She'd love to see Deepa's brilliance revealed.

She wishes she had Deepa's email address, she could write to her right now — 4:44 a.m. She sighs. If only she could see past walls, across distance. If only she could fly through the dark over the narrow streets of the Plateau, lined with rows of brick and greystone duplexes and triplexes. She'd weave through the glass and concrete of downtown, swoop past the offices of Place Ville Marie, towering over their underground shopping mall, then skim the long rectangle of the Queen Elizabeth Hotel. She'd make a whimsical loop around the dome of Mary Queen of the World Cathedral — itself, whimsically enough, a reduced-scale model of St. Peter's Basilica in Rome. According to Nicholas, a miniature monument to Bishop Bourget's desire to thumb his nose at his ecclesiastical rivals. Then, heading west in the quiet night, she'd pass over the geometry of quiet streets, flowerbeds, and bus stops of Verdun, and approach Deepa's house. Hovering, she'd look to see whether there was a light on.

If Deepa were sitting up in bed, hugging her knees, chewing on her anxiety over Nicholas's safety, Julia could tap on the window and attempt to comfort or at least distract her. Or maybe ... Julia rolls over and perches her chin on folded arms in front of her, gaze resting on the dark wall, and allows herself a moment of pleasure: maybe Deepa is awake and thinking of her, Julia, wishing they were together, wanting to be held again the way Julia held her in her kitchen. This time, in bed, where she could nest her head against Julia's shoulder and truly rest. Fall gently into sleep.

AUNT JUDY IS IN THE hospital; she's had a small stroke. She is resting comfortably and expected to make a full recovery, but it is frightening nonetheless. It also leaves Uncle Paul alone in their house, where he is not really able to look after himself. Julia leaves work after the lunch breaks have been covered and picks Uncle Paul up in a taxi. They go to the Jewish General Hospital and Julia walks slowly beside Paul as he thunks his way down the fluorescent-washed hallway toward Aunt Judy's room. He looks sicker than some of the patients, Julia thinks; his skin is a yellowy-grey, his steps heavy and unsure. Aunt Judy is half-sitting against her pillows, and her face creases with pleasure when she sees Julia and Paul enter the room. They talk a little bit, just to keep the air open.

Julia and Paul stay until Aunt Judy gets her early dinner. Julia peels the foil away from the plastic cup of juice, rips open the clear plastic pouch containing the plastic cutlery. She is helping Paul snap his jacket closed in preparation for their departure when a nurse comes in to attend to one of the other patients in the room. She glances over at Julia. "This your daughter?" she asks Judy, in the half-inquiring voice of someone who assumes she already knows the answer.

"Almost," Aunt Judy says, smiling at Julia. Julia feels a heat behind her eyes. It occurs to her that although she has, for much of her life, felt as if she were deprived of a mother, circumstances are now conspiring to offer her a pair of stand-in parents. The fact that Judy isn't related to her by any blood tie at all makes it even better. Julia kisses Aunt Judy and squeezes her hand.

"Let me know if I can do anything for you, Aunt Judy," Julia says.

"You're doing what I need you to do," Aunt Judy replies, nodding in the direction of Paul's back as he pushes his walker through the doorway.

At home, Uncle Paul goes directly to the living room. Julia hears the air go out of him as he sits down in his usual chair. She follows him in and takes his jacket, pulling it off each arm in turn; it reminds her of undressing a toddler. She goes into the kitchen and looks through the fridge, the cupboards, assembling a spare meal for the two of them.

Paul is too tired to get up and move to the table, so Julia brings his soup, in a mug, to the living room. She brings a mug for herself and they sit in silence as Paul spoons food into his mouth with a trembling hand. Julia grows tender toward him, watching him work so hard to eat this small amount. She's almost glad Bill is in Toronto, and won't be arriving until the next day. She wants this: the chance to heat a cup of soup, hang up a jacket.

"I went for a walk in Snowdon," Julia says to Paul. He looks at her sideways, then returns his gaze to his wavering spoon.

"What for?" he says. Julia smiles to herself. She'd be willing to bet he knows.

"Bill remembered the name of the private detective and that his office was somewhere between our house and Steinberg's.

So I went for a walk, to see if I could find it. If it was still there. I thought ... Well, since it was paid for ..." Saying it out loud, it sounds foolish. Julia is embarrassed.

Paul sips from his spoon, coughs wetly, sips again. "Find anything?" he asks.

Julia shrugs. "No. Of course not."

Paul puts his spoon into the mug, turns and looks at Julia. "What did Bill say the name was?"

"Arthur Lemberg," Julia says, "or something like that." She feels a little short of breath.

Paul nods. "I think it was Limburger, now that you mention it — you know, like cheese," he says calmly, turning back to his soup. "I think he would be too old now, he wouldn't still be there. Your mother described him as an older man at the time. But he had a son. He worked with his son."

Julia gulps a mouthful of soup and it scalds her tongue; she shifts it frantically around in her mouth until she can't hold it anymore and then swallows it. It sears a path through her chest. "Do you remember where his office was?" she asks. Her tongue is weirdly leathery.

Paul shakes his head. "That building isn't there anymore," he says. "They tore it down and built a restaurant or something. Few years ago." He lifts his mug and tips it against his mouth, swallows the last drops of soup, then puts the spoon back in the cup and hands it to Julia. "Thank you, dolly," he says. "Now if you wouldn't mind I'm ready to get into bed."

At home, Julia sits by the window drinking a glass of white wine; there is no light but what sneaks in, yellow, from the streetlight outside. Uncle Paul hadn't wanted her to help him change into his pyjamas, but he'd asked her to take his shoes off for him before she left. Kneeling before him, unlacing his black shoes, pulling the socks off his puffy feet — the big toes twisted, the skin scaled white and lizardy by age — Julia had felt her nose filling, and she'd had to keep her head down and blink as she rolled up the worn socks and placed the shoes side by side on the floor of Paul's closet. This is a reasonable thing for a forty-year-old to do, she thinks, taking shoes off the worn, swollen feet of someone long beloved. Halfway through a life and bestowing care upon the ones who came before. She didn't have the chance to perform these small services for her own father. The loss of that small intimacy twinges in Julia's chest.

She thinks about her mother. Carol was still relatively young when she died; she wouldn't have needed the kind of help people need in old age, and there would have been nurses or aides to help her once she was in the hospital, really debilitated by the cancer. Or maybe she did need someone to sit by her bedside, pour water from the plastic jug filled with melting ice chips, hold the pleated straw for her so she could sip from the Dixie cup. Would Paul have been there to do that for Carol? Or did she spend hours lying alone, her head on the white pillow, thirsting, as she watched the condensation collect on the outside of the plastic pitcher, too weak to lift it?

Julia shakes her head, turns her thoughts deliberately back to Paul's puffy feet, whence they wander of their own accord to her father's white face lying on his own hospital pillow. She remembers the purple-yellow bruise in the soft crook of his arm where a narrow channel of metal had, with incidental brutality, been repeatedly opened between the outside world of saline drips and diuretics, and his tender interior. She knows he was probably never conscious enough to feel the pain that contusion signified. This makes her remember the moment, sitting across his sheet-draped almost-corpse from her still, silent mother, when she realized he wouldn't ever raise his papery eyelids again, ever see Julia or meet her gaze. An old wound re-opens somewhere behind her ribs. She grits her teeth, squeezes her eyes shut until the sharp edge begins to dull.

She takes a sip of wine and warmth spreads through her chest, soothing the aching spot where her father's untimely death is pulsing now for the first time in years. She picks up the mostly full wine bottle and twirls it along the edge of the side table. The wine makes it better, Julia thinks, it really does. Easier. She wishes Deepa were here, squeezed into the big chair next to her. They could drink the whole bottle between them, murmuring in the dark, easing each other's sadnesses, old and new. Outside, Julia sees the neighbourhood cat cross-ing the street and she salutes its confidence, its independence, its swaggering grace. She raises her glass in the direction of the window.

❧

THE DAY HAS SEEMED SIMULTANEOUSLY very long and very short. Julia went to help Uncle Paul get ready in the morning and took him to the hospital, went to work for a few hours, then returned to the hospital to bring him home. She is slicing open a microwaved baked potato for him, spreading its inside with the low-quality soft yellow margarine he favours, when Bill arrives, shedding his jacket and bags by the door. The three of them sit at the table while Paul slowly makes his way through his meagre supper, the fork tremoring in between bites.

"I didn't know you remembered that private detective," Paul says, looking curiously at Bill.

Bill shrugs. "I was fifteen or so. Why shouldn't I have remembered?"

Paul takes a moment to dig at the potato with his fork. "I didn't say you shouldn't, I just didn't know you did," he says.

Bill rubs his hands down his thighs. "Well, I did."

Julia watches. She can't tell whether there is tension between them. Bill is wearing a pair of jeans and a maroon button-down shirt; she can see the collar of a blue T-shirt visible behind the open neck of the button-down. She hasn't seen him dressed in anything other than a suit as an adult, since they have seen each other only at funerals and weddings. He looks more like a real person this way, she thinks. More like a person with a history.

Uncle Paul brings his fork to his mouth, a chunk of potato balanced precariously on its trembling tines. His face is thrust forward, his mouth open, his tongue extended to catch the food. It tumbles in and he sits back, chewing. "I think it was Limburger, the name," Uncle Paul says.

Bill considers. "Could have been," he says, and looks at Julia. He smiles sheepishly. "I don't remember exactly."

"Limburger and Son," Uncle Paul says firmly, not looking up from his plate. He is manoeuvring a last shred of chicken onto his fork. Julia and Bill look at each other. Uncle Paul sounds sure.

❧

JULIA SITS BESIDE AUNT JUDY's bed. She has brought magazines — *The Walrus*, at which Aunt Judy nods with satisfaction, and *Vanity Fair*, which makes her grin mischievously. She has always been Julia's best-dressed relative, a woman of taste and grace; Julia thought that if she was too tired to read she might enjoy the glossy ads. Judy's grin is ever so slightly lopsided, and the heavy magazine almost slips out of her left hand before Julia grabs it and tucks it by the pillow.

They sit in companionable silence for a little while, then Aunt Judy reaches over and takes Julia's hand in her own thin, fragile one, holding and appearing to examine it. Julia feels a sting in her nose and must look away briefly. Finally Judy turns to her and says, "I remember when I started dating your Uncle Paul, and he took me to meet your family. I thought, I like that shy young lady. I think we'll be friends." Judy's papery smile is warm and gentle. She reaches up with her free hand and caresses Julia's cheek. "I love you," she says.

⇜✦⇝

JULIA HAS TO GO BACK to work to make up a couple of the hours she has lost, but Aunt Judy is going home tomorrow and Bill will stay for a day to help them get settled, so she is free as of nine tonight. She phones Deepa from a pay phone at the hospital. The line rings once and then Julia hears the clack of the receiver being picked up, Deepa's breathless "Hello?" Julia feels sad; there is so much yearning in it.

"Hi," she says, "just me."

"Oh, Julia, I'm so glad you called," Deepa says, and there is a rush through Julia's belly. "I feel like it's been forever since we talked. I was beginning to think you had abandoned me."

By the time she has closed the store and made her way to Deepa's house it is almost ten. She sees no lights on and hesitates, wondering whether perhaps Deepa isn't there, or didn't really want her to come. She makes herself ring the doorbell and Deepa is at the door in moments, her glossy hair tucked behind her ears, padding over the cold floor in a pair of light blue wool socks. She is wearing a wine-coloured cotton turtleneck and it makes her face look more incandescent than usual, the gold lights in her brown eyes catching on the slim worked-gold beads of a necklace that pours over her chest and down between her gentle breasts. Julia's cheeks are hot as she turns her eyes away from Deepa's front, but when she raises them she knows that Deepa saw her. Deepa is smiling. She takes Julia's hand. "Come on," she says, pulling gently.

They sit in the living room with glasses of reddish beer and a little dish of pistachios; Deepa has snapped on a single lamp. They are facing each other on the couch, their backs against the arms, their legs drawn up. Deepa puts the bottoms of her sock feet against the fronts of Julia's calves; Julia feels the gentle scratch of the wool through her tights. They're bathed in low, warm light; the rest of the house is quiet and dark around them. It makes Julia feel as if they are in a tiny secret room.

"Allen says the people at the British High Commission in Casablanca found a couple of folks who saw Nick arrive, but no one since. There's a possibility Nick hired someone to take him into the desert, but they couldn't confirm that it was him for sure. Allen has to return, but he put a guy on retainer — a policeman who works part-time as a detective for one of the hotels. He's supposed to follow up." Deepa's voice is tired. She fingers the fringed edging of a throw pillow. "I miss him," she whispers. Julia reaches across and pulls Deepa's hand from the pillow, squeezes it. She is going to draw her hand back, but Deepa holds on. She lays their two hands, hooked together, on her bent calf.

"The funny thing is," Deepa says, "If I didn't know there was anything wrong, I wouldn't be thinking twice about it. I'm so used to him not being here. I'm used to having a life of my own," she says, and lifts her head. Julia squeezes Deepa's hand again. They sit in silence for a while. They are looking into each other's faces; worn as she is, Deepa glows with warmth. Her gentle expression sits lightly on her features like a just-set custard, sweet and delicate, soft and rich. Julia imagines Nicholas looking at her; she understands completely how he must have fallen in love with her. The thought makes her smile, and at the same time she can't help wincing; she looks away, lets her gaze pass over the cream-painted cornices, the slate-blue walls, the spider plant in its Delft-blue pot in the far, night-shadowed corner.

The gold beads shine dully in the diffuse light; Julia reaches over with the hand that isn't holding Deepa's hand, and touches them. As she's doing it she worries that this is too intimate a gesture, but she wants badly to feel the textured metal, warm from Deepa's body, under her fingertips. Deepa reaches out and strokes Julia's wrist as Julia runs her finger-ends along the curved path of the beads. Deepa slips her fingers into Julia's palm and they hold each other's hands for a moment. Time corkscrews in, tight, until it only exists in the pulses of blood under their fingerprints, along their lifelines, obscured by the calluses across Deepa's palms. Julia hears herself breathing, hears Deepa breathing. Julia's mouth is hypersensitive; the air tickles it.

Deepa lifts one of Julia's hands and brings it to her cheek, presses it there with her eyes closed. Julia thinks wildly, what if I tell her? What if I don't tell her? Her heart is thudding in her and she imagines it quieting, breathes until it slows. Deepa is peering at her, her gaze firm and intelligent.

Deepa kisses Julia's knuckles and Julia thinks, oh god, what do they smell like? She remembers scrubbing the sink next to the work counter in the back of the store with pine-scented cleaner, thrusting her hands deep into a bag of cedar mulch. Changing the receipt roll in the cash register, smearing the medicinal ink. She thinks Deepa will smell how small her life is. And then, as if someone has pushed her head forward from behind, she leans over and kisses Deepa right at the corner of her mouth. Right on her almost-dimple.

Without moving, Deepa laughs gently. "Coward," she whispers. "It's like this." She shifts her head ever so slightly so their lips are aligned, and she kisses Julia on the mouth, softly. She smells like cinnamon and beer, something like warm fruit. Julia thinks, frantically, she wouldn't kiss me if she knew I was sleeping with Nicholas — and then, almost with wonder: but she knows I know she's married to him. Deepa's tongue is so soft, perfectly damp, a beautiful muscle in Julia's mouth. Julia thinks again, I should tell her before anything happens. Then she thinks, anything is happening, anything is happening — anything has happened, and it makes her want to laugh, but she doesn't want to break the moist seal of their mouths, so she swallows down the bubble of laughter until it disappears. She lets herself sink into this instant in time like a tightrope walker who steps out onto the rope and feels it sag, bounce back a tiny bit, then stabilize under her weight as she leans forward into thin air.

Then Deepa's hand brushes Julia's nipple so softly she doesn't even feel the touch, only the electric shock it produces, and she craves Deepa, and can't bear to risk ruining this moment. A sound unfolds inside her throat but it is trapped; it runs up into her nose and behind her eyes and a kind of panic inhabits Julia's head but she doesn't care, she just wants more of this. She slides her hand around the back of Deepa's warm neck and dips in under the turtleneck, holding her near. Deepa lays her hands flat across Julia's shoulder blades and holds her too. They feed on each other and feed and feed until each woman is the repository of all the other's desires, concentrated in the expanding spaces of their mouths, the air around them holding their heat and their odours, their bodies stretching and furling, bending and levering against each other.

Finally Deepa stands, pulling Julia up without once allowing their mouths to separate, and they step blindly up the stairs and into a small bedroom, clean and spare, and fall across the soft, puffy burgundy spread. For the first night in what has felt like forever, Julia does not think of Nicholas once between coming to bed and falling asleep, and she does not dream of him.

⋇

FOR THE NEXT COUPLE OF days, Julia and Deepa speak on the phone, email each other and meet, intending to eat a meal but falling into a knot on the couch. They sit knee to knee in Deepa's kitchen, leaning forward so their mouths meet. They end up back in the spare room, under the burgundy comforter. Julia doesn't see the conjugal bedroom; that door is kept closed. She is grateful for this, but in spite of the extravagant amount of time they spend together, the acuteness of their attention to each other, the liquid warmth of their persistent touching, she still feels held to the margin of Deepa's life, and it makes her nervous. She sometimes wonders what Deepa thinks, what Deepa imagines brought her here. What Deepa thinks will send her away.

That first morning, Julia woke to find herself alone in the small spare room, hazy light coming through the window over the bed. From where she lay she couldn't see anything outside but pale blue sky. She held herself still and listened. Deepa was moving about somewhere below. Julia lay there, savouring the thrill, managing her fear, impatient for Deepa to appear. The room was, apart from the bed and a chest of drawers, all bookshelves. Paperback novels — Julia saw *A Complicated Kindness* lying on its side in front of one of the tidy rows. A little poetry: Leonard Cohen and Irving Layton, Carolyn Marie Souaid's slim *Snow Formations*. A whole wall of architecture books in English, French, Spanish, Italian. Aldo Rossi, *The Architecture of the City. Les objets singuliers ... Y-a-t-il une vérité de l'architecture?* A book of photographs of the Alhambra. *Moorish Architecture: In Andalusia.* Julia looked at the spines of these books, these *objets singuliers*. Is it possible that these passive, inoffensive objects led Nicholas to his particular death — or to some other path, chosen by him but obscure to her, to others who love him? Is that one

of the truths of architecture, of travel, of love and its repel-
lents, its decay, Julia wondered. That Nicholas's fate followed
from his restlessness, his constant questing, striving for
knowledge and experience excavated spoonful by spoonful,
the space revealed like a tunnel under a wall leading somewhere warmer, more exciting, where there were to be found:
a wine that tasted like flowers; a different image of himself
in the convex lenses of the eyes of comrades new and old;
fresh, more fragrant flesh. It was this urge in him that drew
his attention to her, Julia knew; it is the engine at the core
of him. There was no use wishing it were otherwise unless
she would wish him different, and if he were different he
mightn't have loved her in the first place, albeit so briefly. If
this was her fate, Julia understood, it was Deepa's fate too —
more profoundly. She pulled a pillow up against her chest and
rested her chin on it. She wondered which each of them had
read. Whose are the Eduardo Galeano novels? Maybe they
both read them, lying in bed on Sunday mornings drinking
coffee and shedding croissant crumbs on the sheets, their feet
entwined at the ankles. She leaned out of the bed and pulled
a book from the poetry section, which was nearest, and flipped
through it. *Now You Care*, it was called. That's appropriate,
Julia thought. *This is the work of ecstasy, says Martin, cracking us open so we can shine*, she read. She closed the book,
the covers pressed together between her hands, and closed
her eyes too. Stinging tears seeped out from between the lids
anyway.

This was the way she felt at the beginning with Nicholas,
how she imagined it to herself. You cracked me open, she
thought, addressing Nicholas in her mind in the dark, in the

middle of the night. You cracked me open. She sniffled. She didn't want Deepa to come in and find her crying; she tried to swallow the tears down her throat. She felt the squeezing muscles move down from under her chin to the hollow at the base of her neck. She can see the crack he made in her, the glow that shines up from within. She wanted all that heat, all that intense yellow light to flow out of her. She wanted to feel her own annealing, to emerge stronger, better. More alive.

It's very different with Deepa than it was with Nicholas. Either she's more demonstrative, more affirmative — or else Julia is less afraid of disappointing her. Julia was wound with anxiety that night, afraid to reveal herself to Deepa, but Deepa had been so gently enthusiastic, so appreciative, that Julia had given up her willingness to be humiliated by her imperfections, had allowed herself to relax and be charmed. Deepa is slightly older than Julia and her body shows similar signs of wear and tear. Her skin softly easing, lacking the tautness of youth. Her breasts beginning to settle into softness. She is strong, her back and legs and arms showing the positive effects of years of physical work — hauling wood, sawing and hammering, squatting to carve or paint delicate patterns on the back of some chair or pew. Julia can see how Deepa will have gentle jowls one day, in ten or fifteen or twenty years, and she is charmed. She plants little kisses under Deepa's jawline, christening these incipient slings of flesh before they have even emerged. She suspects her time with Deepa is limited, assuming that when Nicholas returns or when some other closure imposes itself, Deepa will fall away from her. Julia feels provisional. It causes her constant dull pain, but it also allows her to plunge into loving Deepa with an intensity she would not otherwise have had the courage for. So she leaves her traces in places that will exist in future, as if laying away a store of honey for a season when sweetness will be in shorter supply.

Julia lay on her back in the spare room and mused. These days, she was constantly at risk of sliding into sadness. She imagined the bees in their hives and the full combs being lifted away from them, the cells cut so the honey oozed out in an amber fullness, sealed into little round jars for human consumption. She had a pang of melancholy guilt for the bees' sake, having their sweet food stolen from them. Am I stealing? she thought. She heard Deepa's footsteps coming up the stairs toward her, Deepa humming happily to herself, and Julia experienced a surge of joy. I am making my own honey, she thought, almost defiant — but this apiary is much-trafficked, the comings and goings of its bee society painfully complicated.

That evening she called Campbell, and almost didn't tell him about Deepa. She told him about Aunt Judy's stroke. She explained the developments in Nicholas's situation. Allen had phoned Deepa as Julia was leaving in the morning and said that they were going to try to track down the man they thought might have been Nicholas's desert guide. After she hung up, Deepa had put her face in her hands and cried a little, with the pain of hopefulness. Finally, as the conversation seemed to be winding down, Julia couldn't hold it in anymore and told Campbell she'd slept with Deepa. There was a sharp thrill in her stomach as she said it and remembered the acute pleasure of Deepa's warm face pressed between her legs, comforting and intimate and exciting all at the same time; she saw the beautiful dark folds of Deepa in her mind's eye as her own pale fingers carefully separated the pleats of flesh, the aromatic spice of her rising like secret incense to Julia's nose, to her exhilarated tongue.

Julia argued to herself that she has always told Campbell everything; he is a sort of chronicler of the history of her life, and should therefore know everything. The simpler truth is that she couldn't keep her mouth shut about Deepa, and Campbell was the only one she could natter to — he's distant enough, and she trusts him with her mistakes. He received the information in silence, then gave a bark of laughter. "You've got balls," he said.

Julia grimaced. "Actually, I don't. Neither of us does."

"Honey, I said it when you started seeing Nicholas and I'll say it again now, it's gonna end in tears." Campbell's voice was gentle.

"I know," Julia said, her voice low and husky. "I'll deal."

"Well, baby, you take your joy where you can find it," Campbell said, and Julia knew this was as close to a blessing as she would get anytime soon.

❧❧❧

THE NEXT DAY BILL GOES back to Toronto, so after work Julia takes the bus back to Côte-des-Neiges. She buys groceries, picks up a phoned-in prescription for Judy on the way. Uncle Paul and Aunt Judy's house is in an uncharacteristic state of disorder. A blanket left wrinkled on the couch, balled-up tissues on the side table and on the floor around it. Paul is sitting in his chair in an undershirt and a pair of pants, the tongue of his belt loose, his hair uncombed. A dirty coffee cup and spoon lie on the table.

Uncle Paul looks very tired. "Judy's sleeping," he says, waving a hand in the general direction of the bedroom.

"I brought a roast chicken," Julia says, hefting the grocery bag to demonstrate. "Green beans, potatoes."

Paul looks down at his hands. "Thank you, dolly. You have some. I'm not hungry."

Julia puts the food away and pours herself a cup of what smells like moderately fresh coffee from the coffee maker. She brings Paul his pills and a glass of water and sits down with him. She watches him put the pills in his mouth slowly, every movement an effort. His lips are wet from the water. Julia's heart feels swollen, full of an unexpected ache of love.

She does a load of laundry for them. When the sheets and towels are folded and put away, the table tidied, the dishwasher loaded, she goes into the kitchen and pulls slivers of meat from the breast of the chicken with a fork while green beans steam on the stove. She slices a tomato, makes a cup of tea. It makes her feel competent — housewifely, in a funny way — not a sensation she has often. She cuts a wedge of lemon, puts a slit in its straight edge so it cleaves to the rim of Paul's teacup. Julia thinks to herself that she hasn't had to do the series of womanly caretaking tasks that consumed the largest part of her mother's life; to do these things now feels odd. She cooks, does household tasks for herself, but no one has ever relied on her to reproduce the conditions that support their daily existence. The months or years between now and Paul and Judy's deaths are likely to be the only period in her life when she will have to act as anyone's sort-of wife or mother. Even after the one load of laundry, the single pot of beans, she understands how women get satisfaction, affirmation from this work. Unlike anyone else in her life, Paul and Judy need her, at least for a little while.

. She wonders whether her mother felt cheated. The deal Carol made was that she would pour herself into supporting a man she loved, creating children, caring for them every day, and in return she would get a home, a place in the world, and love. Yet she died alone, her husband long gone, her first child pulled from her body and her life before she ever saw it, her second child absent and hostile. Her place in the world pulled out from under her like a rug, in successive destabilizing jerks. Loneliness and loss coming up hard.

Julia's not sure what bargain she herself has been making. Her expectations are not as set as her mother's were, and so her disappointments have been more diffuse. She imagines Deepa's face shining at her in the moonlight from the window over the bed. She has had thrills, pleasures her mother never could have had. She puts a bit of margarine on Paul's green beans. She thinks, on balance, that she is willing to have the pain of loneliness and the rending sadness of the loss of love, in order to have felt the rushing torrents of joy that preceded them.

When the plate is assembled, she brings it out to her uncle. She puts it on the little table beside him and gently pushes the fork into his hand. He twists his mouth to one side in brief, wry protest, then sighs and applies himself with little enthusiasm to the food. He eats about half of it, then lays his fork down. To Julia it's like bargaining with a recalcitrant child — except she can't pretend to know better than Paul. She takes away his plate and returns with a couple of the penny-sized gingerbread cookies she has found in the cupboard. He is sipping his tea and he grins at her when he sees she has brought him this treat.

"Even though I didn't finish my supper?" he asks, eyes twinkling.

"Yeah," says Julia. "I'm a pushover."

"Good," Paul smiles and nods, chewing his cookie.

Later, in the metro, she replays this in her mind. She imagines herself standing on a curb. An arm comes from one side and pushes her off. She falls over, then lifts herself from her knees, brushes herself off, and remounts her perch. The arm appears and pushes her over again; again she falls. The scene repeats itself, and each time it is a particular arm, tan, nicely muscled, strong. It takes her a while before she comprehends that it is Nicholas's arm. She is a pushover and it is he who has pushed her over — pushed her away. Unbalanced her. Brought her to her knees.

She emerges from the pivoting doors of the Verdun metro onto the concrete sidewalk and begins to walk toward Deepa's street. Deepa has pushed her over too, but when Deepa pushed her she fell into Deepa's arms, the softness of her bed, the warmth of her breath. Nicholas is not a pushover. He may allow himself to fall from time to time, but mostly he is a stele, a pillar. An immovable object and an irresistible force. At Deepa's front door, Julia sees a warm light coming from within the house, translated through several rooms, the inner door, the outer door before her. She imagines it emanating from Deepa herself — from her abdomen, as if she were a hybrid of a woman and a firefly, the glow cast from her body illuminating the corner of the world that surrounds her. Julia wants to be within the circle of that glow.

❧

ON HER LUNCH BREAK AT work, Julia googles Arthur Limburger, private detective. There is no listing. She looks in the phone book, calls information, tries alternative spellings, all her efforts fruitless. Until she has really tried everything she can think of, she is unaware of how tense she is. Then the muscles in her back, which were painfully clenched, unlock themselves and the ache mostly drains away. Marie-Soleil's boyfriend comes in and leaves a bag of blue potatoes, small and elegantly ovate, as if laid by a snake. Marie-Soleil grins. Impishly, she pulls the potatoes from the bag and piles them around the base of a purple hyacinth, barely beginning to bloom, on display in the front window. Julia wishes she had such uncomplicated love.

Lauren, who during their breakup accused Julia of liking things fraught, would disagree. She likes to quote Dr. Phil, might say, "Judging by results ..." Campbell would say it differently; having known her longer (and not being a devotee of TV psychology) he'd say, "If you look at your history ..." Julia signs for a delivery and takes the box into the back, using a matte knife to slit it open. She bridles at these interlocutors of her own fantasy. Stewart wasn't complicated, or at least not at the beginning. She couldn't have known how things would change with him, could she? Then Nicholas, and now Deepa — you can't control your feelings, she thinks defensively. She would have liked it better if Nicholas had fallen in love with her and turned out to be as single as she originally thought he might be — although that would have been no guarantee that he'd have stayed in love with her. She tosses aside the sheaf of packing paper and lifts three copies of a book out of the box. How to make twig furniture for the garden. She flips through, looking at the shiny colour photos. Bent-willow benches, woven-branch trellises. It makes her think of the furniture Deepa is making for the garden in Westmount, although it will be nothing so rustic. Picturing Deepa's work-worn hands gives her a quick electric shock to her middle; for a second she can feel Deepa's smooth calluses on the insides of her legs. Then she thinks of Nicholas's beautiful fingers, and then, carried by the momentum of this train, the image of Nicholas's large, strong hands on Deepa's smooth pale thighs intrudes. Julia sighs. She prices the books and takes them to the front of the store. Marie-Soleil is dusting, humming to herself. You're not old enough yet, she thinks in the direction of Marie-Soleil's back, her tumble of golden curls, her graceful arms. You'll have your complications sooner or later.

❧

IT HAS BEEN GREY AND rainy most days since the weather turned. The dim and damp make it hard for Julia to wake up fully. She slugs around work, clutching a cup of coffee that is either cooled to stone or, re-microwaved, too hot to drink. Thoughts of Deepa slip in between her and whatever she's supposed to be doing. She will visit Uncle Paul and Aunt Judy again tomorrow after work, do little household chores for them. Judy is getting around more now, although Paul is tired. His skin hangs looser on his face and wrists. Last night Judy told her firmly not to come today; Julia knows it's partly to give her a break, but she thinks it might also be to give

Judy and Paul a chance to get back to their normal life, uninterrupted by outsiders taking up space in their home, between them. Julia wonders what it would be like to have a marriage that has lasted for decades. She has imagined old people's relationships as being in some kind of stasis, but now she sees that for Aunt Judy and Uncle Paul, at least, their love still requires cultivation, a little fertilizer, some gentle watering. She puts her coffee down on the cash desk and rests her chin against her fist.

Deepa is having dinner with Allen and his family tonight. She loves both Nicholas and Deepa, yet Julia is outside the family circle — now, and forever. Julia sinks into a reverie as she pictures Deepa, her dark hair reflecting chestnut lights from the neck of the wine red sweater she'd been wearing, its soft folds mounted around Deepa's face, a setting for that jewel. Her short, straight nose, her full lips, her single almost-dimple. Julia imagines kissing that nose, the shallow trough of Deepa's upper lip, the rich mouth, Deepa's warm scent rising from her skin to perfume these acts of adoration. Julia blinks.

"What are you thinking about?" Olivier demands, his voice half exasperation, half amusement. Julia feels the beatific expression she was wearing dissolve as her facial muscles awaken to her surroundings. She grins, embarrassed, and turns her head, hoping the heat will evaporate from her cheeks before they get good and red.

Lauren emails and proposes that they go swimming together after work and then have supper together somewhere. They meet at the Schubert Bath, the renovated art-deco municipal pool near Julia's place, paddling along like old ladies in the same lane, chatting, until a second lane empties, then they separate and swim laps for a while. When the adult swim period is over, Julia watches Lauren lift herself out of the water in one strong, controlled movement like a column rising from the sea, her legs bending smoothly to attain a purchase on the tiled pool edge, the muscles in her thighs flexing visibly as she levers her body weight up. Water trickles off tendrils of hair that worked themselves out of her bathing cap while she swam and now lie plastered on the goosefleshed skin between her shoulder blades, the trickle diminishing to individual drops over Lauren's sleek back and generous hips. She turns and catches Julia watching her, treading water, and sticks her foot back in the pool to flick a spray of water at Julia's face, laughing.

Julia is starving, her stomach empty as a bowl; she thinks that if she swallowed a penny it would roll around in there, ringing against the sides. They go to a Vietnamese place on Duluth Street and sit at a table in the plant-choked window crunching spring rolls between their teeth, the greasy golden bits of fried wrapper sticking to their lips. Lauren waits until they've demolished their appetizer, then she looks at Julia. "How's your extracurricular wife?" she asks coyly.

At first Julia hears "extracurricular life" and it strikes her as an apt way to describe all the things that have been happening to her outside her usual routine of *métro, boulot, dodo*. Then she re-hears it correctly in her mind — "extracurricular wife" — and Julia feels heat rise into her face for the second time that day. She is embarrassed by her own reaction, and hesitates long enough that Lauren guesses the answer to her question. Lauren laughs loudly, slapping the edge of the table.

"You vixen!" she whispers loudly. "Tell me!"

Julia cringes. Somehow it feels wrong to peel back the leaves and expose the little warm nest of love she shares with Deepa. She shrugs. She looks down at her hands on the tablecloth and realizes that she feels vulnerable partly because she is transient in Deepa's life. Plus, although social interactions with Deepa aren't nearly as opaque as they were with Nicholas, with his mysterious silences and oblique turns of phrase, Deepa's motivations are more obscure. Julia suddenly feels a little unsteady.

"Come on," Lauren urges, grinning. Julia shrugs again, smiling wanly, placating. She sees the top of her disingenuous face reflected in the window behind Lauren's head, her wide, pale forehead wrinkling in a pretense of innocence, her eyes shadowed by the overhead light. "Oh, no," Lauren says, her voice low but commanding. "You're not getting away with that. Spill, bitch."

Julia smiles for real. She can't resist Lauren, who manages to combine a teenaged girl's lust for gossip with an interrogator's probing force of personality. The truth is, Julia will enjoy being able to talk about Deepa; it's a way of touching her from a distance. She doesn't say much, but it's like eating a pomegranate, each tiny seed of thought bursting under her teeth, each bead of tangy sweet juice rivering on her tongue. She describes Deepa's hair, her hands, her warm voice, the way she transforms the muscular work of wrangling wood into beautiful, minutely detailed objects that can be as large as people.

They eat soup with asparagus tips floating in it. Julia catches one in her spoon, admiring the way it looks like the top of the Chrysler Building sheared off and lying, shrunk to green miniature, in the little pool of broth. She talks about Aunt Judy's stroke. She finds herself breathing deeply, slowly. She hears herself say, "I'm afraid my Uncle Paul is dying," and is very sad to realize that it's true. She says, "I'm afraid he'll die before I've found my sister," and is shocked to understand that she has hoped, all along, to actually find Baby Goodman.

The words run out all of a sudden and she sits. A bubble of silence hovers over their table. Lauren sits back, lays her spoon down, watches. Julia can hear the sounds of the restaurant going on behind her, the clashing of dishes, conversation. A smell of beef and chili peppers wafts past her nose like a finger poking her, goading her to continue.

"Oh, honey," Lauren says, and reaches across to touch Julia's hand, ever so lightly. Julia's brow is furrowed; she is all disordered inside and trying to shake herself back into place. Lauren leans forward. "Did I know you had a sister?" she asks, curious. "And what do you mean, 'find her'?"

Julia shakes her head. Her existence seems to have so many layers, she is starting to lose track of them all. Concealed affairs; unknown, rediscovered siblings; these hidden pockets in her life generating, alternately and concurrently, spikes of anguish and wild joy, washes of melancholy. Meanwhile, on the surface, she has the most ordinary existence, trekking to work every day to sell tulip bulbs to people with four square feet of precious earth in front of their row houses, coming home to a hot bath and a glass of wine. Julia thinks of herself as completely unexceptional, and yet suddenly she almost feels as if she is some kind of secret agent. She hates it. Right now it is much too hard.

Over the noodle course Julia explains the history of her sister/not-sister. Lauren grunts matter-of-factly, coolly receiving and processing the information. Julia gets a kind of relief from seeing that it is possible for the bare facts of her sister's life, and her own, to not provoke anger and grief, feelings of betrayal. When she gets to the end, the part about how she failed to track down Arthur Limburger or his son, Lauren lays down her fork and lets out a gravelly, extended rolling burp.

"I happen to have a professional connection to some people who know some private detectives," Lauren says dryly, patting her stomach. "Let me see what I can do for you."

⊰✦⊱

JULIA WORKS LATE THE NEXT night and goes to see Deepa afterward. On impulse, she uses her employee discount to buy a single paperwhite growing in a glass bowl filled with clear marbles. Its roots thread through the marbles; the glass orbs catch and release curls and flecks of light as Julia carries it out the door, onto the yellow street-lamp-lit sidewalk. The plant's still-blind head reaches upward, unbearably fragile, the spade-shaped bud paler than its reedy stem.

She walks down to Sherbrooke metro station, goes the one stop to Berri and changes from the orange line to the green line that will take her to Verdun. Sitting in the metro car, Julia cups her hands around the paperwhite bud, afraid that it will be jostled and broken by some passenger tipped off unsteady feet as the train rounds a curve or lurches into a station. There will be something funereal about this flower once it has bloomed — its flat, unpleasant odour; the white blossom that emerges, crumpled, from its green hood. Julia has a strange moment of guilt, as if she is bringing Deepa a lovely secret message of death. She actually goes so far as to put the plant on the moulded plastic seat next to her, imagining that when she reaches her stop she will stand up and exit the metro car, leaving it behind. Then she shakes her head and picks up the glass bowl again, cradling it in her lap.

She sees a reflection of her hand distorted along the bowl's curve. Stretched out like that, her fingers look alien, thin and insubstantial. If Narcissus had looked at himself in a glass bowl, she thinks — or the back of a spoon, or a funhouse mirror — how different his fate might have been. He would not have thought himself too beautiful to settle, could have allowed himself to love, would have eased into an ordinary life. Having children perhaps, growing fat in old age. Or maybe he would have seen himself as contorted, deformed, and wouldn't have allowed himself to have relationships at all, for fear of rejection or out of a conviction of his lack of worth. He might have become bitter and lonely, sinking into alcoholism, dying poisoned by his own rage instead of mesmerized by his own perfection.

Julia nudges one of the glass marbles; her fingertip comes away damp. Lovely things can come from destructive emotions, from suffering, from selfishness. She's not sure whether this is a compensation or an irony.

Deepa answers the door wearing a white silk shirt over soft black wool pants. She has a few touches of makeup on.

The mascara and shadow make her eyes seem as if they are set far back in the wells of their sockets; her lips, tinted dark red, are more prominent than usual. Julia, who is used to seeing Deepa with no makeup at all, can tell that she looks more conventionally beautiful this way, but it makes her face look out of balance with itself. They hug and Julia smells a faint cloud of something sweetly cedary hovering in the warmth of Deepa's body. They kiss, their tongues touching briefly, and then Deepa uses her thumb to wipe a smear of lipstick off the corner of Julia's mouth. It is an almost motherly gesture.

Deepa had been out at a *cinq à sept* that lasted until much later, and only arrived moments ago herself. She bustles around her kitchen, pulling a bottle of wine from the door of the fridge, rummaging for a couple of clean glasses, pouring assorted olives into a shallow bowl. Julia watches. As soon as they tumble out of their plastic container she can smell the briny fruits, salty-acrid. They lie in their bowl like the eggs of a mixed-up flock of birds; black and wrinkled, plump and rosy brown, little beige ones with stems and fat green ones flecked with dried chili pepper. She chooses a black one and bites it, tearing the yielding flesh with her teeth. Her narcissistic offering sits on the counter, forgotten. There is something hectic about Deepa's manner tonight and Julia feels it with foreboding; she almost wishes she hadn't come. But she craved Deepa so strongly she would have come anyway, even if she'd known this in advance. Deepa tosses open a cloth napkin and extends it, then pauses for just a second to place it in Julia's palm, closing her fingers around Julia's, still cold from the air outside.

They sit at the kitchen table and drink. The wine is a gris, a rosé made from grapes grown in sandy French soil. The flush pink of it adds a raw-meat glow to Deepa's cheeks, her well-formed chin, and for Julia this, too, is some kind of portent.

"So, there's progress," Deepa begins, her voice strained with impatience. The policeman Allen hired found the family of a man who, he established, had indeed guided Nicholas into the desert. The car they were riding in broke down and they were stranded on the edge of the Western Sahara waiting for a spare part. Then their return journey was broken when Nicholas became ill and could not travel for a number of days. But they know he is alive. Now he is en route to Marrakesh whence he will fly home via Casablanca. Deepa's hands are open in the air as if she could, at this remove, hold Nicholas up, make him safe. "I knew he'd come back," Deepa says fervently. Julia thinks: this is one of those things people only say when they're not true. She doesn't voice the thought. She smiles at Deepa.

"I'm so happy for you," she says, then raises her glass so she is looking into it, at the gently pitching lake of pink wine, instead of at Deepa's radiant face. Julia's chest is tight at the thought of Nicholas returning. She has been waiting for him to come back, hoping and wanting him and yearning for it. But everything has shifted unpredictably during his absence. Without his being aware of it, their affair has drawn to its end; Julia can't see how to be with him anymore, now that she has been with Deepa. Now that she has been with Deepa and loves her and it has been so much easier, so much less angst-ridden than it was to be with Nicholas. Now that she has been inside Nicholas's house and seen the forbidden rooms, the black-and-white tiles of the bathroom where he has showered a thousand times, the little package of spare razor blades sitting in the medicine cabinet, a rectangular trace of his intentions, his habits. The side of his life that made their affair possible insofar as it stayed hidden, the backstage machinery that provided props for, that produced, his life in the world.

Julia swallows the wine methodically, then refills her glass. Deepa is slicing a baguette on the counter, spooning hummus into a little pottery dish decorated with childish drawings of hammers and saws. The happy excitement must be making her hungry — or maybe it's that she can't keep still. Julia looks down at the finely grained surface of the wooden table, perhaps sawn, sanded, stained by Deepa's own small hands.

Julia still loves Nicholas. It aches in her like a constant menstrual cramp — she can't imagine this pain ever disappearing. But her mouth and her fingers and everything that smells or tastes or touches in her want this woman shimmering before her eyes. Deepa comes and sits down again, laying the bread and hummus on the table, topping up her glass and then Julia's almost-full one.

Julia's chest burns with anticipatory grief, with the loneliness of watching Deepa so mired in relief and joy that she does not think of how Nicholas's return is likely to end her love affair with Julia, who sits six inches away from her, molecules of saliva from Deepa's tongue still lying against the mucous membrane inside Julia's cheek. Julia doesn't begrudge Deepa her happiness. She wants Deepa to be happy. She knows their relationship had its own obsolescence built in, it couldn't have lasted; it is laid out on booby-trapped terrain.

At the same time she sees that every turn in this path has left her further outside of Nicholas's life. When there was a crisis it fell to Nicholas's family, excluding her, to find him. Now that the crisis is resolved, the normal everyone will get back to when he returns will also exclude her. She will be at the margin of Deepa's life, too. Every inside she has found has been pregnant with its own outside, every entry the beginning of an arc ending in exit, expulsion. Even her sister — found and then lost again, the very finding of her the discovery of her loss.

Julia looks up to see Deepa gazing at her. "What is it?" Deepa asks, her voice low and quiet.

"I'm so happy for you," Julia repeats, working up a smile.

Deepa frowns, a skeptical twist to her mouth. "No," she says, "really."

Julia feels as if Deepa has reached in and stroked her directly on the heart muscle with her warm hand. "Really," she begins, and sighs. She pushes her wineglass around the table a bit, picks up a piece of bread, breaks it in two, and puts it down. Deepa is demanding an effort from Julia; Julia sees that her habit has been to avoid such efforts, and she is frightened but grateful that Deepa is strong enough to push her to break that bad habit. A practice learned from her parents, by their example.

"Really? Really ... Not that I would wish for a second for Nicholas not to come back. But" — Julia's voice drops to a hoarse whisper — "I think we probably won't see each other anymore after he comes back, and I am missing you already." A sob seizes and wrings her; she is embarrassed by this but can't help it. She is also embarrassed that she has lied to Deepa —

or half-lied, for she has told a partial truth. But the loss of Deepa is the immediate source of this sob, these ragged breaths.

Deepa doesn't rush to reassure her, for this small mercy Julia is grateful, again; instead, she rises and comes to stand behind Julia, puts her arms around her. She leans down so her breath is hot against Julia's ear and says, "Oh, baby," her voice low and rough with passion and compassion, desire and regret. She uses her arms to pull Julia up from her chair and turns her around so they are facing each other. They kiss slowly; Julia feels the snot running down onto her upper lip and tries to rub it away surreptitiously without taking her mouth away from Deepa's warm-fruit one.

They make love in the spare room, which Deepa decorates with candles and a bowl of peach-pink tulips she brings in from some other place; it pinches Julia to wonder whether Deepa has brought them from the conjugal bedroom where she'd put them in anticipation of Nicholas's imminent presence there. They lie mostly naked under the comforter, their flesh pressed together; Deepa is still wearing her panties of elastic lace, fancier than usual to match her cocktail-hour outfit, and Julia slides her fingers under the fabric, feeling the stretch. They have carried the bottle of wine upstairs and Deepa tips her head up to drink straight from the neck of it and then turns over and lets the warmed wine slide from her lips into Julia's mouth, and because Julia is lying down it runs right down the back of her throat and she begins to cough. The coughing catches on something sharp and becomes crying, then rolls over again into laughter, and they lie clutching each other and laugh together. Deepa takes another swig and then holds Julia's head up, a hand at the back of her neck like someone feeding a dying person, and transfers mouth-warm wine to Julia's lips again. This time Julia swallows without choking. Deepa lets Julia's head down onto the pillow and, still holding the wine bottle against her hip, leans down and nuzzles Julia's neck, traces her collarbone, kisses the plain of her shoulder and flicks her tongue at the top of the fleshy fold of Julia's underarm.

"We don't have to decide anything now, baby," she whispers, then tugs gently at the side of Julia's breast, flat-spread like a lake of spilled milk, with her teeth. Julia feels it down to her belly. Deepa's hair sweeps over Julia's skin and Julia touches it with her fingertips, trying to focus on it, on every detail of the way the light plays there, a single grey hair emerging mischievously from the curtain of dark chestnut. Julia thinks she will want to remember this.

"It's not about deciding," she whispers back. "It already is."

Deepa is sucking assiduously at Julia's brown nub, pulling sensation up from somewhere inside Julia and making it rattle and glow. Without raising her head she reaches up with her free hand and covers Julia's mouth with it, her palm open, fingers splayed. Julia lies under her lover, pleasure insinuating itself through her body, and feels herself, under that hand, effaced.

⚜

JULIA ARRIVES HOME MID-MORNING and takes a shower, changes her clothes. She shuffles around in an old sweater, a bit aimless, does laundry, changes the sheets on her bed. Smoothing the sheets, she tries to summon the image of

Nicholas laid out across her futon, head on her pillows, but the picture is faint. He is becoming a ghost. She shakes out the duvet and tidies it. The bed is made. Julia looks at the bed as it really is, empty.

She turns her back and walks away, goes and sits at her small table, not in her usual place but in the chair where both Nicholas and Deepa have sat before, so she doesn't have to see it empty too. She eats a late lunch of bread and cheese. She makes herself a coffee and then thinks to check for messages. There is one from Aunt Judy. Now Uncle Paul is in the Jewish General. Judy gives the phone number and the room number. She'd called the night before.

Julia phones, but it rings and rings. She pulls on her coat and boots and rushes out the door. When she arrives in Uncle Paul's room an aide is serving his dinner tray. He is lying back in the bed looking grey as paper. He moves his eyes in Julia's direction and she is horrified to understand that this is all the greeting he can manage. She and Aunt Judy hug each other tight. Aunt Judy is frail in Julia's arms, hollow and birdlike.

Aunt Judy gestures toward the food. "Help yourself," she says. "He's not going to eat any of it. He's got this," and she gestures toward the IV that ends in a silver spike that lies between the skin and the bone of Uncle Paul's hand like an oven thermometer in a chicken back. Julia shakes her head, reaches for Uncle Paul's other hand. She was going to squeeze it, but it feels too fragile for that. She strokes his palm with her fingers, then draws away. Moving to the end of the bed, Julia perches there, careful not to sit on Paul's slack, bent feet.

They sit in silence for a while in the greened light of the half-pulled curtain, the smells of overcooked meat and salt and coffee lying like a layer of fog over metal, adhesive, disinfectant. Eventually Julia realizes Paul's eyes are closed and the low wet clatter she hears is his breathing in sleep. Aunt Judy turns and smiles gently, tiredly. Julia considers her expression; she looks oddly peaceful. Maybe waiting for this was harder for her than living through it will be. Julia lowers her head and agrees with herself. Anticipation is harder.

"So where were you?" Aunt Judy asks. Julia looks at her and sees her raised eyebrow. She has managed to ask in a tone of voice that is at once friendly and frankly curious without being prurient or critical. Julia loves Aunt Judy.

"Out," she answers, and then meets Aunt Judy's gaze and laughs quietly at herself, at this adolescent evasion. She shrugs. "With a friend. It's a thing that's nice but won't last," she says. Aunt Judy smiles and pats Julia's hand.

"You'll find someone, dolly," Aunt Judy says. She gestures toward Uncle Paul with an open hand. "Look at me, it took me a couple of tries."

Julia is startled. She knew Aunt Judy had been married before, but it hadn't occurred to her to be curious about Aunt Judy's life before Uncle Paul. Julia inclines her head inquiringly.

Aunt Judy nods. "I got married when I was nineteen years old." She looks down, shakes her head. "It was a mistake, but I didn't want to admit it. Not that I regret having my children," she adds quickly. "But, you know, they had to live with it too. I wish none of us had to live with it. In the end Irving died very young, from Huntington's disease, which" — she looks up at Julia — "is a horrible way to die." Julia wonders if this is meant to comfort her, a way of saying that, in comparison at least, Uncle Paul is not suffering much. "I took care of him as long as I could. I'm glad I took care of him. But we wasted ourselves on each other."

Julia chews the inside of her cheek. How many times does she need to be nudged out of herself before she stops being so utterly self-absorbed? How often will she have to relearn the lesson that everyone has a history, currents running at multiple depths, the movements of which have created the visible surface? She knows it about herself — it's one of the things she knows best about her own life; it explains so much of her weakness and her pain. Yet she still sees only the top layer, the static present in other people. If I were more generous, more willing to love … she leaves the thought open.

Aunt Judy stands, leaning on the edge of the bed for balance, and pulls the foil seal away from the plastic juice cup on Uncle Paul's tray. She pours part of it into an empty Styrofoam cup and hands the rest to Julia. Julia sips, the sour juice running rough and piss-warm over her tongue. She thinks of her mother, whose ability to love was too harshly pruned by the loss of her baby, the disapproval of her husband and her family, and consequently wasn't able to bloom. I am my mother's daughter, Julia thinks, and her shoulders drop and sag. She knows this is obvious, inescapable, but every so often it strikes her with renewed force. It is ironic but also logical that the limits to her ability to love leave her craving it; she never feels she has enough.

Has she ever had enough? She thinks of the early days with Stewart. She can suddenly see his face; he used to gaze at her with adoration. She rests her chin on her fist. She probably got enough from him for a while there, at the beginning. But she didn't trust it, and held back herself. Tears are running down over her cheeks and onto her hand, she doesn't know where they came from. Is that why Stewart left? God, Julia thinks, I'm not only my mother's daughter, I'm my actual fucking mother. She feels Aunt Judy's thin hand close around her wrist.

"Let's go get a cup of coffee downstairs while he's asleep," Aunt Judy says quietly. Julia sniffs and nods. Aunt Judy will be one of her role models from now on, she vows to herself. Aunt Judy who not only has sufficient love for herself and for the people in her life, but who has so much that she can allow the people she loves the space to love themselves too. They walk slowly toward the elevator, Aunt Julia's four-footed, post-stroke cane like a third person accompanying them through the wide linoleum-and-fluorescent corridor. Julia is embarrassed to be crying for herself while Uncle Paul lies dying, but she takes a deep breath and tries to let the shame flow out and escape, along with her breath, warmed by her blood.

꘎

BILL ARRIVES AND SPELLS JULIA at the hospital. The next day Uncle Paul goes home. He hasn't spoken out loud since they first admitted him. At home, in a hospital bed installed in the bedroom, he looks almost lively for a couple of hours, then rapidly sinks into a kind of enclosed consciousness. Julia sits with him. When he feels her take his hand in hers, he gives her a tiny squeeze; she tries not to let him hear her crying. She doesn't know if he'd realize it is a kind of exaltation provoked by that fragmentary contact, that miniature pulse of love exchanged.

That night, she goes home exhausted. She stands by the

phone in the kitchen in flannel pyjama bottoms and an old sweatshirt, drinking a cup of camomile tea. She hates the taste but she knows it will help her be calm; she badly wants to sleep tonight. There is a message from Lauren. A cop she works with has put her in touch with Sheldon Limburger, Arthur's son. He is a private detective in Toronto and he still has his father's files. He doubts that anything useful remains but he will check. Alone in her kitchen, Julia shakes her head. This doesn't seem very urgent right now. She erases Lauren's voice. If something comes, she'll deal with it then.

A second message is from Deepa. She wants to see Julia. "Call me, it doesn't matter how late," she says. Julia dials, then hangs up. Then she gathers herself, dials again. Deepa answers, her voice a rush of warmth; she sounds very glad, even grateful to hear from Julia. "How are you?" she asks, and Julia can hear the depth of her concern but also something else pushing behind it.

"I'm just really tired right now," Julia says. She hears the muffled clink of glass on teeth and wishes she were lying in Deepa's warm arms on the couch in her living room, sheltered and supported in the curve of Deepa's woodworking muscles, her head pillowed against Deepa's slackening breast.

"Nick'll be home in two days — on Thursday night. I really want to see you before he gets back," Deepa says. There is a quality to her voice Julia hasn't heard before. It is almost shy. Julia thinks that Deepa has come to see that there will be no way to make space to be together once Nicholas returns. There is something about the near-catastrophic character of his absence that makes his return more emphatic. He has become something of a prodigal husband.

Julia agrees to call Deepa the next day. Everything will depend on Uncle Paul's condition. They say goodbye and are about to hang up when Deepa breathes, "Julia."

"Yes," whispers Julia.

"Julia," Deepa whispers back.

⚜

JULIA SLEEPS LATE, WAKING LUXURIOUSLY drowsy and stretchy in her warm duvet nest, exhaustion having been smoothed away by the gentle ministrations of her newly attentive lover, sleep. She lies under the cover for a while, delaying the moment of rising, when her muscles and bones will have to bear the weight of her flesh. Eventually she becomes fully awake, too restless to stay in bed. She makes coffee, tosses out yesterday's mail — ads and solicitations, menus for souvlaki joints and pizza places. Olivier has kindly told her to take all the time she needs, but she is thinking that if Uncle Paul seems stable today she might spend a couple of hours at work. It's the only normal part of her life anymore, and she could use a little stability.

She dials Uncle Paul's house and Bill answers almost immediately. "Oh hi, Julia," he says. He sounds brisker, more businesslike than Julia expected.

"Hi, Bill. How are things?"

"He's gone."

Julia has a momentary vision of Uncle Paul's rumpled, empty bed.

She realizes that this is not what Bill means.

"It happened some time in the night," Bill says. "I sat with him quite late, and when I left him he was sleeping. But early this morning when Judy woke up, it was over."

"It happened," "it was over." Julia wants to push her hand through the long, twisting cord of the phone and grab Bill by the throat and shake him. Tell me he's goddamned dead, Julia thinks. She says, "Okay. I'm coming."

She sits on the bus, watching the drops of rain cling to the outside of the glass, tracing their meandering paths, each trickle shaking loose under the vibrations of the bus's movement. One by one they travel erratically toward the places where they will merge with what looks like relief into narrow running streams of worked light and shadow, twisted together like handmade wool. Lucky water, Julia thinks, always coming from and going back to some form of being larger than itself. It has no history of its own, only an endless series of transformations and permutations.

She stops at the supermarket near the house and buys a cheese platter and crackers, grapes and olives, small plastic bins of chopped liver and hummus, a roasted chicken and a fresh can of coffee. Soon Aunt Judy will be surrounded by more food than she could ever eat, but in the meantime it will be a relief to her not to have to think about being a hostess. In the house Julia and Bill have the first hug she can ever remember having with him; they stand, her breasts flattened against his white shirt, and he holds her, really holds her with a strength that comes from sorrow. Aunt Judy canes her way into the kitchen while they are standing there and they open their little circle to include her. The three of them stand, touching each other, and say nothing. Julia thinks, none of us is really much related to the others, and yet we are more related to each other than anyone else, at least for now.

She unpacks the food, washes the fruit, spoons coffee grounds into the coffee maker. She thinks about proximity. It seems to be all that counts, in space and in time. She fell in love with Nicholas when they passed within inches of each other, the leaves of a shrub connecting them in a delicate chain of seconds. She fell in love with Deepa because Deepa was strung close to her, suspended between Nicholas and Olivier. Her sister was not her sister because she was never close enough to know; her sister became her mother's constant grief because she was so quickly and so far removed, after having been the object of such a ravaging intimacy.

Men come from the undertakers and carry away Uncle Paul's corpse, strapped down, wrapped up; their gurney rolls, its smooth functionality nearly obscene. Julia watches them slide it out the door and then goes back to the kitchen. She'd do anything now, to have something to occupy her mind. She rummages for cups and spoons and lays them out on the table. She never saw her father's corpse; there'd been no viewing. He'd opted for cremation, against Carol's objections. Julia remembered them arguing about it long before either of them died.

"It isn't enough that Hitler burned six million of us, now you want to have yourself burned too?" Carol cried, and Julia, listening acutely without looking up from her algebra homework, was amazed at the frantic note in her mother's voice.

Her father shook his head, his own voice deliberately low and controlled, as if he could win this argument by demonstrating a superior, reasonable manner — his usual strategy. "That's not the point, Carol. I'm not going to let something Hitler did thirty-five years ago govern my choices now. That would be giving him more power at this late date."

Carol leaned in, hectoring, her manner nearly desperate. "But Raphael," she said, wringing her hands in a gesture that Julia knows she, as an adult, unconsciously repeats, "you're not supposed to. We're not supposed to. Think of your parents. Your father would be devastated." Raph whirled on Carol and, dropping his pretense of calm, shouted, "My father was a narrow-minded old bigot whose religious beliefs were about maintaining his authority, not about what was right." Raph's face red, his breath coming in bursts. "You should know that even more than I do," he said. Carol cried out, and ran from the room.

At the time Julia had attributed the heat of the argument to a kind of inexplicable adult hysteria, but now, lining Aunt Judy's butter knives up against the paper napkins, she suddenly understands the context of this argument in their history. How bitter it must have been for her mother. She'd been forced into the most painful choice of her life in order to honour her father-in-law's scruples and — even worse, as she must have known — to accommodate her husband's fear of his father's wrath and condemnation. (Or does Julia have the balance wrong? Does her mother deserve less pity, more of something else?)

Then, decades later, having suffered the pain of that original decision every day since, to have her husband reject her request to be allowed to bury his body. To lose the possibility of the comfort, such as it was to her, of having his physical self remain on earth for as long as it took for the earth to reclaim it. To make her appeal to the authority that had justified the greatest loss of her life, and have that authority cast aside now as not only empty but wrong, by the man who had wielded it then. A pill bitter enough to choke on.

Julia stands, a forefinger stilled on the lordotic arch of a spoon handle. That must be one of the difficult things about a long marriage, she thinks, living with the knowledge of the way your flaws and your spouse's flaws — cowardice, fear, shame — deformed your life, or someone else's, and yet to love and care for him in the face of those disappointments. She slits the plastic wrapping on a bar of cheddar and lays the sweating cheese on Aunt Judy's wooden cutting board. It would be unkind and unfair to expose Baby Goodman to the knowledge of how her beginnings were so brutally shaped by generations of fear and selfishness, ringing and echoing from life to life — so easily, it seems, overcoming the more innocent impulses of love.

⚘

DEEPA HAS INVITED JULIA TO meet her in a restaurant downtown for what Julia sorrowfully guesses will be an expensive dinner — compensation of some kind. Or if nothing so crude as a payoff, then at least some form of acknowledgement. Cash value as a measure of the importance of their attachment, the rending power of its passing. The thought gives Julia a cold ball in her stomach. Before leaving Aunt Judy's house, she calls Deepa and asks if they can't meet in some less public place. She is afraid she'd feel awkward sitting in the chi-chi restaurant, surrounded by the burghers of Westmount and Outremont in their designer clothes, her sweater ravelling into her denim lap, the smell of funeral cheese on her fingers. Deepa is silent for a moment. Julia resentfully wonders whether Deepa is gauging the possibility that without the stiff formality of the starched linen napkins and truffle shavings Julia will collapse into a formless emotional mess, unpleasant to witness and difficult to manage.

"Look," Julia finally bursts out, "I don't want a send-off. Can we just spend the time together, enjoy being in each other's company, and then say goodbye at the end of the evening?" Deepa begins to reply, hesitates.

"I can't stay late anyway," Julia says, "I've got a funeral tomorrow."

Deepa sounds shocked. "Did your uncle die?"

"Last night."

"Oh, baby, I'm so sorry. I didn't realize. Look, if you don't want to do this ..."

"No," says Julia firmly. "I do want to do this. I want to do it more than anything." As she hears the words march out of her mouth she knows they are true. She knows that if they don't meet tonight they may not get a last time together, and she doesn't want any more loose ends in her life. Plus she is craving Deepa's warm embrace. She wants to smell Deepa's breath again before she goes off in the morning to truck with death.

They agree to get a pizza and eat it at Deepa's house. Julia doesn't necessarily want to go there, to see the kitchen cabinets, the bathroom floor, the doorways Nicholas will walk through the following day while Julia is drinking coffee in Aunt Judy's kitchen, the mud of her Uncle Paul's grave still clinging to the arches of her shoes. Yet her own place feels separate, a sort of refuge; she doesn't want to layer any more memories of Deepa over the ghostly remnants that are already there. Nor does she want to live with any material reminders of the simultaneous ends of her involvements with both Deepa and Nicholas. It would be too hard to step out of the shower in her own apartment and pick up a towel she remembers seeing tucked around Deepa's chest, her skin almost invisibly sprinkled with pale nutmeg freckles.

Julia approaches Deepa's house, dampness making the dark thick and muffled. The streets and sidewalks are plastered with wet leaves in the process of disintegrating into an ochre-brown vegetable slime. She stops at the curb. She has the urge to go around the back, to retrace the steps of her original visit here, to hide herself in the shadowed walk between Deepa and Nicholas's house and the house next door. Last time she walked that path she was in an entirely different relation to both Nicholas and Deepa. It is as if she is on the outer edge of a disc and must continue to walk the rim, while Nicholas and Deepa move about according to the demands of their own trajectories inside the circle. The three of them have made various triangles as they've all moved through time and space. Now the lines between Julia and the two of them will be snapped. Nicholas and Deepa will go back to being two points linked to each other (there may be others — will be others, Julia is sure — but she doesn't need to take them into account). She will go from being one angle of a figure to a single point in space, unconnected except by memories and wayward desires. This is a strange geometry.

Inside, Deepa greets Julia gravely and hugs her. Already, Julia feels, she has passed out of the erotic sphere and into the role of an object of pity. Deepa stands back and peers at her from under the rim of light that traces her hair, scattering along her part, spangling her gentle head. When their eyes meet Deepa steps forward again and kisses Julia long, delicately, with a hunger that fills Julia with gratitude.

At the end of the evening Deepa presents Julia with a handful of burgundy cloth, loosely folded over itself. Julia lays it on her lap and opens it. Inside is the worked-gold bead necklace Deepa has often worn. Julia looks at it spilling across her lap and can't help but see the image of it pouring down between Deepa's breasts, defining the shape of her. Julia looks away.

"This is not a goodbye gift," Deepa says. "I'll want that back."

Julia keeps her head turned. Deepa is so much more courageous than she is, willing to plant the seed of a future connection that Julia was trying to give up in hope of escaping some of the pain of this separation. Julia looks hard across the room, her fingers hooked around the precious metal in her lap. If she is going to become a person who lets herself love, she thinks, she might as well start now. She turns back to Deepa and throws her arms around Deepa's shoulders, plunging her nose into Deepa's sweet-smelling hair, feeling every exquisite atom of the pressure of Deepa's fingers on her back. When they have finished nuzzling and hugging and stroking each other's faces, Julia pulls the necklace over her head and looks down at it, lying against her age-flattened chest. She will wear it tomorrow.

THE FUNERAL IS AT ONE. Julia offered to come over to Aunt Judy's in the morning in case she needs any kind of help, but Aunt Judy's children, Seth and Anya, have arrived from out of town, so Julia's morning is her own. She didn't fall asleep for a long time the night before, returning from Deepa's house nervous, her brain rattling through a series of jump-cuts. Deepa as Julia left her, small and glowing in the light of the lamp next to the couch in her living room, moving into the night that would lead to the day when her husband would be returned to her. Nicholas, thin from his illness, the bones of his face sharp, his eyes set deep and dark as bubbling wells of tar and glistening in the shadows cast by the overhead light, reading a book in the close safety of his seat on the Royal Air Maroc jet. She tried to touch herself, stroked her belly and the insides of her thighs, her sticky folds, but she couldn't concentrate enough to get a rhythm going, much less achieve any kind of calm, climactic or otherwise. So she watched the bars of light on the wall instead, wondered whether her street cat neighbour, who she thought of as a kind of feline spirit companion, was curled up warm some-where or out wandering — its restlessness working in it to move it through the world the way Nicholas's restlessness had moved him toward, through, and then away from Julia; the way Julia's and Deepa's had moved them to find each other, a glancing blow.

So this morning she wakes late. She takes a very long, hot shower, finally emerging when she has admitted to herself that she is only staying under the scalding curtain of water as a delaying tactic. She turns off the water and steps out onto the bath mat.

She finds herself standing before the kitchen counter in her funeral clothes, the same ones she wore to her mother's funeral and, as she thinks of it now, to meet Nicholas. She is wearing black tights instead of summer-weight pantyhose, a black turtleneck instead of the thin cotton button-down blouse, and black ankle boots instead of her black shoes in deference to the on-again, off-again rain. So, she thinks ruefully, not really the same outfit at all. It is a different season. She takes a sip of hot black coffee. In some ways — good ways — she is a different person. In some ways, both good and bad, she is the same.

The funeral service is brief; Uncle Paul would have approved. It is informal. Everyone who wants to, stands up to speak. Bill leans over to tap Julia on the knee, looks inquiringly at her. She shakes her head. There is almost no one here aside from her, Bill and his family, Aunt Judy and her children. The remaining two old men from Uncle Paul's "club," the group of ancient friends, sit with their old wives in the second row. A couple of neighbours and other surviving friends fill out the party. They are in the same room where her mother's corpse was displayed. Julia remembers Uncle Paul saying, "I'll be back here soon enough."

In retrospect, she is grateful that her mother predeceased her uncle, otherwise Carol would be here, and Julia knows she'd be expending all her psychic energy warding Carol off instead of attending to this moment. It's a strangely intimate point in time, her here with the end of her Uncle Paul, the debris left behind in the wake of his exit, the people to whom he has attached Julia scattered around the room. As each person in her life has passed out of it, she has had to renegotiate her relationships with those to whom she was connected through them. Her mother died and she was able to rediscover Uncle Paul — a gift Julia gives her mother credit for, for the first time. Now Uncle Paul has died and she will re-tie the strings that hold her to Bill and to Aunt Judy. She never thought of death as productive, but now she sees it creating and recreating relationships between people. Death, absence, the end of love. They are like the leaves she has been walking over for a week or two now, that turned brilliant and died and immediately began rotting, feeding themselves back to the earth that fed their engendering.

Everyone is standing, pulling on coats. The old men are not coming to the cemetery — the weather is too uncertain, and they cannot stand for very long. Julia moves to one side and watches as Aunt Judy's son, Seth, helps her take her toddler-like steps down the carpeted aisle. She is like an old violin, the wood brittle but the strings still tautly strung. Following them is Bill, walking with his arm loosely slung around his son's shoulders. The boy is just beginning his growth, but his bones are already ranging outward, too fast for the flesh to keep up. His chin, his shoulders, his wrists are all too pronounced for his size, but Julia figures that when he has caught up to himself he'll be big, and handsome; a solid version of Bill, who is himself a well-made version of his father, Paul. Julia waits until they are too far ahead to engage her in conversation and then walks toward the exit herself, in company with her thoughts.

She knows she is, inescapably, a version of her own parents — in odd moments she catches sight in the mirror of her mother's face living within her eyes, cartilage and bones; her father's dark brown hair growing away from her forehead as his grew back from his own. The older she gets the more frequently her parents appear to her in her own image, by some alchemy of genetic memory. She can't help wondering whether Baby Goodman looks like her, whether the attributes got shuffled more or less the same way or dealt totally differently.

Deepa showed Julia pictures of her parents one night, and Julia wouldn't have guessed they had created the woman by her side. She has nothing of her mother's sharp, long face with its large features and wild widow's peak — and she has almost nothing of her father's milk-pale skin peppered with freckles, his thin red hair flying in a feathered crest above an enormous grin. But the more Julia looked the more she saw the shape of Deepa's father's face repeated in her, Deepa's mother's dark hair framing it. Julia hopes, for Baby Goodman's sake, that she has inherited her hips and ass from Raphael's side of the family, her strong teeth and fingernails from Carol. She hopes Baby Goodman has Carol's physical heart, but that her emotional one comes from some hidden depth of the gene pool, a place where love eddies freely, unbounded by fear or shame, sparkling on whoever swims through it as it catches and transforms sunlight.

At the cemetery, the gravediggers have placed a canvas skirt at the edge of the hole, protecting the mourners from the tacky mud that underlies the trodden grass. Bill stands next to Aunt Judy, holding her hand tightly. They all squint against the grey sky. Bill has tears in his voice but he is not crying.

"I love my father," he says. Julia isn't sure whether he said it in the present tense on purpose, but it feels right.

"I love him too," says Aunt Judy, her voice surprisingly strong.

"Me too," Julia says loudly, startling herself; Bill and Judy look over and smile at her. There may be no one standing by the side of my grave, Julia thinks. Baby Goodman will not be there, even if she is still alive when I die. She probably doesn't even know I exist. That's okay, Julia thinks, she has some other life. She feels more peaceful about it than she did before. It's not that it hurts less, but that Julia, somehow, can stand the pain better. She used to feel it as a fresh wound; now she understands it as a loss that has become part of her, a scar that is becoming her skin.

Julia is missing Uncle Paul. It is pulling persistently at her insides like a painful period, and she is glad of it — it's a much less complicated distress than she had at her mother's death, growing as it does from simple love. She is staring at the box lying at the bottom of the hole, dirt clattering onto it, slowly accumulating. This seems to Julia a perfectly appropriate thing to do with the leftover flesh that people become. She takes her turn with the shovel, selecting a clump of damp clay the size of a loaf of bread, tipping it forward into the air, listening for its resounding thud.

At Aunt Judy's house afterward, Julia busies herself laying out food, washing teacups, collecting empty plates left on side tables. Neighbours drop in, a clutch of women Judy worked with before she retired, a couple of Bill's old university friends. Mrs. Yuen from next door comes in bearing a tin of butter cookies and Aunt Judy introduces Anya and Julia to her as "my daughter and ... my other daughter," and it makes Julia happy, satisfaction briefly easing the rawness of sorrow.

She is standing alone in the kitchen, leaning one hip against the counter and eating a piece of an apple strudel someone brought, when Bill's son wanders in. "Hi, Matt," Julia says. The boy looks up at her and smiles quickly.

"Hi," he says. He shoves his big hands in his pockets; his dress pants are loose on his bony frame. He looks around.

"Want a piece?" Julia says, proffering the white box with the golden strudel inside. "It's really good." She leans over and lowers her voice. "I didn't put it out there. I thought we could save it for ourselves," and she winks. She is embarrassed at herself — winking is such a ridiculously adult thing to do. But Matt grins.

"Sure," he says, bobbing his head, shuffling a little in the confined space between the counter and the dishwasher. Julia slices a big slab of pastry and slides it onto a plate for him. He digs into it, shifting a large mouthful of it into the side of his cheek as he chews. She can see the recently-become-familiar gear shaft motion of Bill's jaw in Matt's face. He nods appreciatively while he eats. Julia hadn't thought of him as a person before; he was just Bill's invisible son.

"So what do you do in Toronto?" Julia asks.

Matt looks up at her for a moment. "Go to school," he replies, fork suspended.

"Yeah, I know," Julia says. She supposes he has every reason to assume adults are clueless. "But, I mean, what are you interested in? You must do something besides school."

Matt nods again, swallows a mouthful of food. "Yeah, actually, right now I'm writing a screenplay." Julia stares.

Matt levers the last large piece of pastry into his mouth and dispatches it with a minimum of effort, and then wipes his mouth politely with a napkin. Julia rinses and loads their two plates into the dishwasher and then pours them each a cup of coffee, and they stand together in the kitchen while Matt tells her about his movie. Julia finds she really likes him, his wry confidence, his quirky way of making jokes about himself and his ambitious project. Maybe he will be standing by my grave when I die, she thinks. I could do worse.

When the last visitor has gone, the food put away and the house cleaned up, Aunt Judy stands unsteadily and announces she wants to go to bed. There will be more of the same tomorrow, and the next day, until the week's period of shiva has ended. Sitting, especially in mourning, is tiring. She and Julia hug goodbye. Julia shakes hands with Matt. They exchanged email addresses earlier; she wonders whether they'll actually keep in touch.

Aunt Judy wants to call a taxi for Julia, and Seth offers to drive her home in his rented car, but she refuses; she wants to feel the cold on her skin, to walk down the street alone. Nicholas would have landed two hours ago. By now he should be in the home Julia can picture so well, in the company of the wife whose smells Julia can conjure in her mind as if from a catalogue of earthy perfumes.

The rattling of dried leaves in the wind sighs after Julia as she clacks down the concrete in her boots. The early dark fills every empty space, erasing much of the detail of the street, smoothing the edges of hedges, the gap between the curb and the tarmac. Julia walks until her hands are painfully cold and then stations herself at a bus stop. She can see Nicholas sitting on the couch in Deepa's — his — living room. She puts a glass of wine in his lovely hand, a bowl of pistachios on the coffee table. Then she changes her mind and has Nicholas sitting back against Deepa, her arm loose around his shoulder, her hand flat against his chest. If Julia were in Deepa's place, she wouldn't want to stop embracing him, even while he was sitting down.

She imagines hollows in his cheeks, painted there by illness and anxiety; she smooths his brow with her mind's fingers, letting him relax now that he is home. She creates the aroma of cooking fish for him — no, scallops, he loves scallops — bought and made ready in advance by Deepa before leaving for the airport. Julia thinks of Nicholas leaning his head back against Deepa's lovely small breasts and then lifting his head and asking, where is that necklace you always wear? Julia slips a finger inside her coat, inside the lapel of her jacket; the beads are warm from lying against her body. She rubs her fingers on the complicated surface of one of them. She wishes this would conjure love.

At home she opens the door to find a white envelope lying on the floor inside. She tosses it onto the little table next to the big chair, shrugging her coat off. Without turning on a light she pours herself a glass of wine, the fridge opening in the dark kitchen like an illuminated coffin. She kicks off her boots and carries her glass to the living room, folds herself in between the two fat arms of the chair, facing the window. Flat, distorted planes of light lie around the cold room, sent across the barrier of glass by the streetlights outside. Julia drinks, the wine making her saliva run, the liquid warming as she holds it in the well of her mouth. She thinks of Nicholas and Deepa lying in bed together, exploring each other as if for the first time, in an ecstacy of relief and gratitude. She thinks of her Aunt Judy lying in bed alone. She wonders whether Baby Goodman is cozy in someone's arms — or maybe alone in a hospital bed, with a baby or perhaps a tumour rooted inside her. At her age it could be either one.

Julia is startled from her thoughts by a spattering of water against the window, raindrops thrown hard by the wind like a handful of gravel. She comes back to herself, her window, her chair. Her gaze crosses the envelope lying mute on the little table, white and flat across the grain of the wood. She nudges it with the base of her wineglass until it lies within the stripe of light that slants in from across the way, and her heart thuds. The return address is "S. Limburger," Toronto. Julia picks it up. It is thin, and light. Probably nothing, she thinks, while her breath is coming so thick she can hardly breathe it. She slits open the white paper, tearing the flap of the envelope into a ragged, uneven edge. She pulls out the folded sheet of paper, two lines scrawled on it in purple ink. "Contents of Goodman file: one photograph, provided to my father before investigation closed. Yours truly," and an illegible signature. A single piece of thin, off-white cardboard, almost square, slides into her hand from within the unfolded page. On the square is written "Baby Goodman, 1963." She turns it over.

"So small," she hears her mother saying. It is a black-and-white photograph of a newborn baby, a familiar shock of black hair sticking up almost comically, the faint crust of cradle cap visible at the hairline. Julia laughs, tears coming up her throat in a ball. She presses open palms to her closed eyes, hard, until coloured sparks fly in the darkness. Then she opens her eyes again and gazes at her sister. She shakes her head. This is the photograph that her mother kept in the back of her wedding photo album. The photo she let Julia believe was a picture of herself as a baby.

How ironic, Julia thinks. When Uncle Paul first gave her Baby Goodman's birth certificate, she thought it was for her but it turned out to be for her sister. All those years she looked at the photograph of Baby Goodman thinking it was herself, and now it turns out to be her sister too. As a child she loved that picture — it seemed to be an image of herself before disappointment and sorrow intruded. Now she knows it was neither her nor from a time before sorrow — except, she hopes, for Baby Goodman herself.

Julia looks tenderly upon the tiny baby face. I had you all the time, she thinks. It makes her sad to realize that Baby Goodman might not have this picture of herself. "I'll keep it for you," Julia whispers. "I'll take care of it for you." She thinks of Uncle Paul, lying far below the rain-swept mud surface of the ground. It was he who started the process that brought this image to her, the day her mother's remains were laid into the same safekeeping. Julia imagines the sequence of events as a long, wacky machine. Upon her mother's interment a ball dropped into a cup, which tipped it into a trough, from which it rolled down a tube ... Until, having clicked and clacked its way through the whole rickety mechanism, on this day when her uncle entered the earth himself, the ball finally came to rest, dislodging the photograph into Julia's hand as if it were slipping from the slot of a vending machine.

Julia props the photograph against the windowsill so she and the baby are looking at each other in the darkened room. She lifts her glass in salute, and drinks.

ACKNOWLEDGEMENTS

I am deeply fortunate. Above all, Alisa Palmer and Ann-Marie MacDonald have steadfastly, over many years, given me every kind of support, including a Room of My Own in which to write the first draft of this book. I am constantly grateful for their generosity.

Bruce Walsh has been extraordinarily generous with his talents, not least of which is friendship. I have benefitted from Marc Côté's brilliance, and from the mentorship and general encouragement (by example, among many other things) of David Homel, Claire Holden Rothman, and Neil Smith. My wonderful sister Mical Moser has gone far beyond the call of duty in supporting both me and the book. The Quebec Writers' Federation was instrumental in my development from aspiring

Acknowledgements

writer to published author in many ways. Katarina Soukup gave me another Room when I needed one. Montana, Emma Lynx, and Konrad were companions of my spirit as I wrote. And of course, Claude Lalumière has been essential, and always will be.

The community of book sellers, writers, and readers inspired this story, and insofar as it lives from now on, it will be through them.

The lines used for the epigraph are taken from the poem "I write" by Susan Elmslie and are used by permission of the author. The poem appears in *I, Nadia, and Other Poems* published by Brick Books, London, ON. © 2006 Susan Elmslie.